This is a work of fiction. Names, characters, organizations, places, events, and incidents are either products of the author's imagination or are used fictitiously.

Text copyright © 2020 Wesley Parker

Independently published by Wesley Parker.

ISBN-13 (paperback): xxxxx

COFFEE  and
CONDOLENCES

A NOVEL

Wesley Parker

ONE

COCKTAILS

"Why do terrible ideas feel like they're good? Like, you know...why do they only reveal themselves as terrible *after* you've decided to go all in? I don't get it, an hour ago this seemed so full proof and now...now I just don't know anymore, you know?" I explain, trying to get my bearings, "I'm Miles, by the way. I'm sorry, you were saying?"

"Um...did you want to see a menu?" The bartender repeats herself, her face in a state of shock. She's probably contemplating another line of work, probably thought bartending in an airport would insulate her from the weirdos, with TSA weeding them out one thumb in the ass at a time. She's a petite blonde with bulging breasts that I'm certain are highlighted to bring in tips from horny businessmen.

"A menu would be awesome. I'm sorry, it's been a rough time lately."

She grabs a menu from under the bar and dashes off to tend to anything that isn't me. When her shift is over, I'm sure she'll probably go home to her boyfriend, who—for the purpose of this pity party—I'll assume is a struggling musician waiting on his big break, and tell him about the guy who rambled incoherently before he got a menu. He'll listen long enough to find an opening for sex, and then after they're done, he'll sit naked, strumming "Hotel California" on his guitar while staring out at the city. This is what I've been reduced to; a cheap ploy used for intimacy in a relationship that's probably on the rocks.

My flight doesn't board for another forty-five minutes, so I sit in a brewery near my gate, plotting a strategy. I know that my estranged sister, Lily, is in a Master's program at NYU. But that's all I know. Stalking the campus for days on end is my only hope of finding her, but even that seems sketchy. We share a love of hip-hop, so staking out local hip hop clubs is another option. As I continue to rack my brain, I get a sinking feeling in my stomach. The only person that can help me is our mother. But before I can make the call, the bartender returns and she seems less suspicious of me.

"What can I get for you Miles?" She asks a bit more cheerfully, like she remembered she's working for tips.

"Let me get a Sierra Nevada and a shot of the strongest whiskey you got—actually, make it a double."

"Fear of flying that bad huh?"

"Only way I'd fear flying more than calling my mom was if she was the one flying the plane."

"Well in that case, I'll leave the tab open." She says, before whisking off to make the drinks.

My mother is a complicated woman. She's capable of kindness but, as evidenced by her three marriages, she's the kind of person to be loved from afar. Like two time zones afar, with a long rural drive after landing at the airport. As a firm believer in the mantra "Upward and onward," she has little time for reflection and harping on the past. Add in the absence of a filter in any environment and you can understand my lack of enthusiasm. She taught us that appearance was everything. While that boded well for me in regards to material possessions to win the ever important popularity points in high school, it left a void that I spent years trying to fill.

When my father was still around, she was an entirely different person. But she went into a spiral after he left. Alcohol became a truth serum and on many nights, after finishing a bottle, she'd confess her real feelings. Though she "loved" me, I bear such a strong resemblance to him that I served as a constant reminder of his desertion and, in turn, I became the enemy—a living embodiment of her failure. She made a vow to herself to never love like that again, to never give everything to another person.

After a few years of picking up the pieces she met Greg, Lily's dad. Looking back, a guy with that name never stood a chance with her. Greg was a banking executive who, after the death of Lily's mother, found himself with a teenage daughter he was ill equipped to raise. In my mother, he found a woman that wanted very little sex—or anything for that matter—who was also willing to raise his child. Greg thought he'd hit the jackpot, until six years in when my mother found out he was sleeping with several interns. The divorce was nasty. Though mother had another failed relationship, she had one hell of a consolation prize in their settlement.

I unlock my phone and stare at my mother's contact. The picture is from her trip to Jamaica between her second and third marriage. She said she needed to "find" herself, and three months later she came home with Robert—husband number three. Robert is two years younger than me, which my mom champions as an accomplishment. I finally press call and prepare for battle. She likes to let the phone ring for a bit; picking up at the last second is her way of reminding the caller that she's more important.

"Well, if it isn't my son who never calls me," she coos in a way that makes wonder if staking out Lily's campus was really the worst option.

"Sorry mom, I've just been busy."

"Doing what? It's not like you have anything taking your time anymore."

Almost on instinct, I throw up triple fingers toward the bartender telling her to keep pouring. Most mothers would've mentioned what happened would bring us together, how maybe we should mend fences and start new, because time is short and life is precious. The bartender scurries over and sets my drinks down, giving me pitiful smile as she backs away. I down the double shot and remind myself of the greater purpose. "It's not like I'm about to lose my third husband or anything," she says.

"I was calling becau...wait," I stammer. Everything I know about my mother tells me that I should just get to the reason I called and ignore her comment, but some car accidents you just can't look away from. "Is Robert ok?"

"I'm fine, thank you. Christ Miles, would it kill you to show some sympathy to the woman that carried you for nine months?" she asks.

I'm gonna go ahead and throw in that she only "carried" me for nine months because she got to the abortion clinic ten minutes before they closed. I learned this during one of her drunken story times, and I remind her of this.

"But, I still carried you the full term," she replies.

Another piece of revisionist history... her mother was in a car accident the next day and, by the time she could get back around to it, the pregnancy was too far along. When your mother is an alcoholic narcissist, she can rewrite reality better than a Christopher Nolan film. So, that river you're crying for her should be running as dry as her during menopause. I can only stand being on the phone with her for so long. I always pictured myself as a fighter pilot with his jet going down; pressing the eject button at the right time is key to survival. Usually she says something crazy and I know it's time to hang up. It's a slow build up, but I need information—so I tickle her fancy a little bit.

"Are you ok?"

"It's not working out Miles, he just wants to fuck and play Xbox," she says, "The sex is great, believe me. But, at my age, I need someone more in tune with my sensibilities. I really think bringing him to America has changed him."

The countdown has begun.

I chuckle at this, which makes her click her teeth in anger. It was American culture, not the age gap or the whirlwind three month courtship. No, it was Chick-Fil-A drive-thru and gigabit speed wi-fi that strained their marriage.

"So, what are you gonna do Mom?"

"I'm thinking I need a getaway," she says and my stomach drops. There are only two people who can tolerate her for any period of time; one is on the phone with her now, trying to get the address of the other.

Getting closer.

"Southwest is running specials to Arizona," I say almost too eagerly, hoping to head off whatever she might be thinking.

"Too many migrants," she scoffs.

Ding ding ding! Strike up the band, we have a winner. "Mom, how's Lily doing?"

"Still living that lifestyle, and miserable," she replies, and I can see her putting quotes around the word lifestyle on the other end, "Why do you ask?" She knows why, but I imagine the self-satisfaction of convincing herself that she brought us back together is too tempting to pass up.

"I'm gonna be in New York City and was wondering if she still lives there."

"If you want her address, just ask. If your foreplay is anything like your social skills, it's a wonder that you've ever had sex."

Dr. Felt is likely to make her money from this phone call alone. To keep myself from hyperventilating, I focus on the bartender as she rinses the glasses near the register. We lock eyes and she gives me the thumbs up, as if to say it'll all be worth it in the end. My mother has sensed that I'm not paying attention.

"Miles if you need help you should talk to Robert, he could talk the panties off of a nu..."

An image of my mother in a bar flashes through my mind. She's sitting there and Robert is whispering in her ear with a hand on her thigh, slowly working its way up. The thought makes me wish I were adopted.

"Mom please stop."

"Did you get the gift we sent you?"

The "gift" she's referring to is a six month membership to Match.com and a year subscription to a porn site that encompassed all of their offerings—like a sample platter of smut. "Yes, I got your gift."

"And?"

"And the neighbors kid is going through puberty, so it's getting good use."

"You're so unappreciative, always have been."

I can only smile at the idea that calling my mother would've be different than any other time. If anything, this has proven that no event will ever restore a sense of normalcy for us. We're doomed to snipe at each other on the phone until another catastrophic event forces us into the same room again.

"Look mom, we both know there isn't enough therapy in the world to fix this family. All I want is a way to contact Lily."

"Why?"

"Because, I'd rather repair something that can be fixed than start anew."

"Ok, I'll shoot you her number."

"I was thinking more like her address."

"You're gonna go visit her?"

"I'm at the airport now because, as you said so eloquently, I don't have anything else to do."

They announce over the intercom that my flight will begin boarding. I pull a couple of hundreds from my pocket and place them next to the empty glass. "Look mom, my flight is boarding. Just text me the address and I'll get it when I land." I say on my way out the door.

"She knows what happened to Sara and the kids, take her to a coffee shop and just talk to her."

"I'm supposed to use my pain to rebuild our relationship?"

"Don't act high and mighty. You're using the settlement money to get there."

"They offered me th..." I start but stop myself, knowing she's got a point.

"Just talk with her, play the grief card you've been holding onto. Think of it as life's draw four card."

TWO

SESSION 1: KEEPSAKES LEFT BEHIND

I CAN'T PINPOINT the moment exactly, but I know the blame was placed on my family sometime between me slipping on the toy Batmobile and my bare ass cheeks pancaking the cold tile of our master bathroom—or my master bathroom. No one has written a book on grief that successfully outlined when possession shifts to one person. Someone should write that book, it would establish clear guidelines for us grieving folks and answer vital questions such as:

Can you blame the deceased for your own living failure?

Are you allowed to use your plight to score with that cute co-ed suffering from abandonment issues?

Is using memories of sex with your now deceased spouse while masturbating an acceptable way of bridging the gap between raging hormones and the inability to start over with someone else?

You know...the important shit. I'll stop there, though I need the answer to the last question the most because it makes me sound like some Ted Bundy/Bill Cosby hybrid.

Life wasn't always like this, producing these thoughts and emotions. In fact, it used to be much more simple. I had a wife and children who I loved dearly. But now they're gone, and I'm left alone with keepsakes left behind as a cruel reminder that the grass isn't always greener on the other side. Let me explain.

When you get married, you let go of some of your dreams to take on those of your spouse. If you're like me and can't cook or balance a checkbook, it's a swap that pays off. If you're lucky, children come along and you become more concerned about their dreams and ambitions. Frustrations will arise from time to time, in which you'll wish you could have the single life again. Because the ability to screw up and the repercussions only affect you. Like being able to spend money freely on shit that doesn't matter, because you know your intestines can handle two weeks of Ramen until the next paycheck. While that feeling for most is fleeting, some—like my father—act on it and tear the family apart. I wasn't him and my family was still torn apart. We'll get there, but right now I'm running late.

After collecting myself, I stand in front of the mirror. The steam from the shower hangs heavy in the air, so thick that I can barely breathe. As I start to brush my teeth, my eyes stray to the other toothbrushes in the holder. One is Thomas the Train, it was my son Harry's. It's one of those electric ones, but never quite did the job.

"It tickles, Daddy," he would say, closing his mouth and giggling a laugh of innocence that's painful to think about. I'd turn it off, wipe the toothpaste from his mouth, and watch him run off to eat breakfast just so we could repeat the exercise before he left for daycare.

Next to his toothbrush is a small aqua device that could pass for a finger puppet. That was Grace's. She was so young it would go on my finger, and I'd run it between her teeth before she got tired of it and would bite down on my finger.

"Daddy got a boo-boo," she'd say, as if it was an accident of my own accord. Then she would take off down the hallway, making sure to run her fingers down the air vents to announce her presence to the next room.

I quickly grab some clothes from my closet and head to the living room to dress. Since they left, I haven't been able to stay in our room without falling apart. It's left just as it was the day they went away. The Cars Blu-ray we would use to distract the kids while we snuck away for some time to ourselves still sits on the TV stand.

A Ninja Turtle nightlight is still plugged in waiting for Harry to turn it on, signaling the beginning of our carefully orchestrated bedtime routine. After the light came, a video was chosen; Harry always thought he was slick and would choose something longer than your basic television show. Once a show was agreed on, there were negotiations made on which toy to sleep with. I can't count how many times I woke up with a ninja turtle poking me in the side or some Pixar character coming out of my ass. He would never sleep in his own bed and most nights he would climb in with me and wrap himself in my arm. Over time, my wife and I accepted that our bed was now home to three.

In the distance, I can hear the faint heartbeat from the sound spa in Grace's room. As she became more independent, she wanted to sleep in her own bed. She even decorated the walls around it herself; stickers with characters from various Disney movies covered the walls, and she could name each one in her own baby language. I could never understand what she said but the passion she pointed with clearly conveyed that she knew, and that all that mattered to her. Although she was happy with her own space, nothing could replicate the presence of Mommy and Daddy, so we got the sound spa that simulates the human heartbeat. I'd sneak in while she slept and just watch her. You ever watch a child sleep? There's a peaceful vibe to it, their little faces blank aside from the occasional smile. When she'd wake in the middle of the night, she would stand at the edge of her bed and stare at the door, whimpering until someone—oftentimes me—would come along and rock her back to sleep.

Back in the living room, preparing to leave, I remember that it was in this room that I last spoke to my wife. It was an argument, actually; she wanted me to open up to her, to be the leader of the family that I agreed to be on our wedding day. She was struggling and needed someone to listen to her and comfort her, to let her know that we'd survive it.

"Can you just try to tell me how you're feeling?" I remember her saying.

But I couldn't, all I could do was watch her leave. That was normal with our fights; one of us would leave to drive for hours, threaten divorce, and eventually come back to hash it out. With two toddlers it was easy to make a quick getaway, because we knew the other wouldn't leave the kids by themselves. But this time, she left with the kids. As she put Harry's coat on, he looked to me in despair—he'd seen this before. After she put Grace in the car seat, she opened the door and ordered Harry to follow her on her way out. He ran to the door, his Batman shoes lighting up with each step before stopping to say goodbye.

"Bye Daddy, I love you."

"I love you too kiddo. Mommy's just a little mad, just be daddy's big boy and I'll see you when you get home, ok?"

"Ok," he replied before running to catch Sara, the door slamming behind him.

Those were my last words to him; another request that he accept being neglected, because I didn't have the spine to work things out.

I'd left her alone to deal with the passing of our third child when it was a burden we were meant to share together. I didn't come to this realization until it was too late. About an hour after they left, I decided to take a drive myself. I came home that night to an empty house and her phone going to voicemail. After falling asleep, I was jolted out of my awake by the doorbell ringing at an alarming frequency. There was an urgency to it, but I thought it was just Sara trying to piss me off. When I opened the door, I was greeted by a sheriff deputy, and the look on his face telling me something was amiss.

"Are you Miles Alexander?" he asked with a tremble in his voice.

"Yes, what's going on?"

"Is it alright if I come in?"

"I'd rather know why you're at my door at 2:30 in the morning."

"Your wife Sara, she...she was in an accident, and I...I think we should have this conversation inside," he said almost pleading.

I knew the moment he asked to come in that they were dead. If they'd been alive, there would have been orders of getting dressed and getting to the hospital. I guess if people die there isn't a rush because the bodies are stiff anyway. He'd explained that it wasn't her fault and they didn't suffer. He told me someone was in custody, and I would be needed at the hospital soon but that I could take my time. The way he explained it and tried to soothe me felt like he had a checklist he was taught to remember for times like this. They could call it an accident, but I knew better. It was the postpartum; the depression after the birth and sudden death of our third child. When he died, he took every sense of normalcy with him and took our family down a path that ended with my wife colliding with a drunk delivery driver, who'd run a stop sign.

These last couple of months I've been waiting for the final emotion to come through. First, I dealt with a numbness; like a car that stalled on the highway, motionless and watching everyone else move on with their lives. Some call it denial—the feeling that, if everything stayed the same, I would hear her keys jingling at the door again, that I could again feel the warm breaths of my sleeping children in my ear, or I could apologize and make things right. I refused to cancel her phone line, spending weeks calling her phone hoping she would pick up and tell me it was a mistake. I filled her voicemail with messages of how sorry I was, even though her phone was right next to me. But eventually the reality set in, after the meals from friends stopped coming and the condolences ceased, life decided it was time to move on. There are still reminders; neighbors that grimly nod in passing and friends that are conflicted about inviting you out because they can't take the chance of you breaking down and causing a scene. With that comes regret, and a darker truth that's been lurking beneath the surface all along—a truth that doesn't show up on the autopsy report. That's what grief does to you; it leaves you alone to stir in the guilt, to remind you that even the most mundane transgressions have consequences, that "too little too late" is more than just a throwaway phrase, and that cutting yourself in high school isn't the darkest place the mind can wander to.

After taking a settlement with the drunk driver's company, their deaths left me with more money than I could spend. The irony being that I can buy anything I could ever want, but the only thing I want is what money can't buy.

Time.

Before walking out the door, I survey the living room. It's the only part of the house that's changed. At first glance you would think someone had been squatting there. Small boxes of leftover Chinese food are spread around the room. A stack of discs acting as trophies, showcasing my dedication to the best of what network television has to offer sits on the TV stand. My wife's old Snuggie is tucked into one of the couch cushions. I never washed it and, for awhile, it still smelled like her, but over the last four months it's lost that scent and changed color, as the purple has faded and stains of soy sauce have become the dominant color. The mantle above the fireplace still holds the family pictures. Grace's first steps. Harry's first time riding his big wheel. The engagement picture of Sara and I sitting on a rock at Garden of the Gods. We were told to glance at something in the distance and smile. Those smiles capture a moment that I still hold dear, one in which we had nothing but each other and were content to figure the rest out as we went along.

If I hadn't walked out the door, they would still be here. That truth has led me to this morning, it's led me through an overdose and a possession charge. But, most importantly, it's leading me to therapy.

* * *

The engine slowly hums while it idles in park as I stare at the old colonial home. The address matches the one on Dr. Felt's website but doesn't match my expectations of a therapist charging a hundred bucks an hour. I exit my car and wipe the potato chip crumbs from my jeans before ascending the steps to the yard. The house itself is a single story structure, painted in an odd shade of green that's grown weathered over the years, leaving faint hints of its original beauty. The yard is well maintained and surrounded by a chain link fence with a concrete path leading to wooden porch. On the patio, the furniture sat covered in dust, the layers so thick it could pass for a tarp. The screen door creaks loudly as I open it and tap lightly on the stained glass windows.

I can hear a figure moving closer to the door before it swings open and I'm greeted by a petite older woman.

"You must be Mr. Alexander, I presume?" she offers a hand and a smile.

"Yes ma'am, but you can call me Miles. And you're Dr. Felt?" I grip her hand in a firm grasp.

"Yes, call me Sandra. Please come in."

I step into the living room and survey the surroundings. It's sparsely decorated with a couple of pieces of furniture and an old school television that has rabbit ear antenna protruding from the back. It's the kind of TV that requires pliers to change the channel when the knob wears off. In the corner sits a small computer that I'd bet the rest of my life insurance money on is still running Windows 95. The shag carpet is light brown and probably went out of style around the time the house was built. Sandra leads me into the room she uses to meet with her clients, and it only serves as an extension of the living room. The walls are decorated with her credentials.

Various awards surrounding the diplomas tell me that the woman clearly knows her shit, or maybe she's just full of shit—time will tell. A single chair is placed in front of a couch, and the walls are lined with bookshelves that are filled with books highlighting psychobabble bullshit to feed to the poor schmucks ordered here by some overworked city court judge.

I'm one of those schmucks.

The judge was willing to ignore my significant stash of pharmaceuticals in exchange for therapy and the promise of turning my life around. I had no doubt that he had factored in my grief as a widower after the death of my wife and children. In any case, I'm a newly single male with no children and seven figures of pity money in the bank from the deceased delivery driver's company—on top of what I received from the life insurance policies. After receiving the money, I drove to the nearest Best Buy and bought whole collections of shows and hunkered down in my living room, embracing the depression one bite of Chinese takeout at a time.

I can't work through my own pain, but I can convey a highly articulate argument of why Tony Soprano did indeed live in the series finale of The Sopranos. Television shows are better for dealing with depression than movies. With movies, you have to decide on the next one—leading to an awkward pause in front of a dvd rack that thrusts you back into the hell that you're trying to escape in the first place. Shows allow you to jump right into the next episode, allowing the disconnect from reality to continue uninterrupted.

Sandra takes a seat in the chair across from me, and I finally get a chance to look her over. She's wearing an old, baggy, gray sweatshirt, commemorating a Syracuse run to the Final Four a couple of years ago. Her curly hair is an equal mix of brown and grey that drapes to her shoulders. Her face is creased with lines and wrinkles that highlight overcoming her own life or struggling to carry the burden of her clients issues—burdens that I will undoubtedly contribute to. But, her eyes tell a different story. A mixture of blue and green, they're warm and inviting and, combined with her smile, they beg to begin opening the pandoras box that is my emotions and fragile psyche. But before the mind-fucking can commence, we must deal with legalities.

"Before we start, we should go over some paperwork and ground rules," she says, pulling a folder from the coffee table next to her chair. "Are you familiar with doctor-patient privilege?"

"Yup, everything I say to you stays here...or I can sue you."

"That's correct. Unless you plan to harm yourself or others, then legally I have to report it. Also, the next page highlights the parameters of our relationship. Basically, it states that I won't be having sex with you."

"I guess a hundred bucks an hour doesn't go as far as it used to," I retort as I sign the papers.

A grin crosses her face and she shakes her head. She's never heard the line and appreciates the humor. She inspects the signed forms and replaces them on the side table and takes out her well-worn, leather journal. It's seen better days. No doubt she's going to take notes and have a laugh over dinner.

"So, Miles, why are you here?"

"Because the judge ordered me here."

"Don't get cute. Your file says you attempted suicide. If you really wanted to die, you would've made the adjustments and tried again," she leans forward and stares directly into my eyes, "So let's cut the shit and start over. Why are you here?"

"Because my wife and children were killed a couple of months ago, and I can't move past it." My heart begins to beat faster—a sure sign of anxiety—and, out of habit, I start fiddling with the hospital band. Not going unnoticed, Sandra begins taking notes. And as strange as this sounds, I feel alive for the first time since the funeral.

"So what made you try to kill yourself?"

"You just go right for the jugular don't you?"

"It's your money, but I thought we could save some time and make sure you leave here with a couple of bucks left in your pocket."

"Trust me, I got enough in the bank to afford an eternity in your care."

Normally I'm not like this in new environments, but the fucks I have to give are on backorder, with no restock date. Sandra is staring me down, chewing on the end of her glasses. I know that I'm not the first asshole that's come to her practice, nor will I be the last. Part of me thinks she's intrigued by the challenge of it. Where's the fun in paying six figures for grad school, if every patient breaks down like a bitch as soon as they walk through the door.

"Ok, let's start with something simple. Are you here because you want to get help, or are you doing what you can to get the judge off your back?"

"Well I know I need help, but I'm not the type of guy to come in here on my own. So, let's meet in the middle and call it divine intervention."

"Are you religious?"

"I was but, after all that's happened, I'll file that under 'it's complicated'."

Sandra starts writing again which, of course, leaves me self conscious. I don't think she's writing anything of substance. Hell, she's probably drawing stick figures for all I know. I'm pretty sure it's just a tactic used by therapists to see you sweat. Like when a cop takes extra time running your license after pulling you over.

"I have this recurring dream," I tell her. She looks up, her pen still for the moment, and I decided to continue, "Every night it's the same... and I got tired of it. That's why I tried to kill myself.

"What about the the dream made you want to commit suicide?"

"*They* were in it."

You can tell a lot about people in how they interpret and process information. Dr. Felt passed the first test by understanding who I mean by 'they,' instead of asking me to elaborate. It was an olive branch—subtle—but I understood that she wouldn't ask any questions that would cause me any mental anguish if she didn't have to.

"Can you describe the dream for me?"

"It starts out the same every time," I begin, "I'm in our bed and I hear whispers. When I open my eyes, my kids are at the foot of the bed but they aren't doing anything, they're just watching me. Then my wife comes in and joins them. If I do anything other than watch them, they disappear and I wake up drenched in sweat."

She jots down a couple more notes, "When did you start having these dreams?"

"Never took note of the exact date, but it was soon after they died. Is that normal?"

"It's pretty common to have dreams about lost loved ones, especially if it happened suddenly like in your case," she explains, "One thing that isn't making sense to me is the gap between the accident and your suicide attempt. Care to fill in the timeline?"

"How so?"

"Well, for one, it's a big jump from living with grief to emptying the medicine cabinet. What made you take all those pills, Miles?"

"I just had one of those days, you know? Where you just wanna give up, when you've run out of things to distract you from the darkness, and you finally have to face it."

More goddamned notes.

"It's been months, why now?"

"Not sure. I was watching a tv show, and I didn't like the way a season ended."

"Try to be specific. I'm sure theres been plenty of things you didn't like in your life, none of them made you attempt suicide."

Internally, I felt a begrudging respect for methods. She nibbled around a touchy subject, asked the same question twice and, before I could figure it out, I'd given up the goods and we were moving on. This might be a good match after all.

"It made me think about what kind of father and husband I'd been. Like, putting them off when I could've spent more time. It just spiraled from there and , next thing you know, I woke up in the ICU."

More notes followed by contemplation, and finally her attention returns to me. "Let's switch gears. Your wife, her name was Sara?" she asks.

"Yes."

"Tell me about her."

I wonder if this is a trick question; does she want the obituary version, or is she asking for the exposè? Sara was complicated, but what spouse isn't? She had a passive-aggressive nature that drove me crazy, but she was the best wife I could have hoped to find. Everything was validated when she took to motherhood. She could remember appointments, allergies, and translate the garbled speech of our children. She was so good that if I died, I knew she wouldn't have missed a beat.

"The best complement I could give her is how well she loved me," I fiddle with my wedding band, removing my it and put it back on, before continuing. "She married a boy, with the faith that love and time could turn him into a man."

"Do you think she succeeded?"

"I did, for the longest time. I was never promiscuous, but there's something to be said for loving someone so selfish and getting them to start a family."

"If you were so selfish, what made you jump into domestic life?"

"My father did. Useless as he was, he inspired me to be the opposite of him."

Sandra lights up with that little nugget, sitting up and nodding for me to continue. Like a boxer that's opened up a cut on his opponent, she's found a breakthrough that must be exploited.

"Was he abusive?" she asked.

"Being abusive implies that he was around. He left when I was three."

Just saying that he left is nicer than it sounds. He started his own family and became to those kids what he couldn't be to me. He would schedule a time to pick me up, but he would never show. Mom remarried and though he was a great guy, he wasn't my father. After Harry was born, I called my father on Father's Day. He got to hear me being the father he wasn't, and I got some sense of closure. Ok, maybe not closure...but I figure I'm good for another decade before I have a breakdown.

"So he gave you the blueprint without even being around?" she asked.

"Yup, I mean, it's a sobering thought when your son is born that just by being there you know that you're already ahead of the game."

"Let's talk about your children."

I knew we were gonna get here, but it's still a shock. I break off eye contact and stare out the window, watching a hummingbird bathe on the patio.

"I'm not really ready for that."

"You've run long enough, but we'll keep it simple. I know there was Harry and Grace and a third one at some point."

I stood from my seat and moved to the window. "His name was Edward," I took a deep breath, "He was born weighing seven pounds, and I grew to love him."

"What does that mean?"

"He was unplanned and unwanted most of his pregnancy."

"What changed?"

"He was beautiful..." I trailed off. The tears began streaming down my face as I faced the emotions I had long tried to bury. I whips my eyes and retake my spot on the sofa. "He was perfect but a week after he was born, he passed away."

"I'm sure the timing hasn't made everything any easier."

She was right. The hardest part of this has been the timing. I'd spent months in a haze trying to come to accept our third child. Sara and I had bitter arguments over whether I would resent Edward because he was unplanned. I couldn't even come up with a name for him, but after he was born, it clicked. All the anxiety disappeared just as I knew it would. You can never blame the child; the circumstances are fair game, but never the child. I loved him just as much as I loved Harry and Grace. But, soon after birth he had an aneurism and was gone. Sara had blamed herself, and she would take the kids on long drives to make sense of everything. We'd always been a team, when I'd get overwhelmed with whatever unforeseen bill or circumstance, we'd take the kids to the park and talk everything over as we pushed Harry and Grace on the swings. It was sobering to know that the person you're mourning is the person you need the most.Looking up, I see that the notebook is back on the table and Sandra is nodding politely, urging me to continue. She's the first person that's actually listened, instead of cutting me off with cookie cutter advice from some bestselling, sellout psychiatrist.

"Your home, is it exactly as it was when they died?" she asks.

"Other than the living room, I haven't touched a thing. I couldn't bring myself to do it. The living room looks like I've been trying to occupy Wall Street."

"Because you view any changes as trying to erase them."

"Exactly."

"But, at the same time you're sitting in this environment where everything has a memory attached to it, and those memories are painful." She muses.

"That's not even the worst part."

"You blame yourself don't you?"

"Myself and, if I'm feeling sinister, I blame them as well. They came into my life and then left... just like my father."

"They're not him and you know that."

"Of course I know that, but it's the same principle."

"No it isn't, they were *taken* and he *left*. Yet, you equate them both as abandonment," She removes her glasses and scoots her chair closer. She's so close, our noses are almost touching. "First, it's not your fault," she says. "Second, they loved you as you did them, and you can't let grief make you lose faith in the world."

I glance down at my watch and realize our session has come to an end. I'm impressed with her demeanor and intuitiveness, knowing when to push and when to pull back. She even asked the same shit in a different way, and eventually got the answers she was looking for.

"So where do we go from here?"

"Well, I have you for four sessions. This counts as one of course, but I think we can use the other three to tackle underlying issues. First, we explore your childhood—what it was like, how it affected you. Then, we cover your children and what fatherhood was like for you, never having had your own around. Finally, I would like to explore your marriage and what you were like as a husband."

"Sounds like a breeze."

"It's gonna be rough, and I'm gonna push you to take your mind to places you've long since abandoned or never cared to deal with. But, I promise you Miles, we're on this journey together and I'll be there through every step, but I need you to buy in and trust me. Can you do that?"

I feel like I'm at a crossroads. The idea of drudging up my past is unbearable, especially if we start connecting the dots to the man I am today. But, my current life is unsustainable and, somewhere down the line, I will breakdown again. Except next time...I'll have the knowledge to finish the job. As I stare at Dr. Felt, I can feel her sincerity. If she's willing to work through this with me, the least I can do is try.

"Alright," I agree. "I'm in."

THREE

FALSE STARTS

THE CAMPUS SITS in the heart of the city, with enough space to not feel overwhelmed by the city but close enough to the action to keep tuition rates high. In a lot of ways, it feels like one of those zombie flicks where society has fallen and the only hope for recovery is to quarantine the only healthy people left. Except, in this case, the healthy people are replaced by college students with questionable fashion choices. The pace of the city isn't lost here as the students move with purpose, their conversations muted by the urgency to get to the next class.

My mother gave me Lily's class schedule. If I can find the right building, I should be able to catch Lily in between lectures. I stop a group of students and ask where I can find the right building, but they merely point giving me my first taste of the New York attitude I've heard about so much.

Very few things in life will remind you of your age, like visiting a college campus. I'm only thirty-one but, in this crowd, I feel like I'm at least twice that. However, the overall vibe of a college campuses stays frozen in time, and some of those memories come roaring back. The older you get, the more you pine for your college days. It's the most carefree time of your life; the beautiful sliver of freedom just outside the overbearing reach of your parents, but without the responsibilities of adulthood that greet you the second you walk across the stage at graduation. I was a Communications major—which will forever be in the running for most overused major. Some majors speak for themselves, like Engineering or Nursing, but Communications—with its ambiguous meaning and ever branching tree of emphasis areas to choose from—felt like one of those cooking shows where contestants are given random ingredients and told to make a dish.

I didn't realize how bullshit it was until my first date with Sara. We met in a chemistry class, which sounds romantic in hindsight, but we were just trying to get our science credits out of the way. She was an Early Childhood Development major, which paid dividends when we had children. I, on the other hand, was taking classes like Gender in Film and U.S. History after 1942—the latter in which I convinced the professor to let us watch Forrest Gump because it covered the same time period.

Our first date was at a place called Taste of Philly, the standard cheesesteak place you find in every city but Philadelphia. They'd been in business for over thirty years, the worn upholstery hosting first dates for students dating back to the Carter Administration. Sara talked of how she wanted to be a teacher, about the impact she hoped to make on inner city kids. I still remember the passion she spoke with and the statistics she cited relating poverty to success in public schools—which made me feel guilty because I thought my upbringing was fucked up.

"What do you want to do after college?" She had asked me.

"I honestly don't know."

This would become a central theme in our relationship —my freewheeling ways contrasting with her need for planning and organization.

I find the building where Lily should be and wade through the scores of students to find a surprisingly empty building. Ahead of me is a security checkpoint, the guard is seated at his post next to the metal detector. He's a burly guy with thick shoulders and, judging by the magazine he's reading, he seems disinterested in the job. A student ID is required to enter the building, so this will require some creativity. I remove my wedding band and place it in my pocket, and the metal detector goes off when I walk through. He waves me over and wands me down, the ring in my pocket setting the wand off.

"What's in your pocket, sir?" he asks, tapping the wand against my leg, "I need your ID as well."

"Look, I'm not a student here," I pull the ring out of my pocket and place it on the table, "My girlfriend's a graduate student here, and I'm gonna ask her to marry me."

He looks at the ring and then back at me, unsure of what to do next. I can tell he wasn't trained for a situation like this so I decide to capitalize.

"You a student here?" I ask. He nods in affirmation and I move in for the kill, "I was on work-study once, it doesn't pay much. I just need ten minutes, so how about you hang out with Andrew Jackson while I do my thing?"

I open my wallet and show him the cash. He's mulling the proposition over—and possibly assessing if I'm a threat or not.

He finally smiles, "Benjamin Franklin is much better company," he says, noticing that I low balled him.

"Done."

Cash is exchanged and I set off in search of Lily's class, hoping it didn't get out early. The building space is vast, every sound made carries an echo through the building. The walls are lined with plaques, celebrating the rich people that have made donations, each one bigger than the last. I've always wondered if the plaque was a condition when they wrote the check, or if the school thought to do it on their own. The varying sizes leads me to believe it's the former. I'm always amazed by the fragile egos of rich people.

I ride the elevator to the floor her lecture hall is on. In the excitement of bribing my way into this prestigious university, I forgot the most important factor of all ...

I have no idea what Lily looks like.

It's been about twelve years since we've seen each other, which might as well be a lifetime. Once you leave home, the years seem to roll by twice as fast. Being cut out of some- one's life is an odd purgatory, where time feels like it rolls by faster and slower at the same time. It's faster because life doesn't stop; college graduation, marriage ... and soon after children enter the picture, taking all of the time that was supposed to be the most carefree of your life, and the people that came with it fade away. But in my situation, where my sister told me she never wanted to see me again, it always felt like it happened yesterday. No amount of time had less- ened the sting of her words and, honestly, it feels a little selfish assuming I can pop back into her life on a whim.

I open the door to the auditorium and find myself greeted by a full house of around a hundred students. Their heads all turn in my direction in unison, freezing me in a state of shock. I'm trying to scan their faces as quickly as I can to find Lily, but it's fruitless. The professor stops his lecture to ask if I need help, but I'm too busy looking for a sign.

"Excuse me, can I help you?" he repeats himself.

Then it happens. At the far end of the auditorium someone is packing their belongings and leaving in a hurry. I follow them outside the building, unsure that it's her but with nothing else to lose.

"Lily," I say.

The echo carries louder in the empty hallway and she stops, turning slowly as if I have a gun pointed at her. Her hair is shorter than I remember, with half of her hair shaved and what's left of it colored purple. We're about ten feet from each other. Her expression is blank, giving no indication either way of how she feels about my sudden appearance.

"What are you doing here Miles?" she finally asks.

Not the best opening response to my presence, but I'll take it. She's tapping her fingers on the pins of her messenger bag, waiting for a response. I recognize the bag as the one *Muse* sold on the Resistance tour. I have the same one, or should I say *had* because Sara puked in it during a bout of morning sickness.

"Is there a place we can talk?" I respond.

She shakes her head, "We have nothing to talk about."

"Can you at least hear me out?"

She checks her phone and sighs deeply, "Look, you can't just show up here and expect a warm welcome from me."

"I wasn't expecting anything."

"Really? You flew to New York City, and somehow got past security at one of the most prestigious universities to interrupt my class because you didn't expect anything? How'd you get past security anyway?"

"I told him I was proposing to you ... also gave him a hundred dollars."

She smiles at this, because it's the type of thing she would try too. "You should get your money back."

"C'mon Lily—"

"You turned your back on me—how ever you wanna spin that in your head, is on you—but that's the truth. When I need you, and believe me I'm working hard to avoid that day, I'll come find you."

She turns and heads for the end of the hallway. I follow at a distance, hoping she changes her mind.

"Lily, I need you," I tell her.

She stops at the door, glancing back at me, "I guess we're even now," she says, heading out and leaving me alone in the hallway.

FOUR

YEAH ... IT GETS COMPLICATED

THERE IS something beautiful about the big city, especially ones that are the scale of New York. They call it the city of dreams, and one glance at the skyline helps me understand why. Being engulfed by skyscrapers really makes you feel like the world is yours for the conquering, that life's possibilities are unlimited. The contradiction comes when you look at the city as you trek through it. As great as it is looking up, looking down brings a hard, cold reality of life that I can relate to in my current state.

Sidewalks are littered with homeless people, each holding a sign more depressing than the previous one. Occasionally, you'll see a sign clever enough to make you give away your money. Pedestrians pass by with no acknowledgment to their presence. Manhattan looks to be in a constant state of construction, with signs directing people on unconventional routes through the city streets. Red lights function as a suggestion, rather than a rule, as people assume no oncoming cars is a sign to the cross to the street.

What strikes me is that everyone seems to know their

role in society. The rich walk in lock step with the poor through the streets, each understanding where they're allowed to go. There aren't any signs telling people they're not welcome—like you see in old photos from the civil rights era—and it's not exactly implied either. But, sure enough, when the businessman enters the building, the homeless man that was matching him stride for stride stops at the door and sets up shop outside. I assume it's his way of preserving his dignity by not having to be escorted out, to not be told that his worth as a human being is tied to a dollar amount.

Just north of Lily's school I find a section of the city that's not as bustling. A small coffee shop sits between a wine shop and a bookstore. I consider waiting for the wine store to open, and wonder what pinot would pair well with my failure. But it's too early to start drinking and, taking my disastrous meeting with Lily out of the equation, the morning breeze makes me feel like it's shaping up to be a great day.

The kind of day that makes you forget about the problems of life.

This moment of silent reflection is rudely interrupted as I slip on what appears to be dog shit. A mad cackle catches my attention and I turn to see a homeless man doubled over while holding his coffee.

"You really outta watch where you're going," he reminds me before reaching into his bag and pulling out some napkins for me.

"Thanks. Can I buy you a cup of coffee? You look like you could use some more," I nod toward his empty cup.

"Sure, just tell them it's for John, and they'll handle the rest."

The coffee shop itself is bigger than it looks from the outside. Once you get into the place, the combination of fresh pastries and exotic coffee blends from South America make you feel at home. It's noisy and full of chatter from yuppies ordering complicated drinks before they head off to whatever faceless corporation they whore themselves for. In the back, there's a small stage with a sign advertising an upcoming open mic. The line inches along slowly as every guy in the place took their shot, flirting with the barista behind the counter. And after seeing her myself, I couldn't really blame them.

There are certain times in a man's life that are unexplainable. Being enthralled by someone before a word has been spoken is one of them. Her brownish, blonde hair whipped around her furiously as she moved gracefully from one espresso machine to another. I'd be willing to stand here and order coffee for the rest of her shift. When she lifts her head, I notice a scar on her lower cheek, just above her chin. It's the kind of scar that leads to people avoiding you. To me, it's fascinating. There's a story there. I have scars of my own, just less visible. I'm able to keep staring because the old lady ahead of me is taking her sweet time. , Olga, the barista calls her, seems to be a regular as she jokes with all the workers, asking about their personal lives and the goings on in their respective neighborhoods.

She turns to greet me as Olga leaves and she freezes. She seems almost flustered, like I'm a familiar face she can't place. Picture a movie scene when two characters are introduced to one another, , but they've met already—and usually had sex—so there's an awkward silence as they figure out how to proceed. *This* felt like *that*. Deja vu on her end perhaps. After a couple of seconds staring at each other, she regains her composure and snaps back into barista mode. "What can I get for you sir?"

The name tag reads Melody. Her hazel eyes aren't as

intense as the others I've met since I got here. They're warm and welcoming ... or maybe comforting is a better word. Either way, they're disarming. If she looked me in the eyes and asked, I'd spill my darkest secrets.

This is an important moment of our non existent relationship; If I order some yuppie drink I'm done. My eyes linger on hers for a second too long as I draw a blank, I was so infatuated with her I never studied the menu. Why couldn't I be one of those guys that talks smooth and knows all the right words to say? That guy is probably an asshole in every aspect of his life, but I feel like I could grow out of that.

I suddenly remember John's refill and save face by ordering the same thing.

"I will have a...refill for John," I say with an obvious lack of confidence, "and one of what he's having for myself."

Melody gives a smile of validation as she writes the orders on the cup. "Can I get a name for the cup?"

"Miles."

It happens again. She freezes when she hears my name —more subtle than the first time, but still noticeable. Hopefully she didn't date an asshole named Miles that I remind her of. "I love that name, it's got a nice ring to it."

It's got an even nicer ring with her name next to it.

Thank God my name is in her good graces.

Now, I know that I've been out of the game for years, but I'm pretty sure she's flirting with me. I pay and she tells me she'll will bring the order outside for us. I head back outside to sit with John, my mind racing with possibilities.

"Do you come here everyday?" I ask John.

"Yeah. I usually stay in places I know that have progressive ownership. I can enjoy my coffee without the stares, and the college kids are so idealistic, they leave me be. You from around here?"

"No, just came here on a whim."

"To New York or to this coffee shop?"

"Both."

John chews on this for a moment. He seems to sense that there is more to me, but is content with my answer for now. Melody comes out with our drinks.

"Morning darling," John greets her as she puts the drinks on the table. John, clearly a regular, banters with Melody like they're two old friends that ran into each other by chance. As she talks, she places one hand on his shoulder with the other on her hip. I watch silently as tells her a joke and she collapses her head on his shoulder to laugh. She trusts John, probably because he doesn't gawk at her like the others in the line and, in turn, he trusts her because she sees him as more than a homeless person. I imagine that she's spent many breaks out here with John and if there is an "in" with her, it'll be through him.

"Melody, have you met Miles?"

"Yeah, I took his order."

"He's here on a whim, a real free spirit."

She looks at me with the same compassion as she did when I ordered. Her eyes are apologizing for John's forwardness, and it dawns on me that I'm being pimped out by a homeless person. To ease the tension I pick up my cup to take a drink and notice that there's a number written on it—no name, no clue, just a number.

"Well John, thank you for caring but I can handle it myself," She turns to walk back into the shop, but stops at the door and turns back to us, "Besides, I didn't have to come out here," she says, giving me a smile.

I immediately excuse myself to call Dr. Felt, who answers on the second ring.

"The prodigal client returns," she answers.

"Spare me. My first contact with Lily went terrible."

"How bad?" she asks, a bit too cheerfully in my opinion.

"Mitt Romney speaking in front of the NAACP bad."

Dr. Felt erupts into laughter, "I'm not laughing at you, I'm laughing at the comparison."

"That's really not helping."

"Ok. What did you think was gonna happen, Miles?"

I stay silent, unsure if it's a rhetorical question and she continues.

"You made contact, so the hardest part is out of the way. Did she say anything that stuck out to you?"

I hum into the phone, recalling our conversation, "She said that we're even now... right before she left."

"That's an interesting way to say goodbye, don't you think?" she points out, "Instead of saying she didn't wanna see you again, she highlighted that you guys are 'even'... sounds to me like she's been waiting for you, but plans to make you work for it."

"You're saying if we're even, I should try again ... because technically, we've both been hurt by one another?"

I can hear Dr. Felt clapping through the phone. "Look at you, digging beneath the surface," she says. "She left you at what she thought was your weakest moment—returning the favor—so now it's a game of stamina. Keep pulling at the sweater and eventually you'll find a thread."

No longer feeling like a failure, I tell her about Melody and the phone number on my coffee cup. She congratulates me like a proud parent.

"Miles, that's progress."

Only in a fucked up profession like psychiatry, can a

widower calling his therapist and talking about a woman that isn't his deceased wife be considered "progress."

"I think going on a date would be healthy for you," she sounds like a doctor telling me I'm pre-diabetic, and I should change my diet, "You're going to have to start dating eventually, why not start in a place that'll allow you to slide back into the crowd if it goes wrong?"

"Because, I'm married ..." I trail off.

"Miles ..." she says, trying to find a way to remind me I'm a widower, without being an asshole about it, "It's just a cup of coffee or a drink, I'm not telling you to take her to the courthouse."

She has a point, though I hate myself for acknowledging it. At some point, life goes on but it still feels like cheating. I suspect this feeling never goes away. Like getting a tooth pulled, the hole will always be there reminding me of what was once there, but still allowing me to have a "normal" existence.

With Melody, the first feeling wasn't lust. It was the sense that I'd found someone who had scars of their own and would understand mine. Grief grants almost a sixth sense for detecting the struggles of another person and the belief that, by throwing yourself into their problems, you can bury your own issues and cleanse yourself of the regret you carry.

"So, I should call her?"

"Yes, even if it doesn't go anywhere, you have to start the healing process."

"And if it does go somewhere?"

"Then, maybe our sessions become group therapy."

"You can kiss my ass, Doc."

"Based on our final session, I don't think you're emotionally ready for that," I give her the silent treatment for a few seconds, then she gets serious, "It's just coffee Miles, not marriage. Besides, embrace that you're the Southwest Airlines of the dating world."

"What?"

"You're cheap, relatively easy to deal with, and come with free baggage."

Funny how the last two people I have spoken to on the phone act like these coffee dates are run of the mill meetings instead of watershed moments.

I thank her for taking the call, promise to keep in touch, and return to the table where John is setting up a game of checkers for us—like he knows I have nothing better to do.

"You travel pretty light—"

"Compared to the other homeless people," he finishes for me, "When you're homeless, you have to be ready to move at a moments notice. There's no time to gather your things, you just grab your stuff and move to the next stop."

"Who makes you leave?"

"It could be anybody, you name it; rich folks scared their neighborhood is going to hell, rodents on trash day, flooding … it could be anything, but it doesn't matter because *we* don't matter."

It's sobering to know that we're sharing breakfast but live in different worlds that, whenever I leave, I can go back to my home, and John will go back to the street. He can see the affect his words have on me.

"Don't feel sorry for me, I'm homeless by choice."

Funny how one throwaway remark can lead to more questions than answers. I've always thought of homelessness a consequence of life, rather than a choice. The idea that someone would willingly become homeless makes no sense to me; either my face has contorted to express my confusion, or John is used to telling his story because he explains it all.

He grew up with a single mother, living in a two bedroom apartment in Harlem. His father was never around, so his mother worked different jobs to maintain their lifestyle. Halfway through college, his mother was diagnosed with breast cancer. The love he has for his mother makes me wish I had a better relationship with mine. After dropping out, he worked several odd jobs to make the mortgage payments. As gentrification swept through the neighborhood, his mother was offered several chances to sell their home, but repeatedly declined. Eventually the owner of the building took them to court, and his mother died during that process. Her death only steeled his resolve to stay because it was all he ever knew. Every memory he had was in that apartment.

Eventually, a judge forced him to take a settlement and vacate the premises. The owner went belly up and John was left with only 20% of what he was forced to settle for. No longer able to afford an apartment in the city, he decided to rent a storage unit for the items that were invaluable to him. The building he lived in his entire life is now a Whole Foods.

"Why didn't you just take the money you had and leave the city?" I ask.

"This is all I know," he nods toward to the city. He looks up the street, staring at the city he loves that doesn't love him back. "To leave this place would feel like I was leaving my mother ... that her death was in vain."

"She wouldn't want you to live on the streets."

John smiles, "I think that too, especially on cold nights. But if I leave, I'd feel like I'm leaving her behind."

You never know the life that strangers around you have lived. Mostly, we view people on a surface level—without a thought to understand their journey and how it shapes their actions. John is living in a prison of his own construction, and I totally get it.

"You gonna give Mel a call?" he asks without looking up.

"Maybe."

"Good, there's more to her than what meets the eye."

"What do you mean?"

"Just call her and see where it takes you."

FIVE

IT'S OK, I'M JUST WATCHING

IT's funny how emotions work; when you're riding the high, you feel invincible. Maybe you send a risky text to someone you've been crushing on, or perhaps you tell off the coworker that's been acting above their pay grade. Or, in my case, you fly to New York on a whim to reconnect with someone who made it explicitly clear they didn't want to see you again ... among other choice words.

But, as soon as you send that text or tell that person off, the high gives way to the crash. Rational thinking takes over, and you find yourself lamenting how stupid you are. I'm currently in this stage as I sit in an Uber, eating a bag of Lays somewhere in the borough of Queens. My driver, Jah,—a Middle Eastern man with an affinity for Brit-Pop—sits next to me as I ponder my next move.

You wouldn't think of Queens as being part of New York because it's so different from Manhattan. The row homes connect together and stretch the length of the block, they each have brownstone steps, and I can't help but wonder how many people have sat on them and had their hearts. It's a weird thought to have, but I think of random things like that. They're packed so tight that one assumes the developers were trying build as many units as they could in one space. The streets have one lane going each way and, if you aren't careful getting out of your car, you could easily be hit by a passing vehicle. This is as close to a suburb that I've seen since I landed.

The neighborhood has working class vibes with shops representing different cultures and customs. Mothers shuffle their children along, with laundry carts and spare groceries picked up at one of the numerous corner stores. Life definitely moves slower here compared to Manhattan. The people look you in the eye and inquire about your day, shopkeepers are more likely to engage you in conversation about the Mets pitching woes than whether or not you plan to purchase anything.

Thirty yards from us, right in front of one of the complexes, there's a woman yelling at another woman, who's pleading outside by the steps. It reminds me of Jungle Fever, when Wesley Snipes's character is caught cheating on his wife. Either this is normal or people mind their own business in this neighborhood, because nobody is stopping to figure out what's going on.

I sent Melody a text on the ride over, but she hasn't responded yet. It's these kind of waiting games, that remind me why I was happy to get married.

"You got anymore rides you need to take, Jah?" I ask, crumpling the bag and wiping my mouth.

"No my friend. As of right now, I'm done for the day."

"Alright, look, I need to go have a conversation with that girl over there, the one outside the building," I say motioning to the women in the argument. He looks nervous and I can see him pondering exactly what he's gotten himself into. "It might take awhile, but I'll need a ride back into the city if you're available."

He looks at me and then back at the confrontation and nods his approval, "How much time do you need?" he asks.

"Half an hour," I reply. As I say this we notice the woman preparing to push a television out the window—I'm talking old school tube television with a glass screen and the red, white, and yellow ports.

The television breaks part upon impact on the concrete of the parking lot. Dropping from a second floor will do that to electronics. The broken pieces take their place among the clothing scattered on the ground.

"Better make it an hour," I say with an embarrassed smile.

The woman on the balcony is shouting as she empties belongings onto the ground, Lily frantically picking them up. Her hair is longer than I remember it being, certainly it wasn't as disheveled as it is now. I guess when your stuff is being thrown from a window, your vanity goes right along with it.

I'm not surprised to find her in this situation, monogamy isn't her forte. She could walk into a nightclub and instantly attract people on both sides of the fence—and make no mistake, she played both sides. She had enough sex in high school to satisfy both of us and even set me up to get laid by one of her friends, Jaime Dupree during junior year of high school. Jamie was the only person who could match Lily's sex drive, and when I protested about being entrant number sixteen into Club Jaime, Lily would have none of it.

"Remember when you got your first car?" she asked.

"Yeah."

"You didn't care about mileage right?"

"Nope."

"Well, the same thing applies here. Don't worry about whose driven it before, just be happy it's yours to drive now."

Lily and I bonded over our love for hip-hop and disdain for our parents. When they would go out of town, we'd take the Mercedes on road trips to to hip-hop clubs in other cities. We'd find partners and have make out sessions in the car before dropping them off at home, vowing to keep our secrets with each other. We would spend hours debating who the best rappers were and dreaming of leaving our parents house, starting a hip-hop magazine and contributing to the culture that kept us believing that we could be someone. As I watch her gather her belongings, I feel a twinge of regret for how far we've drifted apart. I didn't realize until now, for two people as close as we were, that indifference was betrayal. Lily needed me to stand with her as she did for me in high school.

I watch from a distance and briefly consider driving back to the airport and telling Dr. Felt that it didn't work out. Knowing her, she'd see right through the bullshit.

As I watch Lily scrounging for her belongings like an animal, I feel a deep sadness.

How did I let it get here? Obviously that question could apply to the last six months of my life, but I mean my relationship with Lily. Why is it that, as human beings, we wait until everything is burned to the ground? Why does it take that for us to realize it could've been prevented? I'm unsure how to approach this though. When someone tells you they never wanna see you again, that's pretty definitive. It's like watching a movie that's great but the main character dies. You want a sequel but, the way the story played out, it's not within reason. Plus, by the looks of it, Lily has enough on her plate without me adding to it.

I step out of the car and, as I get closer, the conversation becomes clear. The woman on the balcony is accusing Lily of cheating. I could've told her that would happen. Lily is way too free spirited to be hamstrung to one person for long.

"Hey Lil," I say.

She whips around greets me with a look of confusion and disgust.

"As if my day couldn't get any better," she says, shaking her head, "what are you doing here."

"Who the hell is that, are you fucking him too?" her partner yells from the balcony.

"Actually, I'm her brother Miles," I give a small wave that's probably more creepy than intended.

"The one with the dead wife and kids?"

I know I shouldn't expect sympathy from someone I just met—especially one being played by my sister—but the bluntness of her description of my current situation is jarring nonetheless. It does get Lily to redirect her focus away from me for a second.

"That's my niece and nephew. I'd choose my words carefully if I were you." Lily's veins bulge out of her neck, which is never a good sign. If Lily is one thing, it's loyal— well to her family, at least. She'd never met any of my children but, even in death, she protects their memory.

"So I ask again Miles, what are you doing here?" she asks, turning back to me.

"I really just wanna talk. You're the only person I have right now... well, you and John."

"Who the hell is John?"

"This homeless guy I met at a coffee shop near your school. I'll explain later, can we go somewhere and talk?"

"I told you already, we have nothing to talk about. Why is that so hard for you to understand?"

I've always marveled at how women can field requests, deduce them, and then ask a question that makes you feel stupid for asking in the first place. All women have this ability. It's like God felt bad for the wage gap and discrimination, so he gifted them this little gem of a skill. "You have no idea what my life is like right now."

"Always the selfish one. Not sure if you noticed, but this isn't exactly the best time."

"I couldn't help but notice this is one of those moments where you might need me."

Her partner seems to have run out of things to throw and joins the fray, "Excuse me ... but we have—"

"Shut the fuck up!" We yell in unison, forcing her partner to retreat inside the apartment.

Just like old times, we found someone that insulted both of us and the dynamic duo rides again—at least temporarily.

"Did Mom send you here?"

"Yes, but I asked for your information. She's getting divorced, by the way."

Lily cracks a smile at this. She wants to hate me, to tell me to get out of her life, but she can't. If the situation was reversed, it would be the same. There's always people in your life you give a pass, no matter their transgressions. You can try to convince yourself that's not the case, but there will always be someone in your life that you need to know is on your side. We'd been through too much together to truly cut each other off. She's gonna make me grovel and there will be the occasional asshole remark but, in the long run, I think we'll be alright.

Out the corner of my eyes I see an object flying toward us and push Lily out of the way as the glass shatters on the ground between us. We take cover behind an old truck as glass continues to rain down.

"You sure still know how to pick them, Lily."

"My life has actually been pretty good lately."

"We're dodging projectiles in the parking lot of an apartment complex, just what part of the good life is this?"

"She's actually a good girl, just a little crazy sometimes."

We share a laugh about it and, for a moment, there's a sense of normalcy between us.

"I'm here for the week at least, and you're now somewhat temporarily homeless. You wanna get outta here?"

"Ok. But this doesn't mean I forgive you and, once we're outta here, you drop me off somewhere," she says as she picks up a brick and sneaks around the car.

"Got it."

I break for the car and, as I open the door, I hear the sound of a window smashing. As we pull up, I notice Lily sprinting away from a maroon Volvo with a shattered back window. Lily hops in the passenger seat and Jah guns it down the street.

Bonnie and Clyde live on.

SIX

BEAUTY FROM THE ASHES

THE ADRENALINE WEARS off with each passing block as we come to terms with what just happened. Lily sits silently staring out the window. Sunlight coming through the window glimmers in the pieces of glass in her hair., I have no idea where we're going or what the plan is. Jah says nothing, driving in silence and probably wondering if he was just an accessory to a crime. After about ten blocks, she finally breaks her silence.

"You can just drop me off at this next corner, at the Walmart," she says, unbuckling her seat belt.

"So, you're not even gonna talk to me?"

"Just let me out of the car."

"I said I was sorry, and I'm trying to make things right."

Jah pulls into the Walmart lot and puts the car in park. Lily thanks him and gets out of the car, quick enough that my goodbye to Jah is rushed so that I can keep up with her. Poor guy got more than he bargained for today. "Thank you for today, couldn't have done it without you Jah," I say before calling after Lily.

"If I forgive you, will you let me leave?"

"Yes."

"Ok. With the power invested in me, you're forgiven and absolved of your sins," she says and turns away from me to walk into the store.

Maybe I should let it go. In theory, I gave it a shot and did what I was supposed to do. But if I'm gonna let her go, I at least need to let her know why I came in the first place.

"I tried to kill myself," I say abruptly, before she gets too far.

She stops in her tracks and turns back to face me, "Why?"

I've learned through the grieving process that saying something crazy disorients people long enough to get your point across.

"I had nobody else and couldn't take it anymore," I shrug, "then I got sent to therapy."

Lily walks toward me, and I can see the tough facade breaking as she realizes that she's is all I have in the world. "I mean why are you telling me this Miles?"

"Because, I promised my therapist that I would try and reconcile with you. That's why I'm here."

"Is that what you really want, or is it to get her off your back?"

"I had to call our mother to get in touch with you. You know I wouldn't subject myself to her verbal waterboarding techniques if I really didn't want to be here."

There's no sense in getting sappy with Lily. We both deal in facts, not feelings. Like going before the supreme court, we lay carefully reasoned arguments with the anticipation of rebuttal. Our mother needs one to grovel for forgiveness; Lily and I communicate through our vulnerability—we're also stubborn.

"I want you to know that I never stopped loving you sis,

even if I didn't know how to say it," I admit, moving past Lily and heading for the entrance of the store.

My phone buzzes and I get excited, hoping that it's Melody returning my text. But my excitement quickly dissolves when I see it's my mother wanting to know how it was going with Lily. She has a terrible knack for making her presence known at the worst time. I respond with an affirmative and check my messages one more time just to be certain I didn't miss a response from Melody.

I should take this as a victory. Whenever you meet someone that you're genuinely interested in, there are moments like this. You imagine what everyday life would be like. How is the pillow talk? Do they bite lips while kissing or just peck away? I want tell Melody everything, start to finish, and convince her that even though I'm broken I can be put back together into something worthy of her companionship. Hell, I'd take friendship at this point.

"Where are you going Miles?" Lily asks.

"I need clothes and toiletries, since I came here straight from the therapist. And seeing as all of your shit is strewn around a parking lot like debris from the Titanic, I can replace yours too."

"Ok, but you need to tell me everything—the suicide attempt, their death—everything," she demands. And before I can agree, she grabs my hand and leads me toward the entrance.

* * *

Walmart is a world unto itself. When Sara and I would fight, I would often go to a Walmart; seeing all the single mothers with sandals more worn than their bodies would remind me that the grass isn't always greener on the other side. As a matter of fact, there was no grass at all; just concrete with roots growing through the cracks. Hollywood makes divorce seem like a fresh start, like you walk out of court and run into your true soulmate in the elevator. But the reality is that divorce is nothing more than choosing the best women the local Walmart has to offer. You might find shit or you might find gold but, just like shopping at Walmart, theres no in between.

I would describe it but every Walmart is pretty much the same. The door is manned by an elderly woman, and I play the game of wondering if she's here because she wants to be or if she wrecked her retirement. The other workers toil along in random conversations, doing the bare minimum of work.

Lily is walking through the undergarments and I try to stay at a reasonable distance. Her first question forces me to close the gap.

"So, what made killing yourself the best option you had?"

"Right for the jugular I see," I speedup to close the distance between us, in hopes that she won't talk so loud.

"Our mother used your porn habits in her testimony at church and you survived that, so it's a wonder that you couldn't power through this."

The event Lily is referring to happened between our mother's second and third marriage, when she was struggling to find "purpose.". It's a miracle Lily and I didn't end up in therapy sooner. Our mother would go rummaging through our things while we were at school and found the cover of a porn dvd that, ironically, I'd found in the garbage with my stepdad's discarded belongings. "Somehow that was more embarrassing than my failed suicide attempt."

"I bet it was, I converted all my porn to digital after

that." She pulls out a leopard printed thong and holds it up, "What do you think?"

"I think your brother shouldn't be the one commenting on your choice of underwear."

She throws it into the basket along with a couple more pairs and moves on to the pants section.

"To answer your question, I had one of those days where it was easier to end it all than to fight."

"So what happened?"

"Season two finale of The Office happened."

"I don't understand."

She doesn't understand because, looking back on it now, I probably could've chosen a better show to push me over the edge. In a nutshell, there was a love story developing during the season between two coworkers. The receptionist, Pam, was engaged and started developing mutual feelings with Jim, a slacker salesman. Over the course of two seasons the writers foreshadowed a love story that had me hooked. Thankfully the show itself had already ended, because I couldn't imagine waiting week after week to find out what happens next. In the season finale, Jim tells Pam how he feels and the camera cuts to black—not in an artsy Sopranos type of way, more in a network television "your ass will be back next season" kind of way. Now, I could've just put in disc one of season three and kept the good times rolling, but it stuck with me. If there couldn't be a happy ending on basic network television, where were the hopeless people like myself supposed to find it?

I walked into the kitchen because I was having an anxiety attack—like I was prone to having during that time. This all took place about six weeks post accident. I collapsed into the wall near the sink, sliding slowly onto the floor as the anxiety crippled all resistance, before settling and rocking slowly, muttering gibberish to myself, hoping it would pass. Eventually I slumped over onto the floor and focused on the refrigerator to take my mind away from the black hole I was staring down.

There was a picture of Harry and myself standing with Batman at a Lego event I had taken him to. He was deathly afraid of people dressing up, but Batman was the exception. It was at that moment I decided I couldn't do it anymore. It wasn't that I *couldn't* live life without them, it as that I didn't *want* to.

Stabbing myself was out of the question. Not because I didn't want to be found that way, mostly because I'm a pussy. I remembered I had sleeping pills in the medicine cabinet so I crawled to the bathroom. The title menu for the Office DVD was doing that thing where the music loops and the menu reloads every thirty seconds or so. I couldn't believe that theme song would be the soundtrack to the end of my life. Looking back, I should've just googled how many to take. I took six because it was a nice even number. Five would've fucked with my OCD and seven had a religious meaning that I wanted no part of. So, I took them and just waited. It was anticlimactic, sitting and waiting for the end. A couple of minutes after I ingested the pills, I decided that I needed to take the trash out. I figured the smell of my decomposing body should be enough, they needn't think I was a slob on top it.

I realized, as I gathered the trash, that a calm had taken over me and the anxiety was gone. Something about knowing the end was coming made everything alright, and soon I would just be a memory—just like Sara and the kids had. As I walked to the trash bin outside, all I could think about was that I'd never see my Eagles win the Super Bowl. I had poured my life into this team, and I'd never see them hoist the Lombardi. I wondered if people who know they're going to die think about these things.

As I got to the dumpster I suddenly felt light headed, the world spinning out of control. There was a ringing in my ears similar to when you leave a nightclub. My legs gave out as I collapsed on a pile of trash bags—because our HOA was too cheap to pay for another dumpster—and it was the night before pickup. The last thing I remember is Mrs. Halsey, our neighborhood watch coordinator, standing over me screaming with a bat in her hands.

Lily is looking at me with a sense of bewilderment after I finish telling her the story. I stand there in the women's denim section awaiting judgment like a convict when she finally renders her verdict.

"Wow," she says as I await her sympathetic take, "that's the most pathetic shit I've ever heard."

"Not exactly the response I was looking for."

"Even you have to appreciate the humor in that, little brother."

"Elaborate."

"Well first, you let a middle of the road show push you over the edge," she says as she wipes away tears of laughter. "And then, you decide to commit suicide but overthink that, and you end up passed out in the garbage like some sort of cartoon."

"Yeah, well hindsight is 20/20."

"No. Hindsight is shitty/shitty. In the future, when you tell that story, just say it was losing your family that pushed you to do it, because Jim and Pam eventually get married and you almost killed yourself without seeing how it played out. Moral of the story, you weren't patient enough to see it through. That goes for your life *and* the show."

"So, you're a philosopher now?"

"I didn't know Sara, but I imagine she would've wanted you to move on," she says, pulling jeans from the shelf, "if you're gonna hang with me, you can't be a fucking downer. Lord knows I don't need any more of that."

"It's not that easy."

"No, it's not. But four people were killed in that accident and, no matter how much you would've like it to have been five, the facts stay the same." "Miles," she looks me in the eyes for what feels like the first time, "at some point you have to let go. It doesn't mean the pain goes away or that you don't love them. Now, go get yourself some clothes while I hit the fitting room."

As I walk toward the men's section, I mull over Lily's words and convince myself that she's right. She's the only person that I won't blow off when she's that blunt with me—though Dr. Felt is definitely making gains on her.

The boys' section is right in front of the men's, and I can't help but stop.

Harry loved this section. He was such a content child; he never cried for the things he wanted, but he got them anyway. He'd stand at the front of the cart like Leo DiCaprio in Titanic, pointing and directing me to his favorite sections. His favorite clothes were the sets—the ones with a pair of shorts and a tank top. Put one of those on him with a pair of shoes that lit up and he was on cloud nine. When Paw Patrol came out he went apeshit for it. It never made any sense to me but, then again, it's not created for the parents. I'm convinced the producers of children's television are horny husbands that can never keep their kids occupied long enough to sneak away for uninterrupted sex. It's the only reason to create such mindless content.

The clothes for men are pitiful. Most of the shirts have some clever line that no male of legal drinking age should be wearing in public. There's an entire section of skinny jeans that make me double check that I'm in the right section. I prefer to have my balls and spare change on separate sides of my pants. I throw a couple pairs of loose fitting jeans in the basket and grab every Marvel shirt I can find. Finally, I decide on a sports coat in an attempt to look like I have my shit together. Just how exactly does one rejoin the fashion world after not caring for so long? Can you start where you left off and adjust from there?

"Think fast," a voice calls from behind me and, before I can fully turn my head, a red, rubber ball bounces off my head and sends me sprawling into a rack of shirts. In an attempt to break my fall, I grab for a shelf only to find out it's not fastened into the wall tight enough, and I bring down the entire supply of skinny jeans on top of me. I can hear the gasps and footsteps of people coming to dig me out of the pile of hipster rubble. As I get to my feet, I hear Lily scolding a worker for not securing the shelves to the wall—as if they were the catalyst for what just happened.

"Lily, what the fuck?"

"My bad! I thought having kids gave you better instincts."

"Yeah, for falls and spills. It didn't give me spider sense."

A crowd has gathered around us to gawk but Lily is having none of it, "Nothing to see here people. Move along gracefully with your day, thank you."

My head is still buzzing as we move through the store, when Lily approaches me with a buzzing contraption. It's shaped like a paper towel roll and, from the open box, markets itself as a neck massager. People use that to massage a neck like guys go to Hooters because the love the wings.

"Put it back," I tell her after she throws it in the basket.

"Well, I figured since you were being so charitable."

"Not that charitable."

"Relax, Scrooge" she says. Before I can scold her, we're laughing like old times. The tears that run down my face are for once from joy instead of pain. Lily comes over and pulls me into an embrace. It's long, but not nearly long enough as I needed it to be.

"I really fucking missed you, more than you could ever know," she whispers. "I don't need the vibrator anyway, I've got...friends."

"This might be the thousandth time I say it, but I *am* sorry," I reply, ignoring whatever it is she has planned from that throwaway remark.

"Water under the bridge. Today, we start fresh."

We head to checkout and I text John to let him know that I'm on the way. Clothing for two—$236.50; destroying the men's section of Walmart and rebuilding a bond that never broke—priceless.

SEVEN

DINNER IS SERVED

WE HEAD BACK to the coffee shop and, to my dismay, Melody has finished her shift for the day. John is sitting in his same spot as earlier and greets us like a doting grandfather.

"Well I knew you had a sister, but you never mentioned how beautiful she was. I'm John and you must be Lily," he extends his hand.

"You're too kind, it's nice to meet you," she replies as she takes his offered hand. "Since we're here, I'm gonna grab a cup of coffee. I hear this is your place John, why don't you show me the best brew."

While they buy coffee I'm left with the task of finding a hotel to stay in. In what's rapidly becoming the norm, I'll be footing the bill, since Lily's financial solvency is more in line with a Bernie Madoff investor. The options seem infinite, but I narrow the choices down to hotels within a mile of Romancing the Bean. I could lie and say it's because John stays close by—at least I assume he does—but that would be bullshit.

It's Melody, plain and simple.

I book a large suite on the top floor that, from the pictures, looks like an apartment. Lily can have her space and, if I'm lucky, the television will have a show that I can binge watch when the inevitable panic attack happens.

Not sure what that looks like.

I've reconnected with Lily which—in theory—means my job is complete. Not sure I'd classify our relationship as *cozy*, but it's getting there. However, there's still something missing. I really don't wanna fly back to Colorado right now; there's nothing there for me. As crazy as it sounds, this feels like where I need to be right now.

Melody still hasn't responded to my text, and I consider texting her again. I wonder if she's waiting for me to call instead. It feels good to be wanted, to know that someone's out there waiting on me to make a move. If I never call her, I'll always know she *wanted* me to call. I haven't dated much but, when I did, women didn't leave their numbers on napkins for no reason. The question is whether I should tell her everything.

Lily and John return to the table, laughing like old friends.

"John tells me there's a woman here that's smitten with you, Miles."

I look at John, he has a sly grin on his face—the same one he had earlier when he was pestering me to call her. He knows something I don't and it makes my stomach turn. My phone vibrates in my pocket and my heart skips a beat. I grab it, a bit too excitedly judging by the stares I get from Lily and John. With one glance at the screen my hopes are dashed. My mother sits on the other end of the line, her sixth sense for detecting an happiness in my life probably set off alarm bells in her living room. *Not now Satan,* I think to myself and press ignore. "She's a barista, and it's just a phone number—no big deal."

"Well, seeing as you're still in your own little Shake-spearean tragedy, I would disagree."

"Am I missing something?" John asks, looking between us.

I'm not sure how to proceed. He knows Melody, so whatever I tell him will likely get back to her. *But,* he's part of this family now and he'll find out eventually.

"My wife and kids were killed in a car accident," I say in a tone that sounds rehearsed—I've gotten pretty good at explaining shit away with the same script—"I tried to commit suicide, and my therapist convinced me to repair my relationship with her." I point to Lily.

"I'm sorry to hear that, I figured you were in a midlife crisis."

"You're not far off, actually," Lily retorts.

As annoying as they're being, I can't help but sit and take it. Today has been one of the few days that I actually have the willpower to get through it.Depression works in mysterious ways; it occasionally offers days that give you a glimpse of what happiness is like—like a prisoner getting his hour in the yard before heading back to his cell.

"Melody is more than a rebound," John says in a protec-tive tone that catches me off guard.

"Two days ago I couldn't watch a starving kids infomer-cial without losing it. I'm harmless."

"He's not lying. He's as harmful as a straight guy at a pride rally," Lily says, forever my protector, "Now, if we were talking about me ... that's a different story."

They laugh and share a fist bump, seeming to have quite the bond—similar to his relationship with Melody. John's demeanor puts me at ease.

"Where are you staying John?" I ask, eager to change the subject.

"I got a tent under an overpass on the Upper East Side. Actually, if I wanna get there before dark, I should be heading out."

"We have a suite at Berkshire. You'd have your own room, if you want."

"It's ok, just come back for checkers tomorrow," he says, before packing up and leaving.

I make a mental note to come back tomorrow; John's the only relationship in my life that isn't on the verge of disintegrating.

"Let's grab some dinner," Lily says, "I know a place that makes great fish tacos."

Before I can refuse, she grabs my hand a hails a cab.

* * *

Our cab driver drives just as bad as anyone in New York. He weaves between cars with little regard for anyone—including Lily and myself. Lily pays him no mind; she's focused on her phone, typing so furiously that it could pass for morse code. Because she's a poor and newly homeless grad student, I'll obviously be footing the bill—not that I'm complaining. I'll pay anything to feel how I do right now.

Alive.

Having my thoughts free, able to imagine the possibilities of the future instead of lingering on the regrets of the past, makes me feel hopeful that I'll find a stage of the grieving process that has a silver lining for me. I know that moment could be fleeting, but I promise myself I'll enjoy it.

The sun is setting, gleaming off the towering skyscrapers.; I've forgotten how beautiful a sunset can be. I find myself smiling, thinking of how—just yesterday—I was going to start a new season of House of Cards with some cajun food for company. Now, I'm reunited with my sister and on the path to normalcy. That path starts with Lily thumbing through the music collection in my phone. She winces, snorts, and frowns as she scrolls through the albums.

"You're situation is worse than you let on." There's a hint of disgust in her tone, "Posthumous Michael Jackson is blasphemy, little brother. I expected better from you."

Now, yesterdays version of Miles would have retorted with a well-timed barb about the pot calling kettle black in regards to disaster and her current life situation. At least on the surface, our individual situations leave no room for either of us to be critical. But this new, world conquering Miles silently agrees that no *real* Michael Jackson fan should have his post death releases in heavy rotation.

"You're gonna love this place, Miles," she gives me wink. I don't know how to interpret that, but it makes me uneasy. "You got cash on you?"

"Yeah," I reply. It's an odd request because, if I didn't, restaurants allow you to add a tip on the bill after you've paid.

"Perfect! Like I said, you're gonna love this place. The waitresses are the friendliest you'll ever meet."she says, her speech so fast it reminds me of the disclaimers at the end of radio commercials. There's something she isn't telling me. She only talks this fast when she's got something up her sleeve. Besides, there isn't a fish taco in the world worth driving like a stuntman for. "There's no way you don't like this place."

Alright, now I know something is off. She's an english major—one of the original grammar Nazis—so if she's using double negatives when she talks, something is up. We turn on to 6oth Ave. and find ourselves driving in one of those neighborhoods you seen in every documentary about New York. Pillars line the streets, holding up the tracks that make the streets rattle when trains roll through. The storefronts are similar to the ones in Queens, showcasing diversity of different languages on billboards and selling everything from iPads to deodorant. A few blocks ahead, a neon sign catches my eye.

As we get closer the light takes shape. It blinks and changes position each time, revealing itself to be the silhouette of a female leg going up and down. Under it the sign announces the name of the place is "Rouge." The building is made of painted cinder blocks, and faces of women with different hair colors stare seductively at us as the taxi comes to a stop in front.

"Lily, exactly what kind of fish taco place is this?"

"The kind where you ask them to hold the crabs," our driver interjects.

A behemoth of a man rushes from the door to open it for Lily.

"Let me help you, Ms. Lily." He takes her hand, helping her out of the car. His voice is much higher that I would expect for a man of his size.

"Thank you Clarence, it's been too long." She gives him a peck on the cheek.

"No way. No fucking way," I say, refusing to get out of the car, "Fish tacos?"

"You haven't even seen the menu yet Miles, and I promised you a good time."

Our driver jumps out of the back with the glee of a child on the first day of school. "If he doesn't wanna go Lily, just let him do him," he says.

"You haven't said two words the whole drive here, and now you wanna be a chatterbox," I say.

"He's been *doing* him. That's the problem." She mimics a masturbation posture.

"Of course, now I get it. The *get-over-something-by-getting-under-somebody* theory," I reply. "All these years in higher education, and you still resort to shit like this."

"At least come in and have a drink Miles." Lily heads toward the entrance with Clarence, "Nobody is forcing you to come in. But you haven't eaten and I know, at the very least, you're intrigued."

She has a devilish smile on her face—which should be every indication that I should get into the car and head straight to the hotel. A small voice in my head is screaming, *live a little*! Lily walks over and grabs my hand to lead me like a child going to timeout. This is becoming a recurring theme, and the jury is still out on whether I like it. The taxi pulls away before I can change my mind. I could follow Lily into the abyss, or I could hang out with Clarence and the ragtag gang of smokers strategizing how to make their money last through the night. I'll take my chances with the former.

Time to live a little.

EIGHT

SALLIE MAE YOU MADE MY DAY

IF YOU'VE EVER SEEN a rap video that's set in a strip club, it looks amazing. There's dollars flying through the air like confetti, a variety of women laid out like a buffet, and a general aura that's enticing. I'm sure it's really like this.

But not on a Wednesday.

On this day, it's more akin to a neighborhood diner during a slow period. Security leads us through velvet drapes into the main room, the dancers wear masks on their faces that give off a Mardi Gras vibe.

Picture the sex party from Kubrick's Eyes Wide Shut with a quarter of the budget.

"What's with the masks?"

"Some of the girls are Bowsers under the mask but they all have great bodies, so no girl gets left behind this way," Lily replies.

"So it's like equal opportunity employment, but for strippers?"

"More like Affirmative Action—leveling the playing field for those less fortunate—but yeah."

"What's a Bowser?"

"Huh?" She's distracted by a dancer that strolls by with a huge set of breasts.

"Focus Lily ... you said some girls were Bowsers under the mask, please explain."

"In Super Mario, there's the beautiful princess you cross the bridge for; well, some of these girls are the Bowser you have to jump over to get there."

"Shit, Lily, you can't be serious."

"I wish I was joking, little brother," she says as we continue our way through the club, "Imagine spending the money I have on what I thought was a beauty, only to end up with Hulk Hogan—mustache included."

In the middle is a stage with a pole extending to the roof. There's a worker, who I assumed just finished, wiping the pole down for whomever is next—at least they believe in a sanitary environment. One dancer appears almost out of thin air, like a State Farm agent, and leads us through the main floor to our booth.

You go get 'em buddy.

We're sat at a table next to the DJ booth and to the left of the stage. Three dancers pounce on us like piranhas sensing fresh chum in the water. Two of them know Lily and take a seat in her lap while the other nestles close to me.

Uncomfortably close.

She's wearing a red thong and nothing on top, with the exception of two hearts placed on her nipples. I know they're there to leave a *little* to the imagination, but it's not leaving much. There's a dragon tattoo on her thigh that runs down her leg and ends at the ankle, where her feet are clad in six inch heels that glow in the dark. Her shade of lipstick matches the red of her hair which makes me wonder if it's her natural hair color. She wouldn't tell me the truth if I asked her anyway. I'm wearing a shirt with the words,

"You're killing me, Smalls" across the front—so I'm an easy target. There's something different about her than the other dancers around us. She seems apprehensive, unsure of herself. If my livelihood consisted of selling a sexual fantasy to complete strangers, I would be a little apprehensive myself. "Hi, I'm Miles." I extend my hand.

"I'm Amy." She takes my hand in hers. No last name, just Amy. I've always been under the impression that dancers took there names from household spices and weather seasons. Amy is giving me the glance over, no doubt trying to ascertain if I'm worth her time. I'm trying to figure out what kind of conversation I want to have.

"So, is this your only job Amy?" I'm not sure what a conversation with a stripper is supposed to entail.

"Yeah, it's my second job while I pursue my Master's in nursing. Gotta pay the bills, ya know. Actually, tonight is my first solo shift."

This makes me think of an old comedy bit by Chris Rock about the myth of strippers needing to dance to get through school. Amy seems authentic though; this being her first night makes sense, giving how uncomfortable she looks with everything. The other dancers work with a sense of efficiency, evaluating every John (no pun intended) like a venture capitalist, wondering which investments will ultimately pay off. This could just be the game she's running, but I doubt it.

"So, you have a bachelors degree and are pursuing a masters, what lead you to a place like this?"

"Sallie Mae," she give me a sad smile. It brings humor to the proceedings but, like every joke, there's a cold truth at the root of it. She drops her head for a moment, like she's rethinking what got her to this point. .

In life, I feel we wear masks everyday. It could be a

mindset or a job but, for most, it's probably pride. We have the need to portray to the world that everything is 'okay'; that, whatever the world is judging us on, is merely a speed bump on a long journey. Some people are better at keeping the mask on than others, but every person has a moment in life where it slips off, even if it's just for a second—like right now—where the soul shines through and illuminates the vulnerability we all have as people.

My mask shattered when I tried to kill myself, and I'm trying to experience life without it for as long as I can.

Amy's mask fell off when she dropped her head. She's staring at the floor while biting her bottom lip, telling herself that this job, this moment with me—or any other male she encounters in this line of work—is just part of the journey. I know, because I had the same look the first time I stood at the door of Dr. Felt's office; it's the look of someone giving themselves a pep talk to keep fighting. That getting to the end of the rainbow is the real reward, not the pot of gold we subconsciously place there.

Business has started to pick up and the music has gotten louder. I slowly scoot closer to Amy, as if I'm approaching a caged animal. She looks down at my wrist.

"Were you in the hospital?" she asks, and I realize that I never took my hospital band off. I'd love to say it was kept as a reminder of what I've been through, but I really just forgot. Before I can answer, Lily interjects.

"He had an allergic reaction to a dick pill he bought at a gas station," Lily says giving her two stripper minions a good laugh and making Amy slide away from me. I lean closer to Amy so she can hear me over the booming bass.

"That's not true," I say loudly for the group to hear, "I actually tried to kill myself. But don't worry, the bills in my pocket are legit and I pose no threat to the safety of you or your coworkers."

They say the truth shall set you free but, judging by the horrified look on her face and her suddenly remembering she's needs backstage before scurrying away, I call bullshit.

"Congratulations little brother, in one sentence you probably made that poor girl switch career paths."

"Don't feel bad, you're probably only the fifth most creepy guy she'll get tonight," says one of the dancers in Lily's lap.

I can't even come in first place in a contest for perverts. Every time I think I've hit rock bottom, I bust through the floor again.

Lily orders drinks and tacos for us, and after they head off I try to take in sheer absurdity of the situation. As I survey the surroundings, a small flash of light catches my peripheral and I turn to see Lily holding her phone up to take a selfie. Actually, it's a Snapchat with the caption, "Look who's back from the dead" followed by three emojis that look like they're crying.

"Is that really necessary, Lily?"

"Given this reunion, it most certainly is", she says as she posts her video. "I see milquetoast Miles hasn't changed much, lighten up."

"Why are we here?"

"I turned both of them," she disregards my question.

"Both of them?"

"Not at the same time." She gives me a dirty smile, no doubt relishing the idea of such an accomplishment. "In strip clubs, consistency is the key. You show up consistently, give more of yourself, and they usually reciprocate. If you're lucky, you become more than a trick."

"Why is turning someone such a turn on for you?"

"Because, there's something arousing about watching them give in to something they've denied themselves for so long, like watching them evolve into their true selves." She's watching the dancers move from one patron to the next, like a lioness watching a herd of gazelle, waiting for the weak one to show itself.

"If you enjoy watching them evolve, why do you let them go so quickly?"

"Because, after it's over, they just don't seem as interesting anymore. They let the world force them to hide who they really are, and it makes me think that if they can't be honest with themselves about who they are, what else will they hide?"

"Do you still like guys too?"

"Nope. Can't deal with the unrealistic expectations of you boys," she says with disgust, "and the egos, my goodness."

"What do you mean the 'unrealistic expectations'?"

"You guys spend years watching porn and substitute that for intimacy, then you hump your little selves out on top of us and have the nerve to ask us if it was a fun experience. This isn't fucking *Best Buy*, there's no customer satisfaction survey. Besides, with women, it's a very intimate experience; actual kissing, more of a give and give situation instead of give and take."

"I've never thought about it that way," I tell her. Looking back, I've done that several times with Sara. Never once did I wonder how sex made her feel but, looking back, I could see how weird it would be. I get annoyed when customer surveys come on receipts, so I could see how irritating it'd be after sex.

One dancer approaches Lily and they exchange hugs. I immediately notice how different this interaction is, compared with the two that went off to fetch drinks.

"Harmony, I'd like you to meet my brother Miles."

I have no idea what her face looks like with the mask, not that her face should be the focus in the current environment. She nods to acknowledge me, then whispers something in Lily's ear before briskly heading towards the back.

"You turn her too, Lily?"

"I tried like a motherfucker, believe me, but she wasn't going for it," she cracks her knuckles. "She's the only one here that's not running game, and over time she's become more like a therapist."

"At least yours is hot, my therapist looks like Bea Arthur," I'm reminding of Dr. Felt explaining that we couldn't have sex. I envision her wearing a one piece like one of these dancers and I want to excuse myself, "I don't think I should be here Lily."

"You want to know why I really don't do the relationship thing?"

"Sure."

"It protects me from what you're dealing with right now. Having someone get close to you and then losing them is a battle I'm not prepared to fight—no offense."

"No offense taken."

My phone buzzes in my pocket, I glance down and my heart jumps seeing that it's Melody. I reread the name and double check the number to confirm that, yes, a woman texted me back.

Sorry I took so long to respond, my other job is crazy tonight.

I don't know how to respond, so I opt to take the nice

guy route.

It's ok, I understand.

I feel like an idiot as soon as I hit send, but soon after, three dots appear, and we're back at it.

What are you up to right now?

Shit. There's no way I can explain to her why I'm in a strip club without coming off like a pervert, but I also don't wanna lie. I decide to try both.

My sister lured me to a strip club under the pretense of fish tacos, so I'm trying to get out of it.

Somehow my explanation looks more idiotic in text that it sounds. Her response is empathetic.

I've been there. You should stay near the main stage if you can, dancers don't like that. I gotta go but come by the shop tomorrow, I'm working the morning shift.

I tell her I will and, afterward, I can only sit there stuck in a place between fear and excitement. I wanna celebrate with Lily but, when I look up, her face is shoved into a stripper's breasts so forcefully that her drink is spilling down her arm.

So much for celebrating.

The other dancers comes back with our drinks as the DJ announces over the loud speaker that Harmony will be coming to the stage next. Lily says I shouldn't miss it, but her tone is more of an order than a suggestion. The two dancers sit in her lap and take turns nibbling on her neck. I take both shots of vodka and feel them burn through my chest before settling warmly in my stomach.

"You're gonna be alright Miles, we'll talk about this later." I'm struck by her tone; on the surface it's an empathetic and caring sister committing to help her struggling brother. However, allow me to translate what she was really trying to say:

"I'm close to having the very threesome we just talked about, and your sour demeanor is killing the vibe. Please move the fuck away and we can continue this conversation at a more convenient time."

After taking another shot, I make my way toward the stage. There's roughly nine seats lining the stage and half of them are full. Mostly old guys ready to throw—what I assume is—social security money at Harmony.

The acoustic guitar of T-Pain's *I'm in Love with a Stripper* comes booming through the speaker as the lights dim throughout the place, and a pink, neon spotlight settles on the stage like an erotic 007 entrance. Harmony appears from the side of the stage, walking slowly to the pace of the bass intro. She knows the crowd is there for her and she plays to them. Turning her back and gyrating slowly while removing her lace top, she approaches the front of the stage, dragging her top seductively beside her.

As the auto tuned vocals begin she climbs to the top of the pole, eliciting whoops and hollers from the crowd as the dollars begin raining down like ashes. She times her summit to the top with a bass drop and splits her legs while spinning like a gymnast. She's got this song mastered like she wrote it herself. I find myself taking one of the seats lining the stage, mesmerized as she slides down the pole upside down, her legs wrapped around securely enough to regulate the speed of her descent. After landing on her palms she stays there, shaking her ass as the catcalls and hollers rises to the same decibel as the music. She walks slowly toward every guy in the front row, collecting every dollar, while rewarding each one with a full frontal view of her ass for their contribution.

She makes eye contact with me and drops to all fours, crawling slowly but deliberately—like a predator moving in on a kill. For a second, I swear I can feel the dollar bills start to crawl out of my jeans like they're being summoned by their true master. But it's just my subconscious unlocking the sexual instinct that has been dormant for so long. She whips her hair back in front of me and shakes her ass before curving her back to the ground, like a kitty when you run your hand from head to spine; it's not the kind of kitty I'm interested in at the moment.

She reaches over the stage and places her hands on the arms of my seat, and now we're face to face—or mask to face. I don't know who this woman is, but in this club it doesn't matter and that's the point. Harmony runs her face up my thigh, her nose tapping on different spots of my body, and soon I feel the plastic of the mask on my cheek.

"Hi, Miles," she whispers. But based on how quickly I'm pulling cash out of my pocket, she might've told me it was a holdup.

I volunteer my bill fold like a sinner that's been touched at his first church service, but she presses my hand with the cash back. "No thanks, first ones free." She runs her hand behind my ear for good measure and heads off stage.

I'm left next to the stage with an erection, a heavy buzz and, miraculously, the same amount of money as when she started her show. The lights on stage descend into darkness —a metaphor for how confused I am entering a this new stage of the grieving process.

NINE

YOU DON'T LOOK LIKE HULK HOGAN

LAST NIGHT WAS A MOVIE.

I heard some kid on the street tell another kid that; I assumed he meant it was *unforgettable*. That's what last night was, at least what I remember of it. I'll give you the rundown.

After Harmony left the stage, I found myself with nothing to do—which, in a strip club, is an oxymoron. I sat at a table alone and was approached by a dancer named Gloria, but I secretly named her Glue. Glue was short for glue factory, because that's where she was headed due to her being past her prime. I told her she reminded me of my mom, which was true. She found it funny, which made me find it funny, and I bought several lap dances from her. She used my version of Freud's *Oedipal Complex* theory—which is the one about having sex with your mother—and turned it into two hundred bucks. I'm remember thinking that maybe she wasn't past her prime. Nevertheless, grinding my erection on a woman that reminded me of my mother was enough for me to order another round of shots.

I stumbled back to our section and Lily asked me for

$300 so she could visit the "Champagne Room" with her two dancer friends. I was confused because they'd been more than happy to bring our drinks to the table. Maybe the champagne stains the carpet or something; either way, I acquiesced and they took off without saying thank you. I ended up sitting next to a random customer, and apparently a satisfied one because he's asleep with one hand in his pants. Don't judge him, the tacos were definitely heavy enough to give you *The Itis*. At some point, Harmony found me sitting alone and stopped to chat. I was determined to not make her a therapist like Lily did, but I failed.

I unloaded on her with everything I'd been dealing with; from losing my family all the way to Melody, I spilled my guts. Then I went to the bathroom to literally spill them before I returned to talk some more. I told her how I was conflicted about calling Melody because of my past, then she pointed out that I had talked more about Melody than Sara. Harmony said I was cute, unlike the other perverts that frequented the establishment. I thanked her, but I told her that it wasn't fair to Melody if I tried seeing someone else. She laughed.

"You really like this girl Melody?"

I nodded like a child in my drunken stupor.

"Well then, ask her out. She's waiting for you."

I asked her how much would it be to take her mask off, and she told me it was against the rules. She told me her shift was ending but that she'd be here tomorrow night, and I should stop by if I wasn't on a date. I handed her some money—maybe forty bucks, I'm not sure—and she left. Everything after that is a blur, I don't even remember getting back to the hotel.

Last night was a *movie*.

* * *

"I'm never drinking again," I say out loud to nobody in particular from the cold tile of the suite bathroom.

I try getting up but the darkness starts spinning and I have to sit back down, smashing my elbow in the process.

"Are you alright in there?" An unfamiliar female voice calls from outside the door. The door creeps opens and the silhouette of a woman fills the doorway. It reminds me of the old Batman comics when he'd appear out of the shadows before beating the piss out of a petty thief.

"Melody?"

The woman—who is *not* Melody—turns the light on and I cower underneath a towel hanging from the tub.

She turns the water on and rinses a towel in cold water before uncovering me and placing it over my face. The coolness helps stop the throbbing headache and, for the moment, my brain decides it's content with staying inside my skull. "You look like shit," she tells me. "Keep that there, it'll help with the headache."

"And you look unfamiliar," I reply, realizing my guardian angel is a stranger in my hotel room.

"My bad. I'm Nikki, Lily's friend from the club."

"Right, I didn't recognize you ..."

"I get that a lot without the mask," she interjects.

"I was gonna say with your clothes on.". Her short hair is mostly black with streaks of purple throughout. I notice her tongue is pierced as she's clicking it against her front teeth, causing just enough noise to make my head hurt again. Nikki has a goth chick vibe; I assume it's probably a hit with the johns that wanted to sleep with one in high school but were scared they'd get mocked or stabbed. "You don't look like Hulk Hogan."

"Fuck does that mean," she asks through clenched teeth.

"Nothing, where's Lily?"

"She's getting ready for class." She gets up and turns the water off, stopping to pose in front of the mirror, checking her hair, and clicking her tongue ring against her teeth again before leaving the room. "There's aspirin on your night-stand," she says on the way out.

I find the aspirin and take double the recommended dose because, in my mind, it should work twice as fast. I look out overCentral Park, the playgrounds and trails stand out like islands amongst the sea of trees. This view is incredible and I understand why people pay for it.

After brushing my teeth I stare at myself in the mirror. Harmony's last words linger.

She's waiting for you.

They play in my head, over and over, like the songs you hear while you're on hold with the cable company—the ones that stick in your head the rest of the day.

She's waiting for you.

"I know she's waiting, but am I ready? Maybe someone else asked her out in the last twenty-four hours and she decided he was the better option. Or she thinks I might be a serial killer and she turns me down after coming to her senses."

She's waiting for you.

"C'mon subconscious, can you let me play devil's advo-cate for a second? You had no problem letting me do that when I was ready to kill myself. You were more than happy to hold the elevator door open for us to go to hell together. Don't you dare forsake me now."

She's waiting for you.

"You know what? I'm gonna ask her out, not because you told me to, so wipe that smirk off your face. I'm doing it so, when she says no,—and she will say no—you'll have to shove it up your ass. Then you can watch me blow enough money on lap dances from Amy, that her books will be covered for the semester. I might even jump on stage and shake my ass for the crowd. All to watch you, my Benedict Arnold of a subconscious, have to admit that you were wrong."

"Miles, who the fuck are you talking to?" Lily asks from outside the door.

"Just thinking out loud," I reply. "Don't mind me."

"Whatever, when you and Benedict Arnold finish your vagina monologues, I'd like to have breakfast with you before I head to class."

"Got it, thanks."

"One more thing. I put your credit card in my Uber app, so don't call Capital One when you see the charges and we can settle up later," she says it like she isn't currently homeless and living with me.

When I get to the table, Lily is already there with a newspaper in on hand, glasses on the tip of her nose, and a cup of coffee in the other hand. She greets me with a naughty, knowing smile that makes my stomach churn—it might just be the alcohol though. "You look like shit," she says.

"I'm aware of that, pass the syrup."

It's the good kind of syrup, I conclude upon tipping the bottle. A thick, slow drip pours onto my french toast before piling up on the edges of my plate. "So can we go over last night?"

"What's there to go over?"

"Well, at one point, your face was so far inside an ass that you could've been passed for being in a pie eating contest."

"Oh, you mean Gloria," she says, like Gloria is an old friend. "Great gal, amazing life story. She oughta be a writer."

Even her name was old. "She oughta be collecting a social security check."

She laughs, banging her hand against the table causing the silverware to rattle—now my head starts hurting again. "I saw you get a dance from her. Hell, I thought she was gonna jump your bones."

"That's the vibe you got?"

I don't know how she got that vibe. Gloria had a maternal presence, like she's the mother hen of the dancers; giving out advice to the younger girls, carrying IcyHot in her purse for the ones with joint pain. Wouldn't surprise me if she could skirt the IRS on her taxes, she did everything but write me a check for my birthday.

"Look, I know what I saw," she says. She takes a long sip of her coffee, moving her cheeks as if trying to root out bread wedged between them, "Not that I'd blame you, her ass feels like it's about half her age."

With that, my appetite for breakfast disappears. I'm stalling because I know what's on the agenda this morning. Lily knows too because she's studying my every movement, waiting for an in. I switch gears before she can get the chance.

"You gonna go back to your apartment?"

"Are you trying to get rid of me?"

"No."

We stare at each other for awhile. "Melody," I say. Lily nods and smiles, ever the master deal maker, "So I take Melody on a date, and you'll consider finding a stable living arrangement?"

"Not just a date. You have to pursue her."

"Why do you care so much?"

"Because you're a good person that deserves happiness. And after watching you last night, you ain't cut out for the single life."

Which is why I tried to kill myself, I think. At least I know my plan of suicide was a sound one. Suddenly an idea hits me fiercely, like it's been there all along. "You know what? I'll match you. Any plan you come up with, I'll go in with you."

"You don't have to do that."

"You really wanna call mom for the money?"

"Good point."

"That's the deal; if I have to grow, so do you."

She mulls this over while pouring syrup on her pancakes in slow circles, syrup oozing down the sides while she mutters incoherently to herself.

"I need a cigarette," she says. "Come join me."

* * *

The cigarette was a ploy to get me out of the hotel, and unfortunately, I don't realize this until we're standing in front of the coffee shop. Lily knew I'd chicken out if we stayed in the hotel room, so the sly devil decided to use the element of surprise. Well played ma'am. The residual effects of the alcohol mixes with the nerves, and now I can't decide if I'm having an anxiety attack or if I have to shit. Lily practically struts to John at his customary table out front, where he greets us like old friends.

"I'll have a large cup of coffee, black. Anything for you, John?," she asks, clearly pleased that her budding career as cupid is rolling along.

"You're a special kind of asshole, Lily."

"Well, if you uphold your end of the bargain, I'll be an asshole tenant." She lights a cigarette, takes a long drag, and waves toward the door. "Your muse awaits."

Having siblings is overrated.

Inside the coffee shop, my anxiety ratchets up another level. There's a group of elderly folks bickering about something, but it's all white noise. All I can hear is my heartbeat pounding like a tribal drum in my chest. Melody is cleaning the bar, oblivious to my presence, presumably still single, and waiting for my phone call. I take mercy on her by heading to the bathroom, letting her enjoy whatever beautiful existence she has left before I wreck it all. My stomach bubbles like a cauldron, and I briefly consider pulling the fire alarm to get out of this situation. I could head out the back, jump in a taxi, and head straight to the airport.

This should be a simple in and out conversation with an order of coffee throw in. She gave me her number for Christ's sake. When I first asked Sara out, I did it through text and even then I wasn't direct.

Passive-aggressive people—like me—are the worst. Instead of telling you how we feel, we throw subtle hints and always leave ourselves an out, never truly taking any risks. It's the human equivalent of eating the crust of the bread but throwing the rest away. That's the life we live; unwilling spectators that hope shit works out for the best.

Back in the cafe, Melody is serving an elderly woman coffee. She notices me and gives me a smile, acknowledging my presence without interrupting her conversation. I wait patiently behind the customer, watching as Melody listens intently to whatever she's saying before finally nodding, giving the cue that the conversation is about to end.

"She was ... interesting," I say.

"Mrs. Colten writes erotic poetry." She looks at me with a frown, "You look like you had a hell of a night."

"You don't know the half of it." I realize two things in quick succession: one, I'm wearing the same clothes from last night, including the navy cargo shorts that are glowing bronze from the multiple lap dances; and two— and most important—my anxiety has subsided and I'm gonna ask her out.

"I bet I know the half of it." She gives me a smile that makes me wonder if she really does know.

"I was wondering, actually hoping that possibly ..." I trail off, realizing I sound like I'm short circuiting.

"I'll go out with you," she interjects. "Monday is my day off here, and I don't work my other job until later. Let's meet in Central Park, near the food trucks."

When we settle the details, I'm saved from further embarrassing myself by a large group of people. As I retreat to the door she calls my name.

"I'm glad you came. I can't wait for Monday."

"Me too."

TEN

TURBULENCE

I TRIED to take my mind off of my impending date with Melody by helping Lily look for an apartment. The idea of me moving in with her was floated, and she kind of ran with it before I could shut it down. Now it's time for me to hold up my end of the bargain. It almost feels like a graduation, a moment of reintroduction to the world.

As my date with Melody approaches, I wonder how people get through first dates?

I ponder this question from a rickety bench at the base of Central Park, its stability as fraught as my nerves. I haven't been on a first date since I met Sara. Since that relationship was going swell, I didn't keep myself up to date on what to expect—you know, since marriage is forever. Back when I worked retail, I had a manager that always talked about "accentuating the positive."; don't dwell on the short-comings of our product against the competition, just show-case the good. It was his way of telling us to shine shit and call it gold, worded to protect himself from HR. But he may have been on to something.

First dates are exactly that, a delicate showcase of positives that sometimes border on fraud; an event where emotional instability passes as quirky, or anger is repackaged as passion. The truth is always just below the surface, but in our quest for a genuine connection, we throw caution to the wind. Like a gambler believing that the next roll of the dice will hit the jackpot, we gamble on people and hope we hit a winner. Sometimes you do find your soul mate in that quirky girl, other times you end up with a junkie that ransacks your apartment while you're showering after sex.

My struggle is if I should tell Melody about my past or not. I was on the fence, so I took it to my tribunal of Lily and John. To say they had differing opinions would be a massive understatement.

The eternally wise John was all for spilling my guts. He argued that Melody was an open-minded gal that wouldn't judge a soul, and that it would serve as a solid foundation to whatever we were going to be. He also threw in some philosophical shit, but I was too hungover, and I tuned him out because my ears were processing his words in the voice of Charlie Brown's teacher. But he meant well and his view was rightfully considered.

Lily's opinion was on the opposite side of the fence. She didn't really make an argument, she just asked me if I was "out of my fucking mind" before heading off to class. She likes to ask that question, which makes you wonder if you've really lost it, eventually leading you to agree with her point of view. Simple but nevertheless effective.

I'm trending toward Lily's side of the fence. I can't think of any scenario where you drop that kind of information on a first date and expect something to develop. You can't bomb the foundation of a structure and expect to build something stable.

A beep emanates from a cross walk, drawing my eyes to

the crowd of people shuffling like a herd of cattle across the street. As the speed walkers separate from the plodding, Melody appears. She's let her hair down, her curls flowing beautifully, and for a second it's almost like seeing her for the first time. Her black leggings fit so flawlessly that I can already tell it's gonna be a struggle to not look down. *God damned hormones.* The track jacket she's wearing is just as snug. Zipped halfway up, it's still showing enough that the guys walking in front of her turn around like they forgot something. Christ, men are such dogs. She's so stunning, it makes me want to hide behind the bench and just so I can watch her; not because I'm a weirdo, but because she doesn't know my story and I don't know hers, so right now we're at the top of the roller coaster.

When you meet a person you're interested in, the version of them in your mind is perfect—almost godlike. We only know what we see, and anything after that brings them down a peg. In other words, they become human. At that point, you start to tally their negatives and figure out if you can tolerate them and for how long. That's all love is, finding a flawed person you can live with.

From the second she hits the sidewalk, her eyes begin searching. It hits me that it's me she's looking for, not one of the many Wall Street types that I'm sure shoot their shot every morning. Fuck them. This must be what it feels like to bypass the line to get into the nightclub, and I'm determined to hold onto this feeling for as long as I can.

Another aspect of first dates that trip me out, is the greetings and general movement.

Do I go in for a hug?

Is holding hands considered moving too fast?

What if it's not a date and she's running one of the network marketing pyramid schemes?

I've had that happen to a friend before. Right after he paid for her coffee, she asked him if he was interested in making more disposable income. Poor guy, Rich was his name, was too nice and sat through her whole presentation. He even took her brochures when he left.

I don't have time to figure it out. She spots me and her face lights up. It reminds me of how my daughter would light up when I'd get home from work. Knowing that your presence holds value to people is powerful.

"Hey Miles," she looks me over, "you're looking better than the last time I saw you." She gives me a hug and I hold on for a long moment, and maybe even a little too tightly. Her scent teases all of my senses, and the intimacy that I'd been missing for so long feels surreal in this moment. For the record, I'm wearing Captain America T-shirt layered on top of a long sleeved shirt—to cover the hospital band I keep forgetting to remove—and cargo shorts. It's not exactly Met Gala worthy, but it's better than this morning's ensemble of sweaty novelty shirt and stripper glitter stained jeans.

"I try to clean up for appearances sake."

"Well, you did a great job. So, what's the plan?"

In all the excitement, I never actually thought of what we'd do on our date; I was just happy she agreed. But now she's staring at me, her light brown eyes piercing a hole through my soul. "We can go for coffee. I mean, I know you work in a coffee shop, so I understand if you don't wanna do that ..." I offer, realizing that the idea was even dumber out loud than it was in my head.

"How about a bike ride? We can ride and chat. Plus, I can show you some cool spots on the waterfront and we can figure out the rest later." We both look up at the clouds moving in. Sensing my apprehension, she grabs my hand, "C'mon, it'll be fun. I promise I won't bite."

She leads me to the commuter bike station and shows me how to unlock a bike. She starts off ahead of me, working to convince me that this isn't as crazy as it sounds—or as dangerous. I'd follow her anywhere, but saying this out loud would make me sound like a creeper.

I can see the waterfront from a distance, but I'm not sure I'll make it because after one block my hamstrings feel like they're on a rotisserie. I catch up to Melody, who's gliding along smoothly and paying no mind to the fact that one errant turn by a car could send her to the hospital. Her hair is whipping in the wind, flowing as freely as her spirit.

"A bike ride is an interesting first date," I say to kick off the conversation.

"Who said it's a date?" She lets her comment hang in the air, like a record scratching to a stop. "I'm kidding Miles, I wouldn't have said yes to going out in this weather if it wasn't a date."

Now that I've established that I am—in fact—on a date, the hormonal male in me takes over and I wonder if we might actually have sex. I feel bad for even thinking about it, but I remind myself that it's natural.

"So, what brings you to the city?" she asks.

"I'd kinda lost my way in life, so I came here to work through my relationship with my sister."

She chews on this for a second, "And where does John factor into all this?"

"He was part of the live audience that witnessed me stepping in dog shit in front of your job."

Conversation comes easy with Melody. Her laid back vibe puts me at ease like Dr. Felt. There's something about her, like she can sense bullshit, so it's not worth trying to hide it. "Alright, my turn. Why did you give me your number?"

The question throws her off. When we get to the water at end of the long avenue, instead of continuing on to the clearly marked trail, we stop. She stares out at the water, pondering my question. The quick-wit has vanishes just as swiftly as the waves do after smashing into the pier. In the distance, I can see the Brooklyn bridge towering above the water between the two parts of the city it connects, a perfect metaphor for our relationship. Two people with a clear attraction to one another just working on a way to make it connect. "You just seemed different than the other guys that come into my shop," she finally answers.

"I feel the same way when I'm buying shampoo. One feels different than the others and I just go for it."

She chuckles and wipes the sweat from her brow, "See, that's what I'm talking about. There's more to you than you let on. Five minutes ago I wondered if you might be developmentally disabled, and now you're cracking jokes and letting your true self show."

"It takes me awhile to warm up to people."

"Well, a little advice, make sure you're preheated before the date starts."

"Noted."

"I'll tell you the real reason I gave you my number, but you gotta promise that you won't mock me."

I'm a twenty-seven year old widower that masturbated himself into an anxiety attack this morning, I'm not exactly in a position to mock anyone. But she doesn't know this, so I agree to her terms.

"Ok ... the universe told me to." She scans my face for any sign of me breaking my vow. "Weird right?"

If I made of list of reasons why Melody chose me among —what I assume were—many other suitors, I could fill ten notebooks and the universe wouldn't make any of them. It's an odd reason but she seems sincere. And, in a weird way, it sounds interesting.

"Not gonna lie, I wasn't expecting that," I tell her. "I've never had someone ask me out because they were told to, maybe you could elaborate on that?"

"I take my cues from the universe," she starts, "I find that too often we focus on trying to control the world around us, so one day I gave up control and decided to listen. You'd be surprised what you find out about yourself."

"I don't mean any disrespect, but I can see a million ways that could go wrong."

"I'm not an idiot about it, but I truly believe that sometimes we miss out on great things because we talk ourselves out of it."

That made my stomach flip. "You think I'm something great?"

"You're getting there."

"What does it feel like?" I hesitate, trying to word it right. "I mean, what tells you that it's ..."

"Time to enter the universe?"

"Yeah."

"Well, first off, thanks for asking. You passed your first test," she laughs. "You know that feeling you get when you're about to have sex? Remember, I'm talking about before, so there's no preconceived notions only possibilities. When your blood is pulsing through you, your breaths become shorter and more controlled."

She puts her bike down and moves toward me, gently placing one hand on my chest and the other behind my neck, massaging my shoulders. I'm in the biggest city in the world and it feels like I'm running out of oxygen.

"It's alright, just relax," she says softly. "Allow yourself to be in the moment, feel it out. Now, take a deep breath." I oblige, inhaling deeply. "Ok, hold it ... and release. Open your eyes."

I find her inches from my face, her eyes locked on mine. "How do you feel?" she whispers.

"I feel ... strange."

"That's how you're supposed to feel. Now, do what comes to your mind first. Don't overthink it."

My hands find her hips like it's the most natural thing in the world, like it was part of the plan all along. I start to gradually move them down her hips but stop myself. Even though I want to go on, I'm scared of her reaction.

She rubs her hand over my heart as it pounds furiously inside my chest. She looks me in the the eye and smiles, caressing my face with the back of her free hand. "*That's* what it feels like."

I pull away and offer her a smirk, hopefully conveying confidence; it's also an invitation to a cat and mouse game for her to discover who I really am. She smiles back willing to play the game, no matter the odds. The moment between us is left hanging like a dinner tab between two frugal friends at an expensive restaurant. She heads off to the restroom, and if she never came back, I wouldn't blame her.

John and Lily swore that it was only a date and nothing more. I know I'm an over thinker, but this is definitely more, and the gravity of it scares me. In reality, I need time to work through my feelings and reconcile everything. If I'm smart, I can hold onto Melody while I figure myself out. One thing is for sure: My life is about to get complicated.

Melody seems to understand this will be a process, but apparently she's game because she actually comes back from the bathroom. Instead of asking me if I'm an idiot, she grabs her bike and asks me if I'm ready to go. We ride for a bit before we get back to our conversation.

"So," I begin, "how does a single girl manage to live in New York City."

"Stripping," she shrugs, and I laugh at her joke.

"I was at a strip club a couple nights ago, you don't seem like the type."

"Oh yeah?"

"They're all running some game, except for one that was a little mysterious. I actually thought she was hitting on me, but then she told me I should call you. It was definitely one of the weirdest conversations I've ever had."

"Really, why do you think she said that?" she sounds intrigued.

"Apparently, in my drunken state, I kept going on and on about you."

She gives me a smile, "You were thinking about me."

"Yeah, and then Lily agreed to look into a permanent living arrangement if I asked you out, so my hands were tied." We both laugh. She tells me there's a vintage record shop not far from us, and we agree to change course.

"This stripper, what do you remember about her?"

"Let's see ..." I rack my brain, trying to remember what I can, "not much. She danced great to T-Pain, wouldn't accept my money until I practically forced her to, and she knew my sister pretty well. They all wore masks so there's not much to remember, features-wise at least."

"I think we were meant to meet Miles, it was destiny."

I'm offended for a second because all I heard was, "your wife and children had to die for me to come into your life." But, I know that's not what she meant.

"I agree. The French roast from Tanzania called out to me like it never had that morning."

"No, I mean it's like the universe wanted us to meet."

"You believe that?"

"I do, actually. Think about it. You could've stopped at a Starbucks because, let's be frank, all coffee tastes the same; but, something made you step in dog shit that morning. Trust me, *all* the pieces matter."

We roll through an underpass where we decide to take a break. To my surprise, there's an outdoor gym tucked beneath it and two basketball courts—one holding a spirited game. Merchants line both courts, selling hats and knockoff sunglasses. It's another beautiful layer in this complex city.

"This city amazes me. Every time I think I've got it figured out, it reveals a new part of itself," I say.

"Kinda reminds me of you. If you decide to stick around, maybe I can show you more of the city."

"I'd like that."

"Me too."

We sit for awhile, resting and watching the games, each one more competitive than the last. Melody grabs my hand and rests her head on my shoulder, telling me again that she's happy I called. For the moment, my world feels whole again. My phones buzzes in my pocket. When I glance down at it, I'm surprised to see that it's a call from my mother. I press ignore.

Not today Satan.

* * *

When I get back to the hotel, I find Lily lounging in a sports bra and pajama pants, looking so comfortable that you'd think she actually lived here. I was hoping she'd be asleep so I could sit in silence and mentally agonize over the first date —like men do.

"Hey, Hey," she says a little too excited, in my opinion. She jumps off the couch and approaches me with open arms, before bending down and taking a whiff of my crotch. "Well, we all can't be so lucky."

"There's something wrong with you. Literally, you're not right in the head."

"You had a pretty girl give you her number—basically offering her ass on a silver platter—you couldn't close the deal, and something is wrong with me?"

"Every date doesn't have to end in sex," I reply, sounding like a guy that got shot down and is trying to save face. But before I can expand on that, Lily pounces.

"I forgot, I'm talking to Mr. Monogamy over here. Why —" she catches herself, giving me a frustrated sigh before relenting. "In the spirit of our rekindled relationship, I'll let you live with this one."

"You're so considerate."

"Did you tell her about your ... situation?"

I hesitate longer than I should and Lily pounces again, "Dude, you didn't tell her?"

Now, I thought my train of thinking was sound. My 'situation' isn't something you just spring on a first date. It's creepy and will likely end up an answer in a drinking game that her friends play when the topic is 'weirdest first dates.' That isn't to say I feel comfortable leaving it out—because I don't— but it's a lot to digest, even for someone as caring and free spirited as Melody.

"There wasn't a right time, Lily."

"I'd love to hear your idea of when the right time would be," she says. "Now me, I'd wait until after we have sex and use it as an escape hatch. But that's not your style, Miles. You're more the wait until the last moment, have it fuck up all your hard work type of guy." She laughs at this observation, and so do I—because it's true. "Remember when you had two homecoming dates?"

"Most bittersweet night of my life," I reply.

Junior year Homecoming will go down as the moment I knew Lily and I would always operate on different planes. My date, Ashley, wasn't my girlfriend but it was trending in that direction, and I was hoping that Homecoming would seal the deal. Only problem was that my Mother couldn't stand Ashley, feeling that she wasn't worthy of being on our fireplace mantel, where she kept all of our pictures. So, Lily set me up with one of her friends to be the "photo date." I ended up spending, what should've been, one of the greatest nights of my life running back and forth between dates—like something you'd see in a sitcom, with my sister and her friends providing the studio audience laughs. Lily watched from the sidelines, finding amusement in my inability to find a middle ground. Ashley eventually got hip to the game, cursed me out, and never talked to me again. I tried years later to befriend her on Facebook, but she declined it and changed her security settings so I couldn't resend it.

"It was like watching a cartoon, Miles," she says. "But that's who you are, the guy who wants to make everyone happy in the situations that require a winner and a loser." She checks her watch, smirks, and continues. "But that's a topic we don't have time for. So, what happened on your date? Did you at least *think* about having sex with her?"

I'm not gonna act like I didn't think about having sex with her, and I'd be lying if I said I would've turned it down. But there are too many moving parts in my life right now, and having sex on the first date would only add to my stress. I tell Lily every detail of the date, wanting to get a female perspective. She makes jokes at the beginning, but by the end of the story she's stone-faced and peppering me with thoughtful questions, making a genuine attempt to help me.

She stops me when I tell her about the moment by the water.

"Did you kiss her?"

"Um, no." She gives me a look of amazement, and not the good kind. More of a "how-the-fuck-did-you-make-it-this-far-in-life" kind of amazement. "I didn't think she wanted me to. She was just trying to demonstrate something."

"Yeah, how she likes to be touched."

It's not surprising that a moment of physical touch is the one she chooses to focus on, in fact, I'd be shocked if she didn't. "Look, I've been out of the game awhile. I apologize if I'm not an expert in romantic cues."

"You play things too safe, always have."

There's a knock at the door and Lily perks up. "Were you expecting room service?" I ask.

"Something like that," she says with an evil smile. "More like a ... study date." She answers the door, and I can hear her exchanging pleasantries with a female. She returns with a girl that looks familiar, but I can't place her. Her hair is short, she's wearing wire rimmed glasses with no lenses, and a full on denim ensemble. If you closed your eyes, she'd be the type of girl you'd see on a subway billboard promoting diversity. I glance at her backpack and would assume it's a study date, but I know better. After a brief shut down—and by "brief," I mean about thirty six hours—Club Lily has relocated and is back in business. "Justine, meet my brother Miles." Lily is behind her, rubbing her hands while looking her up and down.

"Hi," Justine says nervously.

I wanna tell Justine to run and to thank me later. That the subject of the tonight's study session has been changed to anatomy, more specifically her own, and once it's over—

after reality sinks in and the hormones level out—she'll be left alone to pick up the pieces of her psyche. But, all I can manage is a smile and a nod. Lily tells her where the room is and that she'll be along shortly. Once Justine is out of sight, Lily moonwalks to the bar, "Been trying to link that shit for a month," she says. "It's going down tonight little brother."

"Can we just finish our conversation?"

Lily nods, "Look, I'm not gonna lie to you, that universe thing sounds like a crock of shit."

"All I'm looking for is honesty."

"Alright. It sounds like she was trying to get fucked, but she didn't want you to judge her, so she tried tricking you into making the first move."

Wasn't expecting that one. "Can you, for once, act like human connection is a real thing? Go ahead, give it a shot."

"You've been out the dating game too long, Miles. Human connection is a '90s concept that's only adhered to by Evangelicals and the Amish. Access is the name of the game, and right now she's swiping right on some guy named Kyle, who has a little dick and a lifted truck. Now, he's gonna come over and cash in on your ignorance. Congratulations, you've done your good deed for the day."

I'm confused, wondering how many Kyles I know and what they drive. But I quickly give up. "Swiping right? What the hell are you talking about?"

She pulls out her phone and shows me an app called 'Tinder,' explaining how people are matched and swipe left or right depending on their attraction to the person. I can understand why Lily has it on her phone, the easy access with minimal interaction is too enticing to resist. We often laud technological advancements, but never acknowledge that *everything* evolves—this includes the dating world. No more buying drinks, having conversation, learning about each other as people, and building a connection. Just a cursory glance at cropped photos with more filters than a pack of Camels, and the decision to proceed is made with the swipe of a finger. "Ten times the ass, with ten percent of the work," she adds. "It's the world we always dreamed of." I neglect to point out that was the dream of horny high school kids who should have matured enough to cultivate healthy relationships.

This is the world I'm entering—a decade behind everyone else—like I've been released from the penitentiary, trying to learn on the fly but feeling more helpless by the second. I should sell my possessions and live abroad on the fringes of society.

I don't know why I thought Lily would be any different after all these years. Maybe I thought going off to college and living outside the bubble our parents kept us in would change her outlook on life. But Mom's financing her education, so I'm starting to think she never left the bubble long enough to figure it out. Lily loves being the center of attention, and, when you combine that with her short attention span, it creates a toxic cloud that poisons those closest to her.

"So, you've had your date?"

"Yes."

"And you wanna see her again?"

"Yup."

"Then, what's next?"

"I'm gonna text her and see if she wants to go out again," I say, confident that I have the right answer.

Lily frowns, "That's the stupidest shit you could do. You're supposed to wait until she hits you up first."

"This isn't the third grade, Lily. You don't just ignore the girl—"

She stands up, interrupting me. "Show of hands, who

here actually has a vagina?" she mocking me, looking around to survey an imaginary crowd. "Anybody, anybody?" Lily throws up her hand, "Oh my god, that's me! I'm the one with a vagina."

"Just out of curiosity, did you become a relationship expert before or after your ex threw your shit out of the apartment? Asking for a friend."

"Grief has brought out an edgier side of you, I like it. The domesticated Miles would've taken that one on the chin." She pours a shot and slides it across the table, "You know what the difference between us is?"

"About $1500 in co-pays at the clinic." I take the shot of alcohol, and it's the good shit—stiff but smooth, complements of the hotel.

"Ha! That's good, let that repressed, sexual energy out. But no. You fight the current, expecting everything to stay the same. I'd rather ride the wave and find my little slice of paradise within it."

"I know you love philosophy, but dumb that shit down."

She sighs deeply, frustrated with the conversation and the time it's taking away from Justine. "You believe in loving one person; and it's cute, but it's also pathetic. But the world around you doesn't see it the same way, and I'm scared for you—"

"I'll—"

"Let me finish. You're looking for forever, and I hope you find it, I really do. But you're doing it in a world full of people looking for what's next, and that'll only make everything worse when you realize that what you're looking for doesn't exist anymore." She puts the shot glasses away and opens the mini fridge. "You spent years trying to be the perfect family man. Maybe you should, I dunno, use this time to indulge in things you've missed out on."

"Such as?"

"Have unprotected sex with questionable partners, run into a bathroom stall at 2:00 a.m., swear to give up your promiscuous ways in exchange for dodging an STD. I don't know ... the sky is the limit." She fills a bucket with ice and examines each glass, eventually finding two that meet her criteria. "Think of it like this, you've been going to McDonalds your whole life, only eating the fish sandwich. It's a solid sandwich, fills you up, but now there's the McRib. It's a different flavor than you're used to, but it's new and exciting, so you order it a couple of times to see if you like it. There's no worries because your trusty fish sandwich is waiting for you when it's over. You can literally have your cake and eat it too. Just don't catch feelings."

I pour myself a shot of patron, and I can feel my confidence level rising as the liquid goes down. "One minute you're scared for me, the next minute I'm eating fish sandwiches in herpes infested bathrooms. I'm supposed to ignore her, but in the next sentence I'm supposed to have sex with her. I'm not understanding why you're so scared for me. I mean, if it all goes to shit, I'm the one that'll have to live with it."

"But that's where you're wrong, at least partially." She glares at me, and it might be the shots clouding my judgement, but she seems emotional. I'd come barreling back into her life, and I can feel whatever bitterness she held towards me melting away by the minute as she slips back into the role of protector. "I'm not scared of you having feelings for her," she says, recognizing she's in uncharted waters. "I'm scared of what's going to happen if she doesn't have feelings for you."

"It wouldn't be the first time the world let me down."

"The last time the world let you down, you swallowed a

bottle of pills. And even though I wasn't involved in your life, hearing about it damn near broke me. If it goes bad this time, when you have nothing to lose..." she trails off, the unspoken words understood.

"I'm not the same person I was, Lily. I need you to know I can handle whatever is out there."

"You might be right, but I've broken plenty of girls that held the same sunny disposition as you. At the end of the day, she's nothing more than a distraction. I've had several of them, and they're fun as long as you check you feelings at the door." She grabs a bottle of champagne and the two glasses. "I mean, don't you think you've suffered enough already?"

With that, she saunters away, clanking the champagne glasses and muttering the beginning of Craig Mack's 'Flava in Ya Ear.' "Get some rest, we have apartments to check out tomorrow."

The door to her room closes and I sit for awhile. Thoughts of the date are replaced by Lily's observations, which are sound, but hint at something that's always been a problem in our relationship.

Jealousy.

She won't say it, if only to deny me the satisfaction, but Melody is a threat to her. This trip started with her being the main attraction, but a surprise guest star appeared and is stealing the show. Any advice Lily gives has to be viewed through that lens; because with Lily, there's no straddling the fence, no understanding that there's enough love to go around. In some ways, it makes me happy that she never met Sara, sparing me the awkward rivalry that would've developed between them. I've been on one date and Lily has already drawn her line in the sand by labeling her a 'distraction.' And yet, it's my fault because I strangely enjoy having the women in my life jockey for position. I enable the behavior because it soothes my fears of being abandoned, watching those closest to you inflate your worth by going at each other.

After awhile, the laughs in Lily's room become softer, replaced by the rising volume of music, and I know it's my cue to head to my room. My first instinct is to call Dr. Felt, but I'm trying to learn to get through life without her, so I'm on my own. Lily's fear is understandable, as I haven't been the most stable person these last few months. But if it doesn't work out, I have the ultimate wild card—flying back home and starting over again. I have the ultimate license to live life on my own terms.

The anxiety returns the second I hit the bed, it's intensity is matched by it's ability to cripple my thoughts. The pendulum of it swings so wildly, I struggle to keep up.

Did I talk enough? Surely I did, right? The beginning was a little rocky, but I felt we got over that pretty smoothly, enough that she put her hands on my chest and violated my personal space.

Or maybe I talked too much? Now that I think about it, letting her talk should've been the play. But no, I had to talk her right into a bathroom break. Only reason she came back was to avoid the fees for not returning the bike. I'll die believing that.

She wanted me to kiss her. What if Lily was right? She wanted me to kiss her, and I ruined her confidence trying to be the nice guy.

Easy there, you're not George Clooney. Right, my bad.

My phone buzzes on the dresser. It's a text from Melody:

Got a quick break from work, just wanted to tell you that

I had a great time today. I'm at the shop in the morning, come through if I didn't scare you away :-)

My stomach lurches as I read it multiple times, confirming that it went well enough that she wants to see me again. I confirm that I'll stop by in the morning. I try to punctuate my response with an emoji of my own, but none fit the context. With my anxiety under control, I set an alarm early enough to allow me some time at the coffee shop before my appointment with Lily.

After channel surfing for a bit, I fall asleep to a Seinfeld rerun—it's laugh track is the perfect audience for my personal life.

ELEVEN

SESSION 2: HONOR THY MOTHER

I've always believed that most anxieties in life come from not knowing, from not knowing when you're going to die or the meaning of life, to not knowing if you're doing the thing you're meant to do or if you're gonna get laid off. As people, we have a desire to *know*—which is why The Sopranos ending still grinds people. But, life doesn't work that way. It's never black and white, and most of the time we straddle the grey area, so deep in our anxiety that we miss everything. By the time you realize what you've missed, time has slipped away and you make do with the remnants. It's similar to being the last person to the punch bowl, its watered down contents give just enough to let you know what you've missed. That's when depression rears its lovely, little head.

The flip side is, of course, *knowing*. As I sit in Dr. Felt's office, the carpet somehow shaggier than last week, I wonder if knowing was worth it. Today is session two and we're covering my parents. Knowing this was coming has made the last week hell. I haven't tried to kill myself again, so that's good, but every time I would have a moment of clarity or experience happiness, I'd think of this session and my mouth would go dry. When I left for college, I swore that I'd never go back home. I would endure everything life would throw at me, and bury all the feelings I had—like an emotional time capsule. Eventually, I'd have my mid-life crisis and have to confront it. Before Sara and the kids died, I figured I had until the kids went off to college at the very least. But now, I sit in this time warp of a house, ready to dig up memories that were lying peacefully dormant, all in the name of mental health.

Dr. Felt is showing her Duke affiliation this week with a national championship shirt, Duke sweats, and blue and white Nike trainers. She's more casual than the last session and, at this rate, she'll be damn near naked by our last session. But my hundred bucks doesn't cover that. She takes a seat and, for a while, we just sit; me, not knowing where to begin, and her with her notepad in hand, ready to dive into my subconscious.

"So, how was your week Miles?"

Simple question for the start, and I like it. If she does one thing well, it's understanding that going into a client's past is a delicate exercise. "It was good. Started a show called Game of Thrones, and ate a little bit healthier than last week, also didn't try to kill myself again—so that was a win."

She laughs at this but doesn't write it down in her trusty notepad. I wonder if I get to read the notes at the end—like a game show where you get to see if your answers square up with theirs.

"You're a funny guy."

"I'm really not."

"I disagree, you've kept your sense of humor through all that's happened to you."

"Depressed people tell better jokes."

"And why is that?"

"Because the world is already shit, and people not finding us funny won't make it any shittier," I say, wondering if this is some warm up exercise designed to butter me up. If this were a date or lunch with a friend, it'd be cute. But, it's hard to discern what's real and what's part of the session.

"What did you think of Thrones?"

"It's the perfect model of how society works. Little boy climbs window, catches brother banging his sister, and he's pushed out the window like he's the problem?"

"Oh, it gets better," she replies with a grin, and for a second I get a glimpse of Sandra instead of Dr. Felt. "But you're correct, and I'd advise you to not get connected to any of the characters. That's all I'll say."

"I can't even connect to people in my real life, how the hell could I connect with one in a fantasy world?"

"Point taken."

"So, where do we start today Doc?"

If there's one thing Ive been excited for, it's this moment. I'm no longer the new client, so I don't expect her to handle me with kid gloves. But I'm interested in how she plans on transitioning into talking about my mother, and furthermore, her tactics to get me talking.

Dr. Felt smiled at this, and if I were a gambling man, I'd bet she was thinking the same thing. "You mentioned in our first session that you'd been having this recurring dream. Has it gotten any better?" she asked.

"About the same," I replied, thankful for the softball question. "At this point I'm just happy to see my kids again, even if it's only for a second."

She jotted more notes. "Why do you think you're having these dreams?"

I blew raspberries out of my mouth, the specks of saliva shined in the peeking sun. "Because my life has been one big tease after another."

She shook her head, letting me know that the time for jokes was over. "Try again."

"Alright, I think there's some sort of symbolism there," I said. "Like, maybe I haven't reached the next stage of the grieving process yet. Or maybe God is punishing me for the husband and father I was."

"As you know, who you were as a spouse and father is on the agenda...just not today. But as human beings, all we know is what we're taught by our parents, which is a perfect transition into our topic today."

Damnit, she got me. In this moment, I know exactly why the caged bird sings. "Do we really have to do this?"

"I made a commitment to help you get better, and you committed to buy in."

"Fine, where do you wanna start?"

"Let's start with your father. Even though he wasn't around, he seems to have cast a shadow over your life."

"The guy was never around, never sent a birthday card." I could feel the anger rising in me, because it's the first time anybody has ever asked. "I'll forever hate myself for allowing him to live rent free inside my head, that I give him more time than he ever gave me. To call him a father is an insult. At best, he was a sperm donor."

Talking about him is easy. He's the guy that orders a drink at the bar and leaves before trying it. Sometimes I wish I had a dad that was a drug addict, or killed in a tragic fashion. At least there'd be sympathy for him. But when someone leaves and is content to live their life like you never existed, it eats at you. Dr. Felt scribbles furiously in her notepad, her gold bracelets jingling to the rhythm, and I don't fault her for it.

"You mentioned last session that he started a new family. Is that what hurts you the most? Or is it him not being there?"

An interesting question, and one that I've asked myself dozens of times. I tend to lean toward the former; to start a new family—like I didn't exist—kills me.

"I used to think it was him having another family, but after Harry was born I realized it was him not being around. I could never imagine leaving my kids, even if Sara and I decided to divorce. I just don't understand it, and I still feel the collateral damage to this day."

"Collateral damage?"

"My mother was never the same after he left, and I've always felt there was a correlation."

She smiles. It's a warm one, giving me a sense of validation that I've never felt before. "You're a deep thinker Miles. Most people wouldn't dare connect the two. Do you feel like him starting a new family gave you an inferiority complex?"

"Probably. I mean, I was disregarded but knew he's being a father to someone else. So, he clearly knows what he's supposed to do as a man. It makes me wonder if something is wrong with me. Like, why are they worthy of love and I'm not?"

"Ok, let's switch gears. Your father leaves and starts a new family; most kids would develop an unbreakable bond with their mother. Yours is a little more complicated than that. Why?"

I ponder her question for a moment before I answer, "After he left, I feel like her drinking turned her into someone else."

"Be more specific."

"Jesus, alright," I say. My thoughts are processing rapidly, and my mouth struggling to keep up. "Imagine your father leaves and, instead of telling you everything would be ok, your mother turns to the bottle. You watch men parade through your home, and when she's drunk, she tells you that you're the reason he left and that you were supposed to be aborted."

"That must be h—"

"I'm not finished. You wanted a buy in? Well, I'm pushing my chips to the middle of the table." She sits up, her old chair creaking into position.

"She became my roommate instead of my mother. She went looking for love and gave it everywhere else but at home."

"Sounds like she might have Borderline Personality Disorder."

"Yeah, bordering on the line of ass and hole."

"Have you ever told her how you ffeel?"

"Sure," I say, the sarcasm dripping. "Hey mom, I know you've been handed a shit hand, but maybe channeling that energy into being a shit mom isn't an effective coping method."

"I know it would be a hard conversation to have, believe me," she says, and for a second I think I'm gonna get a personal revelation. "But, didn't you even try?"

"Everything I love, I lose. I thought if I pushed her, she'd leave me too. Somewhere along the way, I became comfortable with who she was, and that was better than not having her in my life at all."

Dr. Felt gets out of the chair and begins pacing slowly around the room. I can see why she's so good in her field. She pushes, but not forcefully; she understands, but sees through bullshit. It's like watching Jordan in '98, or a young Tiger Woods. Some people are just born to do a certain job, and watching a master ply their craft is inspiring—even if you're what they're plying.

"Your mother is a woman that—let's say—hasn't experienced a lot of love in her life."

"You could say that."

I don't like where this is going. She's not taking sides, but it sounds like I'm gonna be looking at this from a different point of view. You normally see this in Law and Order; a lawyer starts with a vague line of questioning, leading a witness into a trap.

"So, we have this woman, a new mom, left with a child by herself. Why do you think she blamed you for everything?"

"Because she's a narcissist."

"Did you ever consider that maybe she developed an inferiority complex as well? She expected to have her partner stay with her forever. But, like you, she watched him become that partner to someone else."

I'm convinced that if Dr. Felt spent five minutes with my mother, she'd change her tune about the sympathetic figure she's has created.

"So, I'm supposed to ignore the planned abortion and years of emotional neglect?"

"I'm not saying your mother is perfect, understand. But you also ignore the fact that she *stayed*. You ignore the fact that she raised you when most people would have given up. That's love Miles. Now, it might not be the love you feel you deserved, but it's love nonetheless."

"I don't hate my mother."

"Never said you did. But, I think your father drove a wedge between you, and in your pain, you blamed each other instead of placing it where it should have been all along. Do you have a favorite memory of your mom?"

The question stuns me. For so long, I'd trained my mind to see my mother as the opposition. As I ponder this question, I wonder if my mom had really changed and I'd been too blind to see it. Damn this woman is good at her job—even if she's a Duke fan.

"I have two of them. I had this field event at school in kindergarten. It's where you play games outdoors and your parents come and cheer you on. She told me she wasn't going to make it, but when I walked out of the building with my class, she was there. She was partly drunk, but she was there."

"And the second memory?"

"She flew out for Harry's birth, and the first time she held him she had this ... look. I'd never seen it before, it's hard to explain."

"Try to explain it," she says. It's almost a whisper, and I realize she's back in her seat, notepad in hand. She's leaning forward in her chair, her face about a foot from mine. I imagine if someone were watching, it'd look like an animal activist approaching a tortured animal. The animal is wounded in a corner, untrusting of anything but its instincts; but this one person remains out of all the others, encouraging trust while helping rebuild a damaged psyche.

"She looked like she was validated, like this long journey she'd been on had paid off. I'd never seen anything like that from her. For a moment, it felt like I saw that version of her I knew before he left."

"It was love Miles," she says. "I guarantee she looked at you the same way, even if she didn't know how to show it. People are complex and the alcohol definitely clouded things, but she sounds like a good woman that's had a hard time reconciling her life."

"That sounds familiar."

"Exactly. We all have a need for love, to know that we matter."

"I've tried to show her that, but at some point I didn't care anymore."

"Well, I think you're at a place where you can try again." Dr. Felt picks up her notepad and starts writing again. "At some point, you'll have a conversation with her, but I want you to try something. Next time you call her, I want you to give her all the love you can and ignore your natural reaction of trading barbs. Just listen."

"You gotta be shitting me."

"Not at all, I think over time you'll find that woman you remember."

"I have a better chance of finding Jimmy Hoffa alive with a maxed out 401k."

She gets up from her seat and heads to the door, signaling that our session is over. We share a hug because, after all that, it just feels right.

"Give her a chance Miles, I think you owe her that much."

"I wouldn't go that far, but point taken."

TWELVE

SWEET DISPOSITION

"IT'S ONLY A COUPLE BLOCKS AHEAD," Melody says as we ride to an unnamed record shop in a downpour.

I should point out here that she said that five minutes ago, so in theory there should only be one block left. But, I'm enjoying our date, and I'd rather have it ruined by no fault of my own. My navigation app says we've ridden for five miles, but when you're riding with someone you have feelings for, it never feels long enough.

She's bared her soul to me on our ride. Her life philosophy of taking her cues from the universe struck a chord with me. She talked down on herself—not in a "woe is me" way, but in a humbling, self-deprecating way. She told me of her dream of getting in a car and driving away, and how she uses her love for others as a way to love herself. I got the sense that her family is a sensitive subject, but I didn't pursue that topic because she'd have questions of her own, and I'd rather not lie to her. In some ways, John undersold the person she is. Something about being with her makes life perfect.

But it also makes me sad, because Sara used to give me

that feeling and now she's gone. I feel like it's unfair to give these moments that were earmarked for her to somebody else. It feels like I'm having an affair, even though everyone would tell me I have to move on.

When I think about Sara, I wish I'd never met Melody. Of all the coffee shops in the city, I happened to get a French Roast at the one she works at. She *had* to be working the counter—instead of doing the payroll in the back, or taking a deposit to the bank. Is it really divine intervention if it leaves you worse off than where you started from? But, on the flip side, being with Melody makes me wish I weren't carrying the baggage I have. I don't regret my children, or my years in love with Sara; it's the fact that they will always cast a shadow over my life and the people in it.

During a another restroom break, I gave Lily a call to bring her up to speed and get some advice. I quickly realized I was on my own.

"Well, if it isn't little Shakespeare," she muses, eliciting a laugh from John in the background. It sounds like she was in a jet hangar. "How's your date?"

"It's going well. We took a long bike ride on the water, held hands, and now we're heading to a record shop."

"Holy shit, you held hands?" she asks, her voice fading away. "Hey everybody, they held hands," she yells to nobody in particular, followed by thunderous yelps and whoops.

"Jesus Lily, where are you?"

"We're at The Blue Room." She sounds almost offended that I didn't know. "So, what's next after that?"

"Probably dinner or something."

"Wrong answer little brother. You're taking her to Pound Town," she says as the crowd repeated it in unison.

"Do I even wanna know what that is?"

"Oh, you know what the fuck it is."

"Why are you even in my life?"

"Because I'm all you got left."

"Not anymore, she's gaining on you."

"You ungrateful little shit," she slurred.

"Lily, I gotta go," I tell her as Melody exited the bathroom.

"I hope you shit your pants on the way over," she said just before I hit the end button. Funny how some rekindled relationships pick right back up where they left off. The record shop is called Abbey Road and is nestled in the Soho section of Manhattan. The shop itself is situated in what looks like an old textile mill, the iron bars across the windows take you back to a different time. All the buildings are several stories high, and if it were sunny, there would be no place for it to shine through. It makes you feel small, an insignificant blip in an ever expanding world. The streets are paved with bricks and, since it's on a side street, it hasn't been maintained as well as the main roads. Because of that, I come to a stop in a puddle of water, which is kinda par for the course for me in this city. I remind myself that last time I stepped in something I met John, so maybe some good comes out of it.

The inside is a massive, sprawling compound dedicated to preserving a time that's long since faded away. The wooden floors are worn and creak with every step, the nails holding them down wiggle loosely under the weight of our footsteps. Behind the counter, there's a large sign reminding us that it's cash only. It's well lit with the rows of discs neatly categorized alphabetically within each genre. A stereo with a pair of headphones sits in the center of the rack which, Melody explains, is to allow you to sample before you buy. An acoustic live album, Coldplay I believe, is playing through the speakers as Melody removes her coat and tells me to look around while she hangs it up.

I head over to the "Across the Pond" section and marvel at the collection of bootleg albums they have. This place feels like home, and I make myself comfortable skimming through the different artists.

"Looking for anything in particular?"

I look up and a short portly man in an AC/DC shirt is standing there holding a stack of records. It's important to note that the shirt isn't vintage, it's more like the ones younger people buy at Hot Topic and try to pass as legit. I imagine he tries to woo female customers by showcasing his knowledge of obscure bands, then calls them sluts under his breath when they tell him they have a boyfriend.

"I'm good," I say. "Just looking for the Oasis section."

"It's all organized by alphabet, and we're running buy two get one free."

I nod in understanding and he disappears as quickly as he showed up. I find the section and quickly begin tallying how much money I might spend. They have Oasis' early 1995 Glastonbury performance and their "Live Demonstration" demo, among the highlights. I open the jewel case and pop their first album into the stereo, blowing dust off the top case as it closes. How could a section with so many gems be so neglected? The stereo beeps, signifying the disc is being read, and after a long pause, the first track starts playing. I put the headphones over my ears and now I'm apart from the world—a slave to the faint hiss coming through the headphones.

The first note of "Rock and Roll Star" comes through and I close my eyes to take it in. The fading guitars bleed into the bass that steamrolls my consciousness, and soon my hands are miming the drum patterns on my invisible drum set. The lyrics about running away speak to my present state in a way in never had before. Music is the one thing in the world that has this kind of power. Lyrics written by a stranger can connect someone they'll never meet, giving them the ability to summon strength from within that was previously untapped. Lily and I used to sit in the basement, screaming these lyrics at each other, swearing that one day we'd make it away from our parents and build our own legacy. Life was so simple back then, and then I had to fuck it all up.

I'm no longer a drummer now. I'm the guitarist, shredding my air guitar before millions of invisible fans. I swing my arm like Pete Townsend, damn near knocking over half the shelf, but I'm oblivious to the mayhem because that's rock and roll. I stop moving, flailing for the finale, Liam Gallagher wailing in my ears asking me if it's rock and roll.

Yes, yes it fucking is.

After the song ends I take off the headphones and return the disc to its case. I know mp3's are more convenient, but the experience of opening a disc shouldn't be lost in the process. The wrapping that was always too hard to get into, the faint pause a cd player makes before starting, reading through the lyrics with each song as it plays; I guess it's how our parents felt when vinyl was going out of style. Life is like a relay race, we each hold our baton and run with it for as long as we can, but eventually we must pass it on.

"That was quite the show."

Melody stands at the end of the aisle, somehow more beautiful under the lighting. Drops of water hang off the edges of her curls, the scar that drew me to her shining under the combination of lighting and dampness. She walks over slowly, something about her walk is familiar but I can't place it.

"Oasis?" she asks, looking at the cover. "Great band, I always felt the back half of their catalog deserved more love from the critics. But when you alienate the press, the jig is up. Pop quiz. Smiths or The Cure, go."

"Smiths, easily," I say, thankful for a question that distracts me from staring at her. "My sister and I used to listen and debate their records all the time."

"Tell me about your sister. I find when people our age try to work through relationships, the person must mean something to them."

I think of how to describe Lily, but it's like trying to describe Frank Zappa to a hip hop nerd. Some things just need to be experienced for yourself. "Well, she's my stepsister, frequently profane but in a lovable way. I should've never pushed her away, she was my best friend."

"How'd you push her away?"

"I didn't really, I just felt like she was always the favorite. She got everything—perfect grades, attention, a closer relationship than I had with my mom. When she came out, our parents were ashamed and secretly I was happy, because to them she wasn't perfect anymore. But I should've defended her, and I didn't."

"So you took their side?"

"No, I just didn't take hers."

I didn't take their side. Actually, I didn't say anything at all. My mother raged on about what our community would think, and how Rich would never get to give her away. The look on Lily's face haunts me to this day. Watching them devalue her existence because of what people might think killed me. I decided then, I would choose a college as far away as I could and pretend they never existed. But I stayed silent while Lily looked at me, practically begging me to protect her. After it was over, she told me she never wanted to see me again, and within six months she was off at college. Something about knowing someone is alive and cutting you off, hurts more than if they were dead. Occasionally, I'd find an album that reminded me of her, of a time when it was us against the world, and I'd wish that I could have that moment back.

"Why didn't you reach out sooner?" Melody asks.

"It was too easy to ignore it, honestly. Sometimes, it's easier to ignore the pain than confront it."

She's now face to face with me. We stand on the verge of a moment like we had looking out at the water. The kiss is there if I want it, the moment is perfect.

But life isn't perfect, and I break eye contact.

"So, when are we gonna talk about it?" she asks.

"Talk about what?"

I've been through so much that "it" could mean anything. Everybody wants the scoop on what's going on, my default response is to feign ignorance until I learn their true intentions.

"Well, we can start with the hospital band." She lifts my sleeve, wedging her index finger underneath the plastic. Part of me wonders how much of this she can take before deciding it's a waste of time. "I feel like that's a logical starting point."

"I tried to kill myself ... but failed." I brace myself for her to pull away. Miraculously, she moves closer.

"Well obviously, but go on."

"I'd been going through some things and decided..." my words trail off as my mind races. I try to regain focus and fall back on an old trick I learned in a public speaking class. Find something, anything, to focus on. In this case, it's a single drop of water that fell from one of her curls that's settled on the tip of her nose.

"You decided that you didn't want to try anymore, not that you couldn't. There's a difference," she says while rubbing my head. "We've all had those moments."

"True, but you didn't act on it. I did."

The room feels like it's gotten smaller, the stacks of records pushing us closer together. It's dizzying, but in a good way. I imagine it's what Jim Halpert felt like in the moments after he professed his love to Pam.

Melody smiles at me, but it's a sad one. She lifts her arms to reveal her wrists. There's heavy scarring on the inside, evidence of a mind that traveled to its darkest depths some time in the past. I run my fingers over the healed cuts, each one smoother than the unbroken skin next to it.

"You aren't the only one with scars Miles." She tilts her head and stares into my eyes—the way you look when you put a piece of art on the wall and can't decide if it's straight. "You're just not as good at hiding them." I notice her eyes starting to tear up. "It's nice to finally meet this Miles. I was wondering if he'd ever show up."

"Pleasure is mine, Melody," I reply. "I'm actually really bad with timing, you'll learn that eventually."

I know she has to leave for her other job soon, but I want her to stay. In fact, I want to hit the airport and fly away with her to wherever she wants to go. It's all so vivid to me in this moment. I can see myself fighting anxiety attacks while she massages my back, soothing mew with her words, telling me she understands. Or taking her to meet my mother, and laughing with her about how I survived such a fucked up family as we drive away to nowhere in particular. Maybe the idea of a soul mate isn't as crazy as it seems. But, I keep waiting for the other shoe to drop. This is the life of pessimist, forever waiting to be told the jig is up.

"You should see the al—"

She leans in and kisses me. Her lips even softer than I imagined. I feel the drop of water slide off her nose and settle just under my nose. The mint in her gum travels through my pores, sending a rush to my brain. I'm trying not to overthink it, and I focus on the intimacy like Lily told me to. Her hands are slowly running down my back, so I guess I'm doing ok. She pulls away, rubs my lips, and tells me she's got to go to work. She places something in my pocket, but I'm too focused on her to look.

Because it's dawning on me that this trip just became a lot more complicated.

THIRTEEN

HALF PRICED FLIGHTS FROM HELL

Endorphins work in strange ways.

It's mind-blowing that one chemical has the power of dictating the mood of a human being, swaying one's view of the world from sugar to shit. Random thought, I know. But as I wait in line at a milk and cereal bar with Melody, I couldn't help myself. A couple of hours ago, I was stuck apartment hunting with Lily when she texted me.

Do you like ice cream?

A woman after my own heart. Besides, you can only look at so many apartments before they all start to look the same. She could've asked me if I wanted to get matching Brazilian waxes and I would have said yes—she's that much fun to be around. I'm pretty sure Lily settled on a studio unit on the Upper West Side, but I won't be sure until we see her later. Yes, Melody is meeting my family, which feels weird to say for a multitude of reasons, the biggest one being my bond with each of them is fragile.

So, now we're here in this brightly colored establishment

—aqua blue walls with white borders and baseboards, standard fare, Top 40 radio pumping through the speakers. The draw of this place is that the cereal is mixed in with the ice cream; not on top, but swirled in with it. The clientele is mostly overgrown frat boys, wearing tan Dockers and Sperry boat shoes, all on dates with women whose beauty is their only definable trait.

One thing I notice about Melody is that she's big on touch. Not in a way that makes you uncomfortable, but in a way that lets you know she's there for you. As we've walked the streets, she held my hand at every chance, and I didn't flinch. I guess when you make out with someone in a record shop, holding hands is a given. I mentioned to Lily that maybe we were moving too fast, but she told me that's how the dating world is now. She's wearing a tennis skirt, the kind that's just long enough to hide her butt, but just short enough to make you wish a breeze would blow by. I've lost count the number of times she's caught me looking, but she always smiles—probably because she's used to it.

"I'm thinking of going with the Apple Jacks," she says, as I realize we're one person from the register.

"The Fruit Loops and Crunch Berries are calling out to me."

"Interesting combo. Go find us a booth, this is on me."

"You don't have to pay."

"I'm aware of that, now go grab a booth before we end up sitting on the floor."

The booth I find is in the corner of the place, far enough back that you could easily miss it. I notice Melody pay with all singles as she shoves excess bills back into her purse. She grabs our order and napkins, then takes a seat across from me. This is important to note because there is a seat next to me.

"My God, I haven't had ice cream in so long," she says, scooping a helping into her mouth. "When was the last time you had ice cream?"

"It's been ... awhile." Truthfully, the last time I had ice cream was on a daddy date with Grace. She was the only person in my life I could start out angry with and still end up at Baskin Robbins with. Grace refused to get her ice cream in a cup, arguing that she was a big girl. I also showed her the greatness that is pushing the ice cream to the bottom of the cone.

"What else haven't you done in awhile?" she asks, her twirling her spoon through the cup.

I grin like a fifteen year old boy that just saw his first pair of breasts.

"Why are you smiling?"

"No reason."

"You thought I was asking about sex didn't you?" Melody cocks her head and stares at me for a second, "Ok, when's the last time you had sex?"

Shit. I wasn't expecting that, nor was I prepared to answer it. It honestly depends on what kind of sex she means. When you have kids and nobody to babysit, uninterrupted sex happens about as often as the Olympics.

"Last time was about eight months ago," I say.

"That's a long time," she says, with a smile that suggests intimacy is on the table in the very near future. I wouldn't be opposed to that.

"You told me last night that I was good at hiding scars and showed me your wrists, what made you do that?"

She tenses up, and I feel like a jerk because the conversation was going smoothly. I could see it was a sensitive subject, but it had stuck with me through the night. "Are you asking me why I cut, or why I showed them to you?"

I hadn't considered that. I think hard about what my answer should be, but decided to be honest with her. "Both."

"When I was in Middle School, I was raped by my mother's boyfriend. When I told her about it, she called me a liar and even made me apologize to him. But it continued whenever he got the chance, and after awhile I became numb to it all." She sees how uncomfortable I am, and probably sensed how bad I feel for making her relive her trauma, so she takes the seat next to me.

"You don't have to do this, Melody," I say. She runs the tip of her index finger across my forehead, like she was soothing a child.

"After you decided to kill yourself, what did it feel like when you were waiting for it to be over?" she asks.

Now the ball is back in my court and, even though the subject matter is serious, I feel closer to her—even if her demeanor has changed. But, I should've known there was something there, because having the kind of happiness she carried with her could only be taught by the hard trail she took to get there.

"I remember being at peace," I explain. "This might sound weird, but it kinda felt like waiting at the bus stop. It's the only time in my life I could recall not worrying about anything. I was also alone, and that allowed me to come to terms with everything."

"I did it in the bathtub," she says, matter-of-factly. "I watched the water change color and closed my eyes, calm like you. But, I forgot it was my mother's half-day at work and she found me. Some days, I question if I'm happy she found me or..." She didn't have to finish the thought, because I know what she was going to say. It's the exact thought I had in the weeks that followed my own attempt. What if I would've stayed in the bathroom? What if she chose a different day? Two different scenarios, and if either of them changed, we would never have met and spent the rest of eternity asking ourselves these questions. "I showed them to you to let you know that you're not alone, and that you can trust me."

For a second, I consider spilling the beans about my situation. It feels like everything is on the table, but I don't want to push my luck. It's so much easier to act like everything else is normal. I dance around the question with one of my own, "Is that why you take your cues from the universe?"

Melody takes time pondering my question. "You're really intrigued by that. Well, in a way, yes. With the universe, if something happens you know it's by chance. It can't be manipulated, so after awhile it makes life a little easier because it feels natural."

"That's an interesting way to live."

"It works though. Think about it. Like I said, as people we have this need to control everything. When something happens that's out of our control, we don't know how to handle it. The universe doesn't play favorites. It's why I like working the open mic night, seeing people chase their dreams—even if it's only for two minutes, it's inspiring. We all have intuition, the only difference for me is that I act on it."

"Well, I'm glad you did," I tell her.

"Me too."

My phone rings, and ironically it's the theme from "Curb Your Enthusiasm," and we both laugh at how perfect it is for the moment. What's *not* funny is that it's my mother on the other end. She's called twice a day for the last two days, but I've been riding a pretty good hot streak and I don't wanna ruin it.

"Who's saved in your phone as Satan?" Melody asks,

intrigued. I struggle to find a way to sum up my relationship with my mother.

"It's my mother."

"You guys must have quite the relationship."

"Enough to put a therapist's kids through Harvard."

The phone stops ringing and I try to regain my composure. Something is amiss, she doesn't call that often. Actually, she doesn't call at all unless she's run out of relationships to suck the life out of. "What's your relationship like with your mother now?" I ask.

She stops in the middle of a bite, pushes her cup away from her, and lets out a deep sigh. "We don't really have one. She left when I was sixteen, and now she only pops up when she needs something." Her hands have gotten fidgety, and she's struggling to make eye contact again. My hands find hers—its a simple gesture with a deeper meaning. It says you care, but you won't pry. Or that you don't understand, but you won't make them suffer alone. It's not like I wrote the book on successful relationships with parents.

"Did she ever ask if you were telling the truth?"

Her face becomes stern. "No, she never acknowledged it. That's probably why we'll never have a relationship."

Hearing that made me think of my relationship with my own mother. For all her faults, she was still in the picture even though I contemplate cutting her off everyday. But I could never do that, because I see flashes of the woman I remember, and the fault for the breakdown isn't all on her—though I tell myself it is. But, I'd rather keep her at a distance and know she was alright than see her drinking herself into oblivion and masking it as happiness.

One of the supervisors comes over and asks to take our picture for the first timers wall. Melody gives me a look indicating it's up to me, and I agree. The lady takes two polaroids, one genuine and one funny, letting us choose which one to keep. If you looked at the photo without knowing either of our histories, you'd wouldn't think anything was amiss. My smile was genuine, and it shook me to the core to see a version of myself that I thought was destined to live forever in the pictures above the fireplace back in Colorado. Seconds earlier, Melody had told me about the worst moment in her life; but there she was, grinning ear to ear with her head on my shoulder. It looked so natural that we could pass as a couple, madly in love with each other.

We chose to give up the crazy one, and watched her staple it on the wall with the others. If this all goes to shit—and there's still time for that—I'll know there's a place I can go to see the moment that *normal* became a possibility instead of a pipe dream.

"I think you should keep that," I say. "You know, in case you have a bad hair day and need a reminder of how pretty you are." In my head it sounds cute, but in actuality, it hints at me leaving—a point neither of us want to address.

"Or maybe you could stick around for a bit. It would mean more coming from you than a picture." She laughs and the air seems to return to the room. Humor really does help smooth over tension. She smiles at me, and that beautiful feeling of all being right in the world comes back again. "You wanna kiss me, don't you?" she asks. I grin like a goofball, a clear giveaway. "What's stopping you?"

I oblige and we share a long kiss, her lips just as soft as they were at the record store, but with ice cream mixed in. She runs my hands up her legs and under her skirt, then back down. When our lips part, she softly bites my bottom lip, and the hair on my body stands straight up—among other things.

My phone rings again, and I swear I'm gonna throw the damn thing. It's Lily, which is even more maddening because I'm literally doing the thing she's been pushing me to do, and possibly well on the way to doing something else she says I *need* to do. "Excuse me just one second." I get up from the table. Melody calls my name but I wave her off, determined to nip this in the bud. A hush comes over the place as I walk away from the table to take the call.

"Lily, you had to call right now. This isn't really the best time ... hint, hint."

"Miles, we gotta talk."

"Since I got here, all you've done is tell me that I've been doing myself."

"We have a real problem, there's no time for—"

"And wouldn't you know, at the exact moment I'm about to put that to bed—pun intended—you decide it's time for a powwow."

The silence in the ice cream parlor has turned to giggles and stares, with the occasional finger pointing. I can't blame them. I know I look like a madman pacing back and forth. It's in this moment that I understand why baseball players are constantly trying to replace testosterone, it really does make you feel invincible.

"All I'm trying to do is—"

"—is ruin the moment," I interrupt.

"You know what, fuck it, I tried," she says. "Now that I think about it, it'll be that much funnier."

"What are you talking about?"

She laughs at the sound of anxiety in my voice. Something isn't right, like when we were driving to the strip club, she's up to something.

"Don't worry about it, we're supposed to meet up soon anyway." The cadence of her voice speeds up as she talks.

"Just know, hell is running a special on travel packages. What time you coming over?"

"We're heading over now."

"Jeez, you work quick. I guess it has been awhile."

"So, you're a fucking comedian now?"

"No, the comedy show starts when you get here," she says with a laugh that makes my stomach crawl, "and I've got front row seats to the show."

"What did you mean by hell—"

"See you soon." She hangs up before I can finish.

I stare at the phone for a second, wondering what she was talking about. *Hell is running a special on travel packages.* That's something a Mafia boss would say on a phone that's tapped by the police. Unfortunately, I have bigger problems.

People are still pointing and laughing, but I'm off the phone now. Melody is wearing a thin smile, like she's embarrassed, and sensing my confusion, she points down. I look down and understand it wasn't the conversation that caused the silence.

It was my erection. My old friend, awakened after eight months of lying dormant under an avalanche of grief and high sodium takeout, rising from its slumber like I'm fourteen again and Cinemax late night had just started. The place erupts in laughter as they see me finally arrive at the punchline of the joke. I couldn't feel more alone even if the lights went out and a spotlight shined on me.

Melody gets up from the table, grabs my hand, and we briskly exit the ice cream parlor.

"I'm sorry," I say, because there isn't anything else to say.

"Nothing to be sorry about, it happens to the best of us."

"You have a penis?"

"I meant embarrassment."

We hop in a cab and head for the bar. The underrated part of being humiliated in a city like New York, is that there are so many people, chances are you'll never see any of them again.

And to think, I was just starting to like this city.

* * *

"You seem nervous," Melody says, and she's right.

We're walking through the streets of the Upper West Side, holding hands, but my mind is somewhere else. If anxiety has one benefit, it's that you analyze everything. Once my hormones subsided, it dawns on me that Lily was trying to tell me something. Naturally, as a horny male focused on Melody, I was too distracted to listen to her. Sex really *will* be the fall of man.

"Something isn't right," I say. "She was trying to tell me something important, but I wouldn't listen."

"What do you think it was?"

"I don't know, and that's what's scaring me."

Melody rubs my back, and we walk in silence for a little bit. It dawns on me that we're on our second date and Melody is about to meet my family. Well, what's left of it. For some reason, it doesn't feel like we're moving too fast. Maybe she was right about following the universe.

We turn the corner and see the lights of the bar halfway down the block. As we get closer I become dismayed at the clientele hanging around in front. The short sleeved Hawaiian shirt, khaki shorts that end just above the knees, these are the guys that wouldn't hesitate to sick their fathers lawyers on you. A couple of them catcall Melody as we wait in line but she ignores them Security checks our ID's and we head inside, through the haze of Calvin Klein cologne and cigarette smoke. The entrance is narrow, the bar stretches to the back where it opens up into a restaurant. As we move through the bar I pick up random pieces of conversation.

"...I don't understand why he swiped me if he didn't want kids, my profile was very clear."

"...the quality of the beer doesn't match the prices, how the fuck do you ruin a Miller Genuine Draft?"

"...this is the year Brady falls off and the Jets win the division baby. Book it."

At the end of the bar, I start scanning the tables for Lily and John. It's just a mass of people talking over each other. Remember in Titanic, when Jack slipped under the water and the camera zoom out on Rose in the massive group of people? Just absolute bedlam.

"MILES, DARLING," a slurring voice booms above the others. I couldn't stop any quicker if I'd hit a brick wall. I close my eyes and pray that someone else in the bar shares my name, and that someone in his life—anyone—gets drunk and slurs his name like a Connecticut blue blood. But, as I continue to learn, life doesn't work that way.

I slowly turn around and am greeted by my mother. She stands there, swaying slowly in her designer dress, her trusty Louis Vuitton hand bag dangling from her wrist like a baton. In her other hand, she holds a glass of Chardonnay. I can always tell what she's been drinking by how she reacts. Wine means she's feeling warm and fuzzy. Hard liquor means hard truths, and everyone at the table should strap in for a rough night.

I take a second to examine how quickly my night has gone to shit.

An hour ago I was having ice cream with a woman I'm falling more in love with by the second. I had confirmed that, yes, my penis does in fact still work, and holds no lingering resentment towards me for months of neglect. We were going to come here for drinks—laughing, drinking, and winking at each other—the alcohol fueling our hormones to a critical point. We'd then excuse ourselves and go back to her place, where I'd hopefully last long enough in bed to not embarrass myself. Afterward, I would probably cry and tell her about my family, then head back to the hotel to eat junk food and ponder the future. Even with the crying, that's still a solid night.

Nowhere was this impromptu family reunion in the cards. Melody is oblivious to what's going on, and I fight the urge to grab her hand and jet out of the bar. Just beyond my mother, Lily stands grinning like a spectator at the zoo that just happen to show up for feeding time. I know she tried to tell me, but right now she's the only one I can fairly project my anger upon.

My mother stumbles her way between tables before pulling me into an awkward embrace. I can smell the alcohol, and it takes me back to elementary school and all of the awkward school events she'd attend while drunk—leaving me to hope that we could get out with our reputations intact. We were already on welfare, we didn't need the indignity of being labeled the dysfunctional, alcoholic family on top of that.

"It feels so good to see you," she hiccups in my ear. I mouth apologies to Melody over her shoulder, and she nods that it's ok.

"Mom, this is Melody," I say, very slowly—since I can't tell how drunk she is.

She gives her the once over, the light illuminating off her eyeballs like glass. "Well, she's definitely an upgrade," she says, before shaking Melody's hand. "Helen. It's nice to meet you."

In my head I'm calculating if I have enough money in my account to beat an assault charge that seems inevitable right now. I figure that I have enough money for bail, but going to trial would be a bit too costly.

Why does every greeting have to come with a barb? Introductions are made to Lily before my mother orders another drink. John correctly guesses that that the tension is rising and escorts Melody to the bar to get a drink. Lily decides she wants to smoke, and I follow her outside, and the last visual I have is our mother downing her drink.

It's gonna be a long night.

FOURTEEN

DRINK TOGETHER SINK TOGETHER

"You SET ME UP," I say as Lily struggles to light her
cigarette.

She finally lights it and takes a long drag, the smoke
filling her lungs as she comes up with a response, "Don't be
so dramatic, it's not like I led you into a Mob ambush." She
blows a cloud of smoke in my face for good measure.

"You knew I was on a date, and I'm being dramatic?"

"As I recall, I called you to give you a heads up." She
pulls her phone out and puts it in my face. I stare at her call
log, showing the time and duration of her phone call earlier.
"And what did you do?" She mimes checking a list, "Ah yes,
says here you were too busy getting your balls played with
by your new friend in there."

Something about her tone makes me nervous, like it's
more than me blowing her warning off that's getting under
her skin.

"I see what's going on here."

"You don't see shit."

"You're threatened by Melody." Lily rolls her eyes and
scoffs, an obvious tell that confirms my suspicions. "I go out

with her, like you told me to, and now you're in your feelings because there's someone else that I care about. Does my little 'distraction' threaten you?"

The other smokers are slowly moving closer, trying to be subtle but failing—our family soap opera too good to ignore. "Lily, I need you to get her out of here."

"Our mother needs us." She takes a long drag, "Besides, this should make the night interesting."

If I made up a list of what Helen's presence would make our night, interesting would crack the top one hundred. Interesting is the NBA considering adding a four point line. This was the equivalent of putting a herd of gazelle on the track during the Daytona 500.

"Our mother? The same person who shamed you for coming out? Now she's *our* mother?" I scoff, "She must have cut one hell of a check for your MBA."

"You know I find it interesting that you show up here, begging for forgiveness, but are only interested if it's you that's being forgiven."

A guy dressed like Billy Idol laughs at this. I shoot him a look and he retreats to another part of the patio. She takes a final drag of her cigarette, waving the blue vapors out of the air. "You love this shit Lily, you always have. Just couldn't avoid watching this accident, could you?"

"I thought you'd be used to handling accidents by now," she retorts. Her face contorts, immediately realizing her poor choice of words, "That was uncalled for, I didn't mean it like that."

"I know."

"Look, I'll concede that maybe this isn't the best time for you. But she showed up when you needed someone, so you kinda owe her one."

I think about Dr. Felt and her directives on giving my

mother love, no matter the situation. I think I need an agent because I keep making terrible deals. First, I agree to willingly be my mother's whipping boy, and now I'm financing apartments in exchange for dating beautiful baristas. Granted, the latter deal—as of a couple of hours ago—seems to have great rewards on the horizon.

"Keep the talk away from my family, Melody doesn't know about that."

Lily lets out a howl. "Are you serious? Still? No wonder you're so nervous. This just gets better and better."

"Lily."

"Alright, I'll do what I can. But, if she starts drinking tequila, it's outta my hands."

* * *

The drinks arrive at our table, and outside of my mother, nobody makes a move—let alone any earnest attempt at conversation. My mother sits at the head of the table, Lily is opposite Melody, who's next to me. John, sensing the Titanic was doomed, jumped in the life boat and left us to sink. We sit in silence, unsure of the next move. Like friends standing at the edge of a lake, each scared of being the first to dive in. Melody, naive to dangers of engaging my mother in conversation while she's drunk, takes the first plunge.

"Helen, what brings you to the city?"

And we're off.

"Well, I'm going through a season of change in my own life right now, as is my son."

I shoot Lily a look, indicating that it's getting a little to close to home, and she lurches up like a guard dog, ready to jump in.

"So I decided ... hey, I love the city and I could use an

escape. So, I jumped on a flight.". She takes a generous swig of her wine. "For a fifteen dollar glass of wine, this ain't doing it for me." She begins looking for the closest waiter, and when one fails to appear, she ups the awkwardness. "So, is this thing between you two casual or ...?"

Melody smiles at this, "We're still getting to know each other, but it's been ... awesome." She's dragging her fingertips up my thigh under the table. I want to stop her because we're trying to get outta this unscathed, and I need all my senses to do so. However, I'm also a male that hasn't had intimacy, let alone sex, in a long time ,and all I can think about are her thighs, soft as dinner rolls. I get the sense that, because of her family history, she's used to being in this kind of situation.

"Have you guys ... you know," my mother looks around—as if she's about to give away a big secret—then mimics intercourse, sliding her index finger furiously in and out of the circle of her index finger and thumbs of her other hand.

The rest of us take healthy swigs of our drinks, realizing we're not drinking fast enough to keep up with the insanity. Melody looks at me, and winks. "Not yet," she replies. "But I think it's in the cards."

Me and, by extension, my penis are unsure how we should react to this. On one hand, we both should be happy to know that our long nightmare has a confirmed end date. On the other hand, we both sink solemnly knowing my mother is now privy to this information. Melody's hands have graduated to my balls, and my penis decides to abandon me for the charms of her palm.

Traitorous motherfucker.

"Where did you guys meet?"

"He came into my coffee shop, I gave him my number, and he asked if he could get to know me better."

"I bet he did," mother replies, winking at me.

Dr. Felt said not to trade barbs and to give love, and in this case, love is me holding my tongue.

A waitress appears and a second round of drinks is ordered, giving us all a well deserved break. The three *expected* patrons sticking to beer, my mother switching to Don Julio. If these chair had seat belts, we'd all start buckling up. Once the waitress leaves, Lily decides it's her turn to take the plunge.

"So, Mom, how's Robert doing?" she asks.

I cant' believe *that's* the best she could come up with. You would think after all the years of cheating, she'd be more adept at navigating awkward situations.

It feels like we're in one of those video game boss fights; the three of us battling against a giant sloth, spelling each other once our health has depleted. If we fail, it'll be a long night figuring out exactly who is to blame. If I were a gambling man, I'd take Lily at +250.

"I told him it's over and to be gone when I get back," she croaks, like it wasn't a forgone conclusion to Lily and myself.

"And when might that be?" I say, having found a logical entrance into the battle. It's the two of us, thick as thieves again—just like in high school.

"That's rude, Miles. Are you ok?" she asks, naturally causing everyone at the table to focus on me. "You're falling asleep."

"I'm fine."

"You don't look fine," Melody says, like she isn't doing the Devil's work under the table.

"I'm good, I swear. Everyone just keep on doing *exactly* what you're doing," I say, specifically speaking to Melody. She obliges.

When dealing with a narcissist, an alcoholic one at that,

it works best for everyone to keep that person as the focus. By boxing them in, you prevent toxicity from spreading to everyone else. But it requires everyone to do their part, like working on a Ford assembly line in the '60s. If one person leaves their post, the whole operation goes to hell and somebody gets hurt.

Our drinks arrive, and while my mother is complaining about something moot, I turn to Melody deciding to give her part of the truth.

"Anything that might fly out of her mouth, I need you to know there's an explanation for it," I say. She gives me a quizzical look, but nods in affirmation. If there was a chapel and a minister in this room, I'd marry her on the spot. Ok, probably not, but she's definitely winning major points with me. She's matching wits with my mother, and I think that's turning me on more than her work under the table. Jury is still out on that one.

"So, how long are you staying Miles?" my mother asks.

Melody brings her hand from under the table. She's got more to lose in this question, because her connection with me is more tenuous. We'd been living in a fairy tale together, but the question was a reminder that the train back to the real world would be boarding soon, and we haven't bought our tickets yet. Lily could see my mind working through this realization and jumps in for the save.

"He's actually decided to stay an extra week and help me find an apartment."

I can see the relief in Melody's face, her smile returns and life goes to normal for the moment. But her question brought our relationship to the forefront. Soon enough, we're gonna have to figure out what the future looks like—if there is one. I'd be lying if I said I hadn't thought about a future with her. But with every glancing thought of us being together, comes another one reminding me that I'm broken. My mood swings on a pendulum, violently back and forth, leaving me confused. One minute, I'm wishing I'd thrown her number out; the next minute, I'm imagining what a lazy Sunday would look like with her.

"You always try to do the right thing Miles. I've always loved that about you," my mother says. I close my eyes for a second, before opening them to see if this is really my mother. My eyes meet Lily's and we silently agree that, yes, this is our mother, and yes, that was a compliment about who I was as a person.

The tension is slowly evaporating, and we could almost pass for normal. Helen is now telling stories of her travels, some that Lily and I have heard and some new ones. The laughs are flowing as freely as the alcohol, and I imagine that we look like any other family in the city to the other tables around us. Lily and I exchange looks of relief, acknowledging that she's a different person—at least for now.

I think back to the funeral, and how she held my hand as the caskets were lowered into the ground, tears rolling down her face as she buried her only grandchildren. I thought she was there for show, and now I feel bad because I never acknowledged the pain she must've felt. She had lost her only grandkids, and with with my age—and Lily being Lily —likely her only chance at being a grandmother. After the funeral she stayed with me for awhile, catering to my every need, and all I could do was make snippy remarks. The love of my life had perished, and it never occurred to me that after watching my father leave, she was the one person in my life that could understand how I was feeling.

Dr. Felt asked me to give her my favorite memories of my mother. Right now, this moves to the top of the list. This woman is my mother, the one I thought was long gone.

She rises from her seat, glass in hand, ready to propose a toast.

"To old friends, new lovers ..." she shoots a lightening quick glance at Melody, caught by both Lily and I. We exchange looks, no doubt both of us wondering if we'd imagined that. She focuses on me and Melody, her eyes shining from the alcohol and chic lighting.

"... and to coffee and condolences."

FIFTEEN

RECKONING

THE DOOR of Melody's apartment creaks open, piercing the silence as we step into her living room. A faint beep of a triggered alarm requires her attention, and while she steps away to enter the code, I stand looking around, silently judging her belongings—like humans are known to do. The space is small, which is to be expected in New York, but it doesn't feel cramped. Her bedroom is at the end of a hallway, the door slightly ajar like I'm getting a slight glimpse at her soul. She enters the code and goes through the normal paces we all do after arriving at home, flipping on lights, and going through mail. I take a seat on the couch and let her do her thing.

There's no sense of urgency toward our plans for the evening, and I'm thankful for that. I'm still trying to process the dinner with my mother. I can't figure out what her angle is and it's killing me. Maybe Dr. Felt was right; maybe she has changed and I've just been stubborn in my view of the woman she's become.

"You thirsty?" she asks from the kitchen.

"No, I'm good."

"You're clamming up again."

I'm not clamming up, I'm playing defense. Let me explain.

Men, as a gender, are all the same. Of course we look different and speak differently as well. But when it comes to sex, or in this case, a situation where sex is guaranteed, we're all the same. We go into self-preservation mode.

Men by nature are stupid, and thus prone to saying stupid shit at the worst time. As you can imagine, this is a problem when trying to convince someone of the opposite sex to engage in intercourse. So what do you do?

Well, if you're smart, you realize there's only one thing to do.

Shut the fuck up.

Now, this can be done in many ways. For example, when I was was married and I knew that sex was in the cards, I would do housework. Yard work isn't as grueling when you know theres a pot of gold at the end of the rainbow. When I was single, that wasn't an option, so I stuck with the military drill—speak only when spoken to. Imagine the end of a close football game, and your team is up and has the ball. They stop taking unnecessary risks. As a man, it's the same principle, just run the clock out. If you're a female, think about the next time you're on a date or out with your husband. Pay attention to his mood shift, and ask yourself: Has it been established that we're going to have sex? If the answer is yes, it'll all make sense.

Melody scampers by on her way to the bedroom, running her fingers on the back of my neck as she passes, a subtle reminder of what's to come. I briefly contemplate joining her, but I lack the confidence required for such a feat. This whole scenario doesn't feel real, and I keep glancing at the door, expecting Dr. Felt to walk though it and pronounce that I had passed the final test and am free to move on with my life. To pass the time, I skim through Melody's record collection.

It's meticulously organized for mood, each section individually labeled. It's like a political convention with each section represented by the best candidate. Depression is represented well by The Smiths, while happiness is highlighted by The Cars and Tears for Fears. Stevie Wonder represents the housekeeping section along with Pat Benatar. Naturally, I pay attention to the intimacy section—just to get an idea of where her head is at. Teddy Pendergrass dominates this section, bookended by The Isley Brothers and Dru Hill. The takeaway from that section is she's a passionate lover; but I also wonder how many guys have stood in this very spot, looking around at the furniture, wondering what positions match well with the playlist. My eye catches a sheet of paper, a list of songs labeled 'Work Playlist.'

I open it expecting a mix of indie rock and Top 40 hits, but it's surprisingly hip-hop centered with a sprinkling of modern R&B. At the top of the list, circled in black, is T-Pain's 'I'm in Love with a Stripper,' immediately taking me back to Harmony—and I suspect it always will. It's a well thought out playlist, songs sequenced to mirror the ebbs and flows of a work shift.

Melody returns to the living room in classic lounge clothes—baggy sweats and sweatshirt. Removing her hair tie, she falls on the couch with a deep sigh which makes my heart drop. When Sara would take her hair tie out and sigh, that usually meant sex was not happening. But I'm confident that we've consumed enough alcohol to render that thought moot.

"Well, that was an interesting evening," she says, "Given

what you told me about her, I figured there'd be more fireworks."

"Dinners with her usually are. In fact, given our history, it went better than I expected."

"You seemed to change your tone with her as the night went on."

"It's funny, I thought I had our relationship figured out. But, like everything else in my life right now, it's all evolving."

"It's interesting how we lock people in these roles, isn't it?" she asks before heading to the kitchen. "I've always found it fascinating that we ask the people around us to understand that we're evolving as people, but we never give that same courtesy."

She makes a great point. But the combination of alcohol, hormones, and general panic at the idea of having sex with someone that isn't Sara, refuses to let me soak it in. Melody asks if I want to split a pot of coffee with her, and I agree as a stalling tactic. From behind, she could pass for Sara— masterfully multi-tasking without letting any one task be neglected. The memories of those nights come flooding back.

The kids would demand attention, but she had a way of keeping everything running as scheduled, even allowing the kids to help with the less dangerous aspects of dinner. Grace loved nights when dinner required a mixing bowl, knowing she'd get to lick the spoon was like having a two desserts. Harry loved anything that allowed him to go into the fridge. He'd bide his time, waiting until Sara was seemingly distracted, and try to steal a yogurt. He'd always get caught, wait about fifteen minutes, then rinse and repeat.

This isn't the best time to take a stroll down memory lane, so I decide to make a move to get my head back in the game. There will be plenty of time for anxiety attacks and emotional breakdowns later. I approach the kitchen as quietly as I can, coming up behind Melody as she's rinsing mugs for the coffee. I make note that she doesn't have a one of the newer coffee machines that use pods, and I judge her silently while figuring it'll make a nice gift in the future.

Whatever that looks like.

I start by massaging her lower back, and for a second she tenses up before realizing it's me. She turns the water off and turns around to jump into the fray. We stand kissing for awhile, finally able to take our time without worrying about ice cream customers or nosy record store workers. She softly nibbles on my neck, just like Sara used to. I decide to change it up to block Sara from my memory. I lift her up on the counter, parting from her lips just long enough to get her shirt off.

"I like it," she says with a naughty grin.

I don't respond because I'm trying to stay focused. Feeling guilty wasn't part of the plan when I came here, and the only way I know how to fight back against the sinking feeling in my stomach is to keep going, continuing to up the ante until it's too far to turn back. Melody takes my jacket off and starts untucking my shirt. I should be thanking whatever god there is that she's willing to have sex with someone who tucks their shirt into jeans. As I feel my shirt coming above my stomach, I stop her. Even though I've stopped her, I'm just as surprised as her. She stares at me for a second, and I swear she's gonna ask me to leave her apartment, and her life while I was at it.

But she doesn't.

"It's ok," she says, her tone one of comfort and sympathy instead of disgust. "We'll just take it a little bit slower."

"Ok," I respond, because I can't think of anything else to

say. I'm in territory that's foreign right now. An hour ago this was a slam dunk, the final chapter in my story of redemption. It wasn't a question of *if* we were gonna have sex, more of when and how long I would last. If I'd was to explain anything, it would be that I don't suffer from premature ejaculation.

Melody pulls me into an embrace and we stand there for awhile, swaying in each others arms as we both contemplate the next move. She begins to try a different angle, her pace more slow and deliberate. She's a very sensual kisser, rolling her tongue against mine and nibbling my lips while massaging my back with her hands. My heart is racing, but I can't tell if it's from arousal or the beginning stags of a panic attack.

In marriage, sex is well choreographed. You know when to start, what positions each person will like, and you have a keen sense of when to try something new and erotic. You know how they kiss, and what little tricks they use to keep the magic flowing. If you have kids, the process is simplified even further. I could tell you which piece of hardwood creaked in my home because that's how we knew the kids were about to burst in. It's like watching one of those dance competitions, except you skip to the final round where all the kinks have been worked out. Efficiency is the name of the game, as every body part and yelp has its place.

But sex with someone new isn't about efficiency. The fun is in the discovery. Feeling the persons body quiver when you try something new, making a mental checklist of what's working and what isn't. You're getting to know someone in their most primal form and it's intoxicating. The goal being to win their mind as well as the body.

My issue right now is the former. I pull away as my

breathing becomes heavier, and when Melody rubs my face, I realize tears are flowing.

"I'm sorry," I say, hoping that I don't have to explain myself. Melody is still on the counter, unsure of what to do next but still being supportive. I step away and try to get ahold of my breathing, like Edward Norton when he played Hulk. I fumble around in my pockets until I can find my phone, and I open a breathing app to help calm me down.

"I'm sorry about this," I say again, and by my calculation, I still owe about a thousand more apologies to explain what just happened.

"It's alright," Melody says, hopping down off the counter and taking a seat next to me on the floor, placing her head on my shoulder and rubbing my hands. "But I need you to know something, I'm not trying to replace Sara."

The look on her face is one of embarrassment, like she let something slip that she shouldn't have. We both know a line has been crossed, and our little fairy tale is coming to an end. It was her desperate attempt to win my mind, and in another time and place, that might have worked.

But it didn't. The only thought in my mind right now is both unexpected and painful.

It's the sudden feeling of regret in marrying Sara and having children; and, to me, having that thought means I should be alone for the rest of my life.

It's an insult to Sara's memory because her only crime was loving me. Ditto that for the kids. Melody deserves someone who can give her the undivided attention she deserves, and as much as I want it to be me, it can't be.

I managed to find another person I cared about and ,in a world where most people can't even find a first love, mine wrecked what was starting to feel like a second chance before it even started. It's maddening how loneliness pushes you into the arms of another person while also making you feel unworthy of love in the first place. I let my guard down and allowed myself to believe in love again, but not only did I get hurt again, I'm breaking Melody's heart in the process.

Life is so unfair.

"I shouldn't have said that, I'm so sorry Miles."

Now she's crying and I'm feeling more like an asshole by the second. Two minutes ago I was on the brink of ecstasy, and now I'm stumbling trying to figure out what the hell is going on. There are so many questions I need answered, but I'm also unsure if I can handle them. The most pressing question is how did she know? If anything, I went to unreasonable lengths to hide my past. In my heart, I know it was John. It's the only thing that makes sense, but I need to hear her say it.

"Was it John?"

She doesn't say anything. I glare at her, looking for any kind of sign to confirm or deny my suspicions. She just stares at the floor—still topless—and now I've been upgraded to horny asshole.

"Was it John?" I repeat with more bass in my voice.

"If I told you the truth, it would only make things worse. But no, he had nothing to do with it, and it's not important. What's important is that I know, and it doesn't change things or me."

I can only muster a sad smile, if only because the idea of us hitting a lower point than *this* is laughable. I had allowed myself to believe in this pipe dream of the possibility of starting a new life, one that included Melody, John, Lily—and even my mother after tonight. But if life was that simple, the world wouldn't be such a shitty place.

"I didn't sign up for this," I say, the cold reality that the fairytale is over.

"Neither did I, but I rolled with it and found something I didn't think was even possible."

"Please don't throw that in my face."

"Throw what?"

"Your whole 'let the universe figure it out' schtick. Life is too real to believe magical shit happens on a whim."

"It led us to each other Miles. I know what you're recovering from is tough, but I also know that what we have is real."

She takes my hand in hers, but I pull away. My mind takes me back to our first date under the bridge, and the sadness I had in the pit of my stomach wishing I had met her without the baggage. That first date feels an eternity away right now, like we'd been dating for years and skipped to breaking point that happens in every relationship.

I get up from the floor and pull her up into a long embrace, taking in her scent one more time before kissing her forehead. Looking in her eyes I want to tell her everything, or at least fill in the gaps, but I can't bring myself to do it. "I'm broken Mel, everything I touch turns out worse than when I found it."

"That's a chance I'm willing to take."

"But I don't want you to, and I'm not sure I can handle whatever this is," I say, gesturing between us. "I'm sorry."

The only positive in this situation is that being fully clothed allows me to escape before she can talk me into staying and dealing with this like a mature adult. I grab my coat and head for the door, knowing that my life will never be the same once her door shuts behind me.

"Miles," she calls as I open the door. "If I told you everything ... about me ... would you stay?"

The question stops me because this whole time I've

been the one holding something in the dark. She's throwing me a life line, one more chance to figure this all out.

"Let's not do this," I plead. "This is hard enough already."

She gets up from the floor but doesn't come any closer. Her shirt stays on the floor, a cruel reminder of a night wasted. "Look me in the eye, Miles," she demands. "Look me in the eye and tell me there's nothing here. Because we both know that would be a lie." She starts slowly moving forward, and I match her by taking a step back. "I know you're scared, believe me, so am I. But you can't let fear control you, because even if it's comfortable now, it'll eventually abandon you. Picking up the pieces hurts more when you're alone."

"You were a distraction," I blurt out. It was the only thing I can say that will get me out of her apartment. It hurts because I don't mean it, but I'm out of options. If I don't do something drastic, she'll convince me to stay, and one day, when I least expect it, Melody will come to her sense and leave like everyone else. For once, I want to know how it feels to be ahead of the curve.

When I was about eight, one of my mothers boyfriends left her in a bloody pulp after one of their fights. He'd left the house and, as I held the ice pack to her forehead, I asked her how a man could treat girls like that.

"When you become a man, you'll realize there's always an easy way out," she had told me. "But taking the easy way doesn't mean you'll be the better man."

That's stuck with me my whole life. Outside of the suicide attempt, I've tried my best to ignore the easy way out. In the interest of being a better man, I have stretched myself in every way possible. But being the better man only seems to benefit everyone else, and honestly, I'm tired of trying.

"Goodbye Melody," I said, closing the door behind me.

I lean against the wall in the hallway, listening to her cry on the other side for a long time. I fight the urge to knock on the door and try again. She'll pick herself up and eventually forget about me. One day, for all I know it could be tomorrow, the universe will send her someone worthy of all she has to offer. As for me, I will take the fact that I left her before having sex as a sign of growth. It's not much, but it's all I have to suppress the heartache.

Riding back to the hotel, I'm annoyed by my cab driver and his incessant need to have conversation. It feels like New York City cab drivers have a sixth sense for detecting despair in their clients. I grunt standard one word answers until he leaves me alone with my thoughts. About halfway through the ride sadness turns to disbelief, as I mull over the idea that John could do this to me. This is the problem with being alone in the world after a traumatic event. You stew in the same negative thoughts without anyone there to talk you out of irrational solutions. The same thing happened the night I tried to kill myself. Having someone there would probably lead to a different outcome.

We hit a snag arriving at the hotel when Mark informs me that his credit card machine isn't working. An argument ensues as the alcohol and testosterone that were earmarked for sexual activity reroutes itself into anger. After minutes of bickering culminate into me dramatically opening my pockets to demonstrate a lack of cash, I find forty bucks in my left pocket that leaves me confused. Embarrassed, I attempt to save face by giving him all of it to cover the twenty dollar ride.

Maybe my luck is changing for the better.

SIXTEEN

SESSION 3: SINS OF A FATHER

"You didn't have to do that Miles. Thank you," Dr. Felt says, genuinely appreciative of the sandwich I brought for her.

"Well, I figured since you were so gentle in making love to my fragile psyche, the least I could do is buy you lunch," I reply, but immediately felt like a jerk. "Sorry, today's topic is is a rough one for me."

"These sandwiches are from Passkey?"

"Is there any other option?"

She shakes her head and takes a bite, humming to herself and mulling my anxiety. "So I was thinking, what would you think about putting the notepad away for this session?"

I wasn't sure if she was being serious, or testing my mettle. I'd had sleepless nights wondering what her observations were. Maybe she thought I was broken beyond repair and she's drafting a nice way of telling me to just play the string out, or she's planning to recommend more sessions because my situation has the potential to be her golden goose.

"Are you being serious, or is this a test? You love torturing me with that thing," I said, nodding to the notebook sitting on the coffee table. Her pen of choice this week is from a real estate company that advertises everywhere and has a B- rating from the Better Business Bureau.

"No, I'm being serious," she says as she takes a bite of some fries before tossing me the notebook. "Read through my observations while I finish my food, I think you'll be surprised."

"About what?"

"About me, you ... hell, your prospects."

The offer was too tantalizing to resist, So, while Dr. Felt loaded peppers onto her sandwich, I examined the notebook for the first time, wondering if I really wanted to know. My name was written across the front in her immaculate handwriting. Seeing my name and knowing it only contained observations about me gives it a personal feeling. Curiosity eventually overcame fear and I dive into her observations of Session 1:

> *Very punctual. Clearly skeptical, but also intrigued by the idea of what therapy has to offer. Uses humor as a way to break the ice. Quick to be witty, but able to get serious when the time calls for it. Tough facade, but quickly shows a heart of gold. Financially secure from tragedy, yet uncomfortable with the strings that were attached to it. Doesn't seem prone to rash decision making, which makes the suicide attempt a perplexing event. Obvious love for his deceased family, possibly a deeper love in the wake of their deaths. Very protective of them. I sense his grief is magnified by his perceived mistakes while they were alive. Will explore in future sessions. Deep hatred for*

his father, hasn't mentioned his mother much, but
hints at a complicated bond. Definitely a topic for a
future session.

"Wow," I say, "I was not expecting that."

"What did you think?"

"I think I couldn't see myself more clearly if I were looking in a mirror," I tell her.

Having someone analyze you and be so spot-on has a dizzying effect. I imagine the people who have portraits painted of themselves have the same feeling. Giving the world—or in my case a therapist—a shallow version of yourself and having her figure out who you really are, boggles the mind.

"Keep reading," she says.

Seeing how accurate she was in describing the first session, which covered nothing, made me cringe at her observations of my childhood. If there was any recommendation about patching things up with my father, I would politely tell her to fuck off. But I read on through session 2:

More at ease this week, really letting his true self
show. Feelings about his father are confirmed, recon-
ciliation is off the table. Keen sense of how childhood
trauma informs relationships later in life. Resent-
ment toward his mother for how he was raised, but
also sympathetic to her circumstances. Professes
indifference on the surface, but clearly cares deeply
for her.

I looked up and noticed Dr. Felt watching me, reading every twitch and movement before I continued reading:

So used to being alone, he buried the good memories of his mother to shoehorn her into a role that's comfortable for him. Blames father for his relationship with his mother falling apart. That combined with what he experienced in being a father himself, cements his position. When pushed, Miles finds positive memories of his mother, though he struggles with articulating them. With a little encouragement, I think they can figure it out. Scared to love because everything he loves, he's lost. So, I can only imagine how hard it is for him to keep trying. Comfortable with ignoring the flaws in people he loves as a way of holding onto them. Avoids conflict and revealing true feelings, brooding on them until it's too late. Has a stepsister that's estranged, a sore spot for him, but I sense this could be a potential launch point. Will explore when the time is right.

I sat the book on the table and rubbed my temples, trying to stall for time and process Dr. Felt's analysis of me. She finished her sandwich and cleared the table, signaling that the session was about to begin.

"So, what did you think?" she asked, no doubt curious on my interpretation.

"You got a lot right, the father part, being scared to love again. That was good work on your part. But, you were wrong about my mother and sister."

"Was I though?" she asks, and her glare is burning a hole through my soul. We sat with our eyes locked on each other for what felt like forever.

She'd hit the nail on the head, and we both knew it. Mind you, this is before we even got to the actual topic of the session.

"So, why did you ask about putting your notebook away?"

"The goal is getting you to open up, and with your paternal relationships that was easy. With you being the child, the only thing you could do was talk about how it affected you."

"I don't get it."

"You weren't in a position of authority because *you* were the child. So, any discussion about changes would be with them, and they aren't my client." She tosses the book in a drawer. "You also have an antagonistic relationship with them, so it was easy for you to let the shit fly. With your children, it's gonna be tough, and I felt writing notes while you work through some of this would be distracting."

"I wish I could just be fixed, that this could just fix me," I say to nobody in particular.

"Your idea of therapy is wrong. Therapy ain't fixing people," she explains. "It's about finding ways of dealing with and accepting the burdens we carry."

"Not sure I follow."

"Think of it like this," she sits up, relishing the moment, "*fixing* implies that the problem has gone away, that everything is back to normal."

"Ok."

"And the only thing that could 'fix' you Miles, would be your family coming back. Since that's impossible, one could argue that you can never be fixed."

"So, if I cant be fixed, shouldn't I just save you the time and leave?"

"No. Like I said, therapy isn't about fixing people. It's about accounting for the trials of life and learning to cope with them. It's also more than just meeting with me. You have therapy every morning when you wake up and decide to keep carrying on, hoping that it hurts a little less each day."

"So, if I can do therapy at home, why do I need you then?" I asks, sounding more like an asshole than I intended.

She smiles at this. "Two reasons: one, because I have no connection to your life. It's the same reason a spouse could never be your therapist—"

"Because she's dead."

"No, because they naturally project their feelings onto you, and in effect, it becomes more about their feelings than yours. The second reason is more about you. Think of every breakthrough we've had. It was *you* that came to the conclusion, I just helped you get there."

"That's pretty insightful Doc. So, what's the launching point about?"

"That's for our last session, we still have work to do."

She rises from the chair and led me to her office, an indication that shit was about to get intense. I sink into my normal place while she washed her hands, and I realize we only have one more session after this one. The thought alone brings a sense of dread over me, but it's not about having to face the world again.

It was knowing that Dr. Felt wouldn't be in my life anymore. I didn't have time to explore the thought, because soon she was back in her customary seat, without the notebook as promised.

"So, I know this is going to be a rough subject for you. But, I hope you understand why exploring who you were as a father is important."

"In a strange way, I'm at peace with it," I say with sincerity. "Where do you wanna start?"

"I'll start with a question. When you think of your children, what is the first thought that comes to mind and why?"

The word appeared immediately like a State Farm agent. "Regret."

"Tell me more. What do you regret?"

I had so many thoughts race through my head. "I used my own father as a crutch. Whenever I would feel bad about not spending time with them, I'd tell myself that at least I was coming home."

"If you felt bad, why didn't you just change?"

A great question, and one I asked myself every time I walked into their rooms.

"I always told myself that I had more time. They were young, and with so much life left, it was easy to assume I could make up for everything."

"What would you do instead of spending time with them?"

"Anything ... I mean, sometimes I would just sit in my car. Once I was home, I'd feel bad about not spending the time and vow to do better."

"Did you do better?"

"No, just the same excuses."

"You do a great job of analyzing yourself. Did you ever know why you found it hard to spend time with them?"

I fiddled with my wedding ring, my eyes focusing on the grooves to avoid looking at Dr. Felt.

"I thought about death, all the time," I start, struggling to convey an answer to a question I asked myself everyday. "Fatherhood was the first time I understood how my childhood would have consequences later in life."

"Expand on that a little bit," she says, earning her money by the second.

"Everything I love, I lose. With my mother, I was so connected to her, and eventually I had to learn that the woman I loved wasn't coming back. I never wanted my kids to have that kind of love stripped from them. So my thought was, if I pushed them away, they'd—"

"—find it easy to move on."

"Exactly."

"Did you talk with Sara about it?"

"What do you think?"

Dr. Felt laughed at the question and rose from her chair. She did this last session, right before she took a verbal sledgehammer to the wall I built around my relationship with my mother. She paces back and forth, swaying her head and muttering to herself. "I think you tried to pacify her."

"What do you mean by that."

"In all of our sessions, I've had to pry everything out of you. Once you get on a roll, you're fine. But you don't show your hand out the gate." She draws the blinds closed, like the start of a bad porno. "Am I correct?"

"You're in the right neighborhood."

Actually, she might as well have been a roommate with how accurate she was. Explaining to a spouse why you had trouble spending time your children is a delicate conversation, one that must be handled with care and maturity. Neither of the required ingredients are my strong suit. Instead of explaining how I felt, which would have deepened our bond, I claimed fatigue about work. In some ways, I was merely a sperm donor. I'd see her Facebook posts with pictures of their adventures together and get angry because I wanted to be a part of it, but I didn't know how. I grew to hate myself because I was becoming the man I despised with all my being, but that little voice in my head convinced me I was better than him because I was still around. It only got worse after Grace was placed on the autism spectrum. Sara began openly wondering if vaccines were the cause, and every night became a fight. She was also pregnant at the time, and given how we struggled with a surprise pregnancy, the issues were only magnified.

It was the only time in my life I could understand why my father left, and the thought of having empathy for him made everything worse. To make up for the absence, I would spoil them with material things. That was a page right out of my mother's book. It got to a point where the kids didn't want dates with Sara because they expected a gift. This only compounded our problems. I was becoming my father, no matter how hard I tried to avoid it.

"Let's say in the future, however long from now, you meet a woman," Dr. Felt let that sentence hover between us, just long enough to make me uncomfortable before finishing her thought, "and you fall in love with her. Would you have children again?"

"No."

Dr. Felt stopped pacing, and I could tell my answer surprised her. We'd been on cruise control up to this point, on the same page with just the formality of her closing arguments left.

"Why not?"

"I don't have that kind of love in me anymore. Any love that's left, wouldn't be enough."

"Don't *have* or don't *want* to have? Because I think it's the latter."

"Who the fuck are you to think you know what's in my heart?"

"I'm the person that was a mirror to you twenty minutes ago," she shoots back. "That's who the fuck I am."

I jump up out of my seat and get in her face, close enough to feel the warm air flowing from her nostrils. She's pushing like she promised in that first session, and her unwillingness to even flinch lets me know that this was part of the game.

Shit was about to get real.

"So, you're gonna throw that in my face?

"Let it out Miles."

"Fine! I failed the first time around, and everyday I have to live with that," I scream, my deepest sorrows bubbling to the surface. "Everyday I have to wonder if they knew I loved them! How sick is that?!"

"Keep going!" She's matching my decibel level.

"I see fathers with their kids everyday and wonder why I couldn't be that guy? Why I couldn't make the library trips, or the movies in the park?"

"Don't hold back, keep going." We circled the room like UFC fighters in the octagon. "Why couldn't you do it Miles, tell me."

"Because I *am* him."

I back into a wall and slide down, exasperated. Dr. Felt drops to her knees in front of me, wiping the sweat from my forehead, her fingertips soothing my throbbing veins. She pulls my head onto her shoulder and whispers something I'll never forget.

"You're *not* him."

I'd had people tell me that before, but this time it held weight. For once in my life, I believed it. It wasn't said to pacify me, or make me feel better about myself. This was a reconstruction of my identity as a human being, and I had one hell of a foreman. She holds me in her arms and sways, repeating the phrase every few moments as if my survival depended on it. For a second, I thought she was reading my mind because every time doubt would creep in, she repeats the phrase and soothe my soul.

"I don't think I could ever give another child the love I withheld from them. "

"Because you're not him Miles. Think about it, he started a new family without blinking an eye right?"

I nodded.

"And you're scared to even consider replacing the one you lost. That alone proves you're different."

"You wrote that my grief was harder because of the mistakes I made."

"Perceived mistakes..." she corrects, "I wrote about your *perceived* mistakes."

"Huh?"

"I wrote that your 'perceived' mistakes magnified your grief."

"What's the difference?"

She lets me go and sets next to me. "You beat yourself up for not spending time with them, without realizing that most parents struggle with that, men especially. You guys can't breast feed, so you start out at a disadvantage in the connection department. Given what I know about your childhood, I would've been surprised if you didn't have those issues."

"I don't know how you do this everyday," I tell her. "Getting cursed out, shouldering everyones problems, you have a gift Dr. Felt."

"Gift of what?"

"I don't know," I say, pulling us both up. "But whatever it is, the shit is worth more than a hundred dollars."

SEVENTEEN

ALL FALLS DOWN

THE ELEVATOR RIDE UP to my room is taking forever, like God is giving me to time reconsider my approach—but it's too late for that. A family shares everything, right or wrong, good or bad. I lost Melody, and I refuse to be the only person with a broken heart.

As I walk to the door I feel a peace rush through me, like the one that hit me after I took all those Ambien. I've gotten so used to saying goodbye that it's routine at this point in my life. It's always been me on the receiving end, left to wonder what it is about me that made me unfit for love. There's a part of me that's relishing this moment, knowing that a relationship is ending on my terms. That I'm the one holding the hammer when the music stops. I could hear them on the other side of the door, laughing and enjoying each other, almost like a real family. Part of me wants to forget about the whole thing.

But I think of Melody, the one sure thing I had left in my life, and the anger comes back.

Their voices get louder as I approach the main living space, Mom's telling a story from her childhood. The room erupts in laughter as she hits the punch line, and I'm greeted like a king as I join them on the couch.

"I wasn't expecting to see you until the morning," Lily says. Judging by the bottles on the table, they'd been going strong for awhile. Her eyes are glassy, the lighting beaming off her corneas like an engagement ring. "I guess it must've been weird having sex with someone else for the first time, I get it. I wanna know every detail, as nasty as you can describe it."

Someday I'll look back and find it hilarious that my sister wanted me to describe a presumed sexual encounter in front of our mother. Today isn't the day for that. I'm frustrated already because I deviated from my original plan. I even played it all out in my head on the ride over. I wanted to yell and curse, but that isn't who I am. Part of me even wonders if it's a big deal that Lily told her, since I would have to explain it eventually. Hell, I even wondered if it was my fault. How could I blame someone else for my issues?

But then I think of Melody's beautiful skin, and the way she'd run her fingertips gently behind my ears, making my body jump before she would pull back and make me want her even more. And her kisses—good lord, the kisses. They were so passionate, from the way she rolled the tip of her tongue against mine, to how she'd bite my lips and stare into my eyes, knowing I would do anything she asked me to do. Finally, that glorious music collection with the section dedicated exclusively to sex. I knew what songs I wanted to mix with certain positions—or the humor, like having sex on the counter to "In Between the Sheets" by The Isley Brothers with no bedding in sight. When I remind myself that I walked away from that, plus the companionship going forward, I think they're lucky I don't kill everyone in this goddamned room.

"Maybe later," I deadpan.

"I knew you two would be perfect for each other, what did I tell you?" Lily says, slapping me on the knee for good measure.

"Yeah, you're a real matchmaker," I say, my blood boiling just looking at her. It's funny how the little things people do irritate you when you're pissed at them.

"Tell me something I don't know, told you we'd get you right little brother. Damnit we want details. Don't we?"

My mother agrees, eager to hear about my exploits and pat themselves on the back for the part they played in it. It's like when someone gives to the homeless but records it on their phone to show the world. You wonder if they did it for the right reasons. Me having sex with Melody is more about them, so I decide to play their game.

"Alright," I agree, "but if we're gonna do this I'm gonna need a drink."

"I'm on it." My mother stumbles getting off the couch but makes it to the bar in one piece. "Vodka on the rocks, right?" She asks before going to work like a surgeon. I've never had one of her drinks, but I'm assuming that years of drinking has at least made her proficient.

My mother hands me the drink and takes her place on the couch. They sit on my left, right, and center respectively —like children at the door of a stranger while trick or treating.

"Ok. So we get to her apartment, and I'm ready."

"I bet you were," Lily says.

"Lord knows it's been too long," this from my mother. She's nodding, with this creepy smile, reminiscent of Jack Nicholson in Anger Management.Being in a suite means higher quality alcohol in the wet bar, but vodka is still vodka and it burns all the way down, giving me just enough courage to continue. I laugh at the absurdity of the situation and they soon join in.

"Anyway," I continue, "we get inside and we're trying to play it cool, you know, be adults about the situation. She went to get dressed and I checked out her record collection, putting on some Isley Brothers to set the mood."

They agreed with the choice of record before chiding me to continue.

"So, she comes from the bedroom and she's got this baggy sweatsuit on that's just begging to be taken off."

"She did that so it could slide off easily," my mother says, her commentary making the moment all the more awkward. I quickly continue because I don't want to know how she learned that.

"Then she goes to the kitchen, and at this point, the small talk is just building our anticipation for the main event."

"You see, that's why you need me in your life, teaching you little things like that. She was just waiting for you to get that shit started," Lily says, drawing laughter and toasts between the three of us.

They think this is a joke, that I am the joke.

I don't know why the thought came into my head. Laughing with someone is different than being laughed at. This is the latter. The combination of vodka and having to recite the moment I walked out on someone I truly cared about is making me emotional. And when I don't have the space to process emotions I get angry. But, I have to hold it together just a little longer, reflection can wait.

"So what did you do next?" Mom asks.

"I jumped her bones in the kitchen. First I pinned her to the stove and took her shirt off—"

"Boy, it had to be the best sex you ever had," Lily interrupts. "Got you crying just thinking about it."

The fact that I'm crying and they assume it's from the quality of sex instead of wondering if maybe they'd pushed me to my breaking point is disheartening. I came back to the hotel to make them feel my pain, yet somehow I'm the one hurting again. Even the justice system, fucked up as it is, has rules in place to make sure you don't get screwed twice for the same shit.

There's a lump in my throat and I'm struggling to keep it together. I use a breathing exercise on the fly, funneling all the air through my nose. Some book I read about dealing with grief said it should allow me to recenter myself and stay in the moment. I'm gonna guess it was never tested in this scenario, and I don't remember a money back guarantee, so I'm shit out of luck.

They need to feel your pain. "Anyway," I say, trying to get back on track, "I lifted her onto the counter and took her shirt off."

"Will you get to the good shit?" Lily drains the rest of her glass.

"So we're making out, but I keep stopping her."

"Performance anxiety happens to the best of us," Mom says, opening another can of worms that I want no part of.

"Not exactly."

The breathing exercise isn't working anymore. I sit in front of them like a science project, each of them having done their own part and waiting to see the final grade.

Do it, Miles. No sense in holding back, the damage has been done.

"So what happened next?" Lily asks.

I wiped my tears away and giggled, savoring their ignorance.

"Well, she pulled me close, and you know what she said?" I asks. "She said that she would never try to replace Sara."

Their faces couldn't have changed any quicker if they been shaken in an Etch-a-Sketch. My mother raises her eyebrows, unsure of where I was going with this, but knowing it wasn't going where she thought it would. Lily, on the other hand, jumped straight into panic mode, forgoing a shot glass and taking a long swig from the bottle. *Drink up Lily, the ride is just getting started.*

"I know guys, it surprised me too." The pendulum had swung, and I was now on the offensive, while they sat being scolded like schoolchildren. "Because I went out of my way to make sure she *didn't* find out about my situation."

They stare at each other uncomfortably, confused by the sudden turn of events. If I wasn't so angry, I'd probably feel sorry for them. Lily rises from her seat and darts to the bar, deciding the vodka on the table wasn't strong enough—like she'd gotten outside the blast radius. In a way, I should be thanking her; it was her theory of me being distracted that got me out of Melody's apartment in the first place.

"You always had to be the center of attention, Lily," I say. "You just couldn't live with another woman being in my life—"

"Excuse me," Mom interjects. "What am I, chopped liver?"

"You'll have your moment in the sun too, trust me," I shoot back. "But let me get back to Little Miss Sunshine over here." I turn back to Lily, feeling more confident that I have in months. "So why'd you tell her? I mean, I already left her crying on the floor of her apartment, so it's not like we have to spare anyone's feelings."

Lily laughs, "I didn't have anything to do with that."

"I didn't have anything to do with that," I mock her. Not the most mature thing I could do, but the alcohol is making everything feel alright.

"Enough!" Mom yells. "Why are you so angry, Miles?"

I take another shot, and this time it's tasteless. Under normal circumstances, they'd have ganged up on me, suppressing my arguments until I gave up. But the alcohol has made things even, acting as a truth serum this family has been lacking.

"Angry? I've never felt this good in my life ... Helen." The look of shock on her face lets me know I was getting somewhere. No matter how angry I would get, there was always acknowledgement that she was my mother, but tonight is different. Jabs have been replaced with full fledged haymakers, each more venomous than the previous one, thrown with bad intentions and little regard for anybody—myself included. "Is this the kind of liquor you guzzled through my childhood?"

"Miles, you need to calm down," she says, sensing something is off.

"I'm calm. I'm calm," I say, clearly not calm. "Just let me know if it is. If so, it helps explain why you were such a shitty mother."

The look of horror on her face makes my heart jump. She quickly regains her composure, but she's already giver herself away, so she opts for damage control. "You're just a little mad, I know you don't mean that."

"How would you know what I'm feeling? You haven't been sober since I was in Kindergarten."

"Maybe I haven't—"

"Don't do that," I stop her.

"Do what, Miles?"

"Rationalize your faults like that." I tell her. "I'm not

sure you know this ... actually, I'm sure you don't, because you're a narcissist ... but copping to your faults later doesn't make you a less shittier person. Believe me, I would know."

Lily tries to jump back in the melee, but I shoot her a gaze and she stays quiet—at least for the moment.

"That's no way to talk to your mother," Helen says. "I understand what you're going through."

If there's *one* phrase or saying I could go the rest of my life without hearing, it's that one. I'd heard it countless times the past six months. Everyone, from neighbors to acquaintances I'd run into, felt like because they knew someone that died, it qualified as them as an expert on my grief.

"Stop saying things like that," I yell. "You can't just show up unannounced, have a few drinks and think that it makes up for everything." I can see she's speechless, but I press on, "I spent my adulthood running away from you, and I did well—at least I was. And now, it turns out I actually need you, both of you," I say gesturing to Lily, "and the thought of that literally makes me sick to my stomach."

Lily steps in between us, having decided Helen had taken enough punishment, and was now on the verge of tears. "If you didn't want me in your life Miles, all you had to do was say the word." She downs the rest of her drink, grabs her overnight bag and heads out the door.

"And then there were two," I turn to Lily.

"That was cold of you," Lily says, once the door is closed. "You didn't have to be that harsh, Miles. She's not the same woman we knew back in high school."

"I'm surprised you didn't go running after her. But then again I'm not, since that would blow your cover, Benedict Arnold." The vein bulges in her neck as she stands there, seething with anger but showing amazing self control. "Oh, don't act like it's some big secret, you've always been in cahoots with her. Anything to make sure your expenses are covered, right?" I stumble to the mini bar and scrounge for more alcohol, any alcohol.

"You really are a fucking asshole, you know that?"

I give a shrug and take a drink, straight from the bottle. "I am, but at least I'm secure in who I am. That can't be said for both of us. But hey, we are who we are right?" I take another swig and it barely goes down, a clear sign that my breaking point was near—which is par for the course at this point. "Now that she's gone, tell me why you had to fuck up the only thing I had going for me."

She takes the bottle from hand and matches my swig with even bigger one. "I already told you, I didn't—" a grin etches its way across her face, "—I did it because you eventually would've fucked her life up. So I decided to save everyone some time since, you know, it's not something we can get back." She moves closer, enough so that I could see the wine stains on her teeth. "So yeah, I told her your sob story, about your little panic attacks every morning, and how you cry like a little bitch in the mirror just to get your day started."

"Our deal is off," I'm too angry to think straight.

"So, you're just gonna throw me out, huh Miles?" She takes another drink. "I don't have anywhere else to go."

"I'm sure you'll land on your pussy just fine," I retort. In my drunken stupor, I was impressed that I was able to come up with that line. "It's time for you to leave."

She goes to her room and I can hear her cursing me from the living room, but I don't take the bait. Instead I start cleaning, an oddly therapeutic exercise for me, except this time I'm not waiting for the pills to kick in. Minutes later she returns, the backpack I bought her from Walmart slung over her arm, and I instantly regret everything I said. She's eerily calm, which gives me hope that I could talk her into staying. Lily was my Dr. Felt before Dr. Felt, helping me filter my raw emotions into cohesive arguments, acting as a sounding board and buffer between me and the world.

And I managed to fuck that up. Again.

She hands me the room key and turns to leave, reminding me of the night Sara left, but she stops at the door and faces me. "Let me leave you with a piece of advice, Miles," she says. "The next time you feel like checking out because life gets too hard, do us all a favor..." her face is still blank, but a twisted smile slowly creeps up, "...make sure you take the whole bottle next time, the world will be better off for it." She lingers for a second soaking in my reaction, and then she's gone, slamming the door and leaving me to be swallowed by the loneliness.

I used to think I hated arguments because I was scared of confrontation, but that's only half right. It wasn't the confrontation that scared me. What I feared was saying hurtful things in anger. Even after you apologize, and both parties agree that all is forgiven, it doesn't take back the words. I've never understood how people could say such horrible things to the people they care about, knowing they'd have to see them again. To my Mother, I'll be the son that kept her at a distance, harboring a resentment that kept its foot on the neck of our relationship—cold, watching the life drain from it. For Lily, I'm the brother that abandoned her—whether that's true or not is open to interpretation—then weaseled back into her life to open a fresh wound. And Melody, that's too painful to think about right now, but it's fucked up too. I held up my end of the bargain with Dr. Felt, and now its time to find shelter in the only coping method I know.

It's time to run away.

EIGHTEEN

SESSION 4: CHECKMATE

THE DAY of my last session with Dr. Felt was easily the scariest day of my life, and for once it wasn't because of the subject matter. Not that diving into my marriage didn't scare me, because it definitely did. It was reality sinking in that I wouldn't be seeing her anymore. Over three sessions, this woman held my hand as we walked through hell together, though the beginning was more me being dragged hesitantly. But she held firm, keeping her word to be there every step of the way, encouraging me to embrace the process, and in turn molding, me into a better person than I was the day I showed up on her doorstep.

And now she was leaving me.

My mind could only process the end of our sessions as abandonment, even though I knew this was part of the game going in. But there was comfort in knowing that there was gonna be another session. That no matter how bad my week would go, there was someone committed to making sure I was gonna be alright. It's moments like this, when the mind can sense the end of something, that I become hyper-sensitive to my surroundings—my senses trying to inventory every scent and visual one more time.

Dr. Felt greeted me like usual, leading me to the office with the shag carpet, giving no indication that she was struggling with the same emotions that I was, or that anything was amiss. I assumed this was normal for her, walking in and out of the lives others making her numb to the goodbye. But I wondered, maybe even hoped, that I was different. As people, we want to believe that there's something different about us, like the john that visits the same prostitute over and over, hoping that he's proven himself to be different enough to make her forget about the job.

I take my customary spot on the love seat, the dust mites floating softly through the air, shining in the glare of the sunlight creeping through the drapes. She takes her spot and waits patiently, getting a sense of my mood before she begins.

"So, we made it to the end," she starts. "How are you feeling right now?"

I'd come to love the start of our sessions. The simple questions she'd throw out, knowing damn well the hard stuff was coming in hot behind it—like a boxer setting an opponent up with a jab while masking the hook.

"It's kinda scary, to be honest."

"That's actually a pretty common emotion. What scares you?"

"You've been a major factor in my life," I tell her. "I know you have other clients, but you make me feel like my recovery is the pinnacle of your life's work. Sometimes I feel like my effort to live is more about not wanting to let you down than actually moving forward. It's just scary knowing that I'm losing that."

She smiles at me. "A lot of my clients thank me, but few

admit the fear they have at the end of our time together. Most play brave and act like they never should've been here in the first place."

I shake my head and grin, remembering our first session and how quickly she snuffed out my bullshit.

"So, with that being said Miles," she begins, "are you ready to dive into who you were as a husband?"

"Yes."

"I'll start with a question. Do you know why I chose Sara to be the last session?"

That's a loaded question. But with Dr. Felt, she always put the candy in the medicine. Her question's so brilliant that while you're wondering why she asked it, your guard drops around the answer itself. She operates on the the fringes of your psyche, leaving precise cracks in the right places, so that you can be put back together without any outward scars.

"I really don't know," I offer up.

"Take a guess and, at the end of the session, I'll tell you why."

"Alright. I think it's because she's the easiest subject to talk about."

She leaned back in her chair, the old rocker squeaking under the pressure. "Tell me more. What do you mean by 'easiest'?"

"Well, you knew my childhood was a sore spot, and talking about my children was a somber affair." I twiddled with my wedding band. "So, I guess for my sake, you figured the end was the best spot for her."

"Oh, you were on the right track up until the end there," she said. "You said in our last session that you wonder if your kids knew you loved them. Do you have the same feeling with Sara?"

"You're just jumping straight in for this last one aren't you?"

"Answer the question Miles."

I sucked my teeth. "I think she knew ... or I hope she did. We weren't exactly the best at showing our feelings. Communication was always an issue with us, and we were incompatible in some important areas."

"Such as?"

"She was naturally passive in nature, and I can be self-ish. There were times I'd just do what I wanted to do because I knew there'd be no pushback."

"You were unfaithful?"

"No, I'd spend money on stupid shit without talking it over like normal married couples do." I sit up, the room feeling stuffier by the second. "Or I'd spend time away from home, claiming to need time to myself."

"That's interesting," she says. During our sessions, that phrase has wreaked more havoc on my mental state than anything else she's said. Just once, I wanna get up and scream, *Why the fuck is everything so interesting?!* It might be the most impressive tool in her arsenal. The way she enunciates the word *interesting*, each of the four syllables get their shine, indicating you're about to go somewhere uncomfortable. Like when your wife says something is "nice", or a husband says that he's "fine", clearly something is there. "Based on your life, I've found you to be passive as well," she observes.

And so it begins. "How so?"

"Well, you craved a better relationship with your mother but could never have the conversation you needed to have with her."

"Because she an alcoholic narcissist an—"

"—and you naturally avoid conflicts out of fear of abandonment." She shifts herself in the chair. "I need you to do something for me in this particular session.I need you to stop protecting Sara."

"What does that mean?"

"I mean you need to be honest about her flaws. With your parents that was easy to do, and your children didn't really have any." She stops rocking, the silence of the room increasing my anxiety. "You have your flaws. But Sara had hers as well, and pretending like she didn't have any, won't help you."

"She's not here to defend herself."

"I'd imagine if she knew you were using them to help you move on with your life, she wouldn't have a problem with it."

"I'll help how I can, but if it gets uncomfortable, I'm outta here."

She chuckles at this. "We both know you won't leave."

I'm not naive, but I didn't think our last session would go like this. I thought it'd be more like the last day of school. We'd go over where we started, talk about how proud she was over my progress, maybe even take a selfie. Even knowing that we were gonna talk about Sara, I figured it would cover my failures.

"Have you ever wondered if you saw some of your mother in Sara?"

I'm not sure if I'm offended by the question or impressed that she had the courage to ask it. In my mind the two weren't even in the same stratosphere. Sara was a representation of everything my mother could never be. Kind. Loving. Empathetic. Take any word to describe Sara, and my mother was the antonym, the polar opposites.

"You've gotta be kidding, right?" I asked, knowing damn well she was serious.

She smirks. "Humor me."

"I don't know why you would try to compare the two, they're nothing alike."

Dr. Felt nodded, as if to agree with me. "You're thinking on the surface level. But look a little deeper. For example, you said Sara didn't push back against you; you also watched men walk in and out of your mother's life without her putting up a fight."

I grip the cushions of the couch so tightly that my knuckles look like they're going to pop out of my hands "It's not the same thing," I say through clenched teeth.

"But in a way, it is. Think about everything you've told me in our sessions." She gets up from her chair and paces back and forth. "You basically walked in and out as you pleased. Does that sound familiar to you?"

I knew in my heart that she was speaking the truth, but accepting it was too much for me. Throughout our marriage, I always made the connection between my childhood and the man I ultimately became. But the silver lining for me was in the differences. I always came back—no matter how far I fell into my worst impulses, I always came back to her. Or maybe she just stayed, and I talked myself into believing it was me that was showing growth. I couldn't bring myself to admit it, and Dr. Felt sensed that, so she let it go and moved on.

"Let me put it in another way," she says. "I think your mother cast a shadow over your marriage, like your dad casted one over who you were as a father."

"You didn't tell me you were an Olympian in your younger years."

"What does that mean?"

"It means you're taking Carl Lewis size leaps in your logic."

She rubS her hands together and smirks, "Am I though?"

If there's one thing I wouldn't miss about our time together, it would be the subtle ways she let me know that I was full of shit. Like when your parents say they're disappointed, and you just wish they'd yell. Her telling me that I'm full of shit didn't have the same impact. Before I could retort she went on.

"You knew firsthand what a bad mother looked like, so you found someone that would be everything to your children that she wasn't to you," she says. "So in that sense, when thinking about it from the kids perspective, she was different."

There's the jab, landing flush, stopping my momentum just enough to line up the kill shot coming over the top.

"But consider this, strictly from the perspective of a spouse," she explains. "You trend toward the familiar, which is normal. And Sara had qualities you found comfort in because they were familiar. That doesn't mean you wanted to have sex with your mother, or anything weird like that, so stop looking at it that way."

"I never went looking for someone that ... look ..." I struggled, thinking back on specific instances Sara would remind me of my mother. "... I'll concede you the similarities, but it wasn't part of my plan. In fact, I didn't realize it until we had Harry."

Dr. Felt nods, pleased with my answer—which only meant further exploration. "Did you ever tell her?"

The laugh came before I could stop it, "I'm not an idiot, Doc," I reply. "I wouldn't trust myself to broach that topic if you were in my ear feeding me the right lines."

Our mutual appreciation for humor brings my anxiety down, marking something else I would miss about her; the understanding that getting the most out of her clients didn't require constant pressure.

"What I'm trying to understand is this: you seemed to find everything you were looking for—beautiful wife, kids that adored you—but you were still unhappy. I have an idea, but I want to hear your thoughts."

"If I knew the answer to that question, they'd still be here."

She raises her eyebrows, surprised by my answer, like I'd just opened a door she'd been trying to unlock. "Let's explore that a bit."

"Let's not," I shoot back.

"Fine, we don't have to go there."

That means we're *definitely* going to go there, she's just waiting for the moment I let my guard down.

The session was feeling more and more like an emotional obstacle course, getting through one task to be greeted by an equally difficult one. Almost like the previous sessions were practice runs for the real deal. All preconceived notions I had about this final session were fading like the color from the old ass carpet.

"Let's come at this from a different angle," she says, as if we'd hit traffic and needed to find an alternate route on a GPS. "Do you think Sara loved you?"

"She stayed with me through three children, that's gotta be a yes, right?" I'm not sure if I'm trying to convince her or myself.

"That's not exactly ... convincing," she admits, the pause in her cadence cuts into my psyche with the precision of a surgeon. "People stay in relationships they're unhappy in all the time. Why do you question her love for you?"

"In all fairness, I question why anybody would love me."

That stopped her pacing, setting in motion the game we

play where I try my hardest to throw her off. "We'll get to that, but let's focus on Sara. Why do you doubt her love in particular?"

"She could never open up to me, no matter how hard I tried. It always felt like she was holding back."

"Can you remember a specific example?"

I rub my knuckles together, trying to find an example she wouldn't be able to manipulate. "There was one time I found a text message. It was to a number that wasn't saved in her phone. She told them how she'd been writing more since they'd met, and I didn't even know she liked to write."

"Did you ask her who it was?"

"Not directly," I said. "I just mentioned that I didn't know she liked to write."

"So you *didn't* ask her then. Were you afraid of what the answer would be?"

"Yes. But instead of knowing for sure, I just kept it in the back of my mind. I'd end up using it to justify my shitty behavior. It felt like that was an even trade. She got to have an affair, and I was absolved of all guilt."

"Sounds like par for the course on your part," she says, throwing in a grin for good measure.

"Well this oughta be interesting. How do you figure that?"

"I think you know."

"Let me guess, because I'm scared of confrontation?"

"Maybe. But think about my notes you read, anything stick out?"

She's pulling out all the stops, and I begrudgingly appreciate the thoroughness of her work. I'd obsessed over her notes from the moment I closed the journal, marveling at her insight into my life, like she'd been a fly on the wall there all along. She wouldn't move forward without an answer so I threw one out.

"I'm gonna go with fear of abandonment," I say, bracing for her laughter.

You know that moment in an action movie where the hero is diffusing a bomb? Usually he cuts a wire and there's about two seconds of silence as he waits for the explosion. That's what these moments of our sessions feel like; me cutting the wire on one of her questions and hoping that shit doesn't blow up in my face.

She wagged her finger at me. "See, you're more intuitive than you give yourself credit for. You put up with the worst of people because you think that'll make them stay. It's natural for someone with a history like yours." She's stopped pacing. "But it's also unhealthy. You questioned why anybody would love you. Elaborate on that."

"Everyone I love seems to end up in a worst position than before they met me. My mother, my kids, my sister ... the fucking mailman." I stands up. "In every situation, I'm the common denominator."

"It's not that you're the common denominator, it's that you don't verbalize your feelings. You harbor anger towards your mother, but can't bring yourself to tell her how you feel. Meanwhile, you guys are drifting farther apart in the time you need each other the most. And Sara—"

"Don't." The tip of my index finger is so close to her nose, I can feel the warmth of her breath. "That one isn't on me."

"You sure? Tell me about the night she left?"

She knew I wouldn't hit her, just like she knew I'd never leave our sessions early. I was starting to understand why she waited until the end for this session. There was something I could sense she was trying to get through to me, but I couldn't put my finger on it. Like some sadistic version of Marco-Polo, I felt my way around, following her clues while struggling to contain my frustration.

"We were having an argument, which was ..." I struggle to catch my breath, stomach queasy as the session lurched into a territory I wasn't comfortable with. "... let's just say it was common during that time."

"What were you arguing about?"

It had been about nothing, like all of our fights during that period. We never talked about the child we lost, and some days I even pretended that he never existed. But his death became the tipping point in our marriage. The home that we built together had become a prison, each of us shackled by feelings we'd ignored for too long. On that day, we'd gotten a check in the mail, a refund from the daycare center from our deposit for our third child. I remarked that at least some good had come from everything. It was one of those moments in life when you say what you're feeling before the mind can filter it. I tried to play it off, but the damage was done. Standing in front of Dr. Felt and seeing the disappointment on her face as I told the story made me feel even worse.

"I didn't mean what I said, Dr. Felt."

She places her hand on my palm, the softness of her touch relaxed my hand.

"I know you didn't, Miles. I know you didn't. But why'd you say it?"

"We didn't recognize each other anymore. On our best days we were co-parents, and on our worst, roommates. I thought if I said something hurtful enough she'd open up to me."

Dr. Felt wiped a tear from her eye and took my other hand in hers. Our relationship had reached the point where some things didn't need to be said. I was about to walk through hell one more time, but she was making sure I wasn't alone.

"You used the only tactic you knew. I can—"

"That's not all I said, Dr. Felt." I breathe heavy through my nose to keep me in the moment. "That's not what made her leave."

"There's more?" she asks, genuinely surprised.

"I told her I wanted a divorce."

The look on Sara's face when I yelled that will haunt me for the rest of my life. The kids stood next to each other, and Grace was screaming like she did whenever we yelled. "Too loud," she repeated over and over—one of the coping methods the autism specialist taught her to help verbalize her feelings. Harry just stood there with a look of calm on his face that was painfully familiar. The look of a child being forced to grow up too fast. It was the look I wore when my mother would argue with whatever random guy she brought home from the bar, after she realized the sweet nothings he whispered in her ear were to get into her bed instead of her heart.

"She was their everything, my everything," I said. "And the last memory they have is me telling their mother that she wasn't good enough anymore."

"How did she respond?"

"That's the crazy part, she didn't say anything. Just looked at me and started getting the kids dressed and headed for the door."

"And you?"

"I was fuming. She wouldn't even look at me anymore, and of all the times we needed to talk she wouldn't say anything." I break off eye contact with Dr. Felt, my eyes darting around the room, which suddenly felt like it was spinning. "She just took our babies and left when we should've worked it out. She gave up on *us...*" my voice trails off as I try to catch my breath, the breathing exercises ill equipped to deal with anxiety of this magnitude. "...she could've come back—"

"And you could've gone after her," she says, finally landing the kill shot she'd been setting up the entire session. "You could've let her know how you felt. And who knows, maybe she still leaves—but you wouldn't be carrying this misplaced sense of fault that's crippling you."

"You see, you just proved my point," I sob. "They'd still be here if I just spoke up—"

"It's ok to have regrets, Miles. That's part of life, and without them, we'd never grow as human beings." She tightened her grip on my hands, enough so that I could feel her rising pulse. "But what isn't alright, is carrying the regrets of the people you love and taking them on as your own. That's been your defense against abandonment., but you need to understand that your worth to people isn't defined by carrying their problems. I know that's hard to wrap your head around, because you feel alone in the world right now."

"I am alone. All I have is a trail of fractured relationships —" her glare silences me. She wipes the tears from my face with one hand, the other still grasping me tightly.

"It's not your fault," she whispered. "You didn't ... kill them, Miles." Both of her are on my face, and now it's her turn to cry. "You can't blame yourself for the mistakes of others, even if you do so out of love. It's unfair to their memory, and it caps your recovery before it can begin."

"It's hard to see it that way. It's hard to see anything in my life as progress."

"Well, let me tell you what I see," she says. "I see a man who loves so deeply, he acknowledges his mistakes when others might sugarcoat them. I see a man that wakes up everyday with a void in his life, who decides to keep fighting, even when the war with himself seems like a lost cause."

I can see in her eyes that she means every word, determined to make sure my last moments as her client are spent preparing me for the world without her. In my peripheral, I can see the base of her palms, placed there specifically to keep my eyes locked on her. We go through breathing exercises together, deep inhales through the mouth, hold, then slow release through the nostrils.

"And most of all," she adds, "I see a person with a heart full of love who just never learned how to harvest it."

More breathing exercises, followed by positive reinforcement, and my mind gradually starts to feel normal again. "So," I say, finally able to produce a coherent sentence, "where do I go from here?"

Dr. Felt smiles wide enough for me to count every tooth. "We go find your launch point. Follow me," she says, leading me out of the office.

* * *

"I haven't lived in this house for many years," she says while making a pot of coffee on the counter.

The kitchen was stuck in a time warp like the rest of the house. The tiles are colored in an aqua that reminds me of the seventies. In the center, there's a small wooden table with a tin of what was originally danish cookies, that I assumed was now full of crafting supplies. The refrigerator shows no markings to indicate usage, making the place feel like a model home you'd walk through in a new development. What does strike me though is the artwork. Posters depicting covers of albums from the seventies decorate the walls.

On one wall, Marvin Gaye in a red beanie, hands on his head in frustration is the cover of his Let's Get It On album. Next to it is a colorful album cover with various characters draped in psychedelic galore—Sgt. Pepper's Lonely Hearts Club by The Beatles. The opposite wall showcases her wilder taste in music. Rick James standing on a corner, guitar in hand with bright red boots on his feet, with a look on his face conveying that your lady friend would be his next conquest. The other is black and white with a figure sitting on an old motorcycle, a cape on his back, staring into the abyss with four faces floating around the side lights of the motorcycle. It's a classic album cover, known to anyone who's a fan of rock music. Quadrophenia by The Who.

"You're a fan of The Who?" I'm genuinely impressed. I figured with her being an academic, she'd be more partial to Mozart or Beethoven like other smart folks that act better than everyone else.

"My love for the '60s and '70s goes deeper than the decor of this house," she says with a smile. "You a fan?"

"They're probably my all time favorite band. Actually, I'm lying. My favorite band is Oasis. But The Who is at least top five," I tell her. "I mean, two of their albums were basically audio movies played through headphones."

"I saw them in their heyday, with Pete jumping around and smashing his guitars. This was back when Roger could still hit the high notes and Moon was still alive," she says, heading over to the fridge. "What's your favorite album from them?"

I love conversations like this, because there isn't a wrong answer. "Gonna have to go with Quad, it was the first record that showed me how powerful music could be. I also discovered it in high school, struggling to find my place. So I guess it just spoke to me. But if you named any of their first seven, I wouldn't argue. What about you?"

"It changes daily, but I would go with Who's Next at this moment. It's just the sound of a band reinventing themselves in the '70s while thanking the '60s for molding them. You're in your twenties, not exactly in their target audience so—"

"—so how did I find them," I say, cutting her off.

"Yeah."

People of older generations love to know how younger folks got into the music of their youth. It's a genuine curiosity where the right answers grant you passage into their secret society. Maybe they let you see an old ticket stub or, if you're really lucky, snippets of a bootleg recording. Imposters, such as people who can only name the hits are quickly discovered and ridiculed. But if you have a genuine love and respect for the music, it leads to bonds forged and stories untold.

"I was in a record shop one day, sophomore year of high school. I heard this sound, almost like a video game score, then the piano and drums. It was Baba O'Riley. I only had enough money to buy one cd and Quad had a cool cover. One of the best decisions I ever made."

"It is a neat little cover, isn't it." She admires it, no doubt reliving her own memories of a time when music was all that mattered.

In keeping with tradition, she prepares the coffee with little technology. A single pot of boiling water on the stove followed by two scoops of instant coffee in a small mug. She's in her element as she glides gracefully from one part of the kitchen to the next, never neglecting any task long enough for it to become a fire hazard. She places bagels on the table, and I assume if I want butter, there's a shed out back where I churn it myself.

"What made you become a therapist," I ask, jump-starting the conversation again.

"Part accident, part yearning to help others," she says before plopping into her seat.

"If I have to elaborate, then you should too—unless your love for the '70s extends to gender equality as well."

"You've got a sense of humor and it's appreciated," she says with a chuckle. "Well, I grew up in a broken home, and I used the thought of living in poverty as fuel to go far academically. Between bad relationships in college and having to confront my past, I found my passion working to help others that are stuck in a rut."

"Does it ever get overwhelming?"

"Not at all," she says, placing her coffee cup on the table. "I feel if you choose a profession, you have to accept everything that comes with it. It's frustrating that clients sometime leave, and I never know what happened to them, or if I really helped them."

"What do you mean? Nobody ever comes back to update you?"

She sips her coffee for a moment. "Typically, no, but it's complicated. For example, if you leave here and I call you next week, that could plant a seed of doubt in your mind about how you're doing. Which could foster dependency, running counter to everything we've done; and I think we'd both be alright with not doing this all over again. So I usually don't call, because at some point, my work has to speak for itself."

"So this is it for us?" I ask, my fear slowly morphing into anger.

"Miles—"

"You're just gonna leave like everyone else, after every-thing you know about me—"

"I'm not going anywhere, like I said, it's complicated." She knew this moment was coming, I surely wasn't the first client to panic at the idea of leaving the nest. For all the jokes I made about the house, there was something comforting about it that I would miss. "My phone is always on, Miles, but I would be doing you a disservice as my client to keep bringing you back to rehash the same memories that brought you here in the first place. At some point, you have to stop being a spectator and get in the game."

In my heart, I knew she was right. Life was always going to move on, whether Dr. Felt was in my life or not. I came into therapy thinking it would make my problems go away, like they never existed. But it doesn't work that way. You come into therapy enslaved to toxic behavior and coping methods. Therapy is about acknowledging them and building up a resistance, because the world will test you, and those toxic methods—so familiar—will welcome you with shelter. The rest of my life will be a daily challenge to accept that my family is gone, whether I accept that challenge and use the tools Dr. Felt has provided, is on me.

After I woke up in the hospital, I figured I would up the dosage and complete the job. I was right about completing the job, it just wasn't the one I set out to finish. One thing for sure is the feeling of resilience inside me. Maybe there was a future. The feeling will pass, but as of right now, I'll fight on. I owe Dr. Felt that much at least.

"You had a therapist?" I ask.

"I did. Sometimes you need someone with no connec-tion to your life to help you get your shit straight. Friends are cool, but at some point, they think it's about them, or just give shit advice."

She had a point. I've experienced said shit advice. It's easy for people to give you advice when they're not invested. Like a sports fan calling their local radio station after a bad game trashing the coaches. They're on the outside looking in, where it's easy to say run the ball, but it's not their livelihood on the line. While grieving, friends of mine—perhaps unknowingly—treated me like a karmic tollbooth. Stopping out of obligation to drop kind words, before briskly moving back into their own world, while patting themselves on the back.

"So, what are you gonna do?" Dr. Felt asks as she takes a bite of a bagel.

The question hung there awkwardly, like a fart on a first date in a movie theater. In all honesty, I hadn't thought about it. I spent so long ignoring everything that no thought was given to the future.

"I don't know," I say, honestly.

A long silence envelopes us. I sit, eating my bagel and drinking coffee, unsure of what was about to happen.

"What you need," she says finally, "is a break. You can't squander your second chance in front of the television."

"Second chances are for convicts and deadbeat parents with a terminal illness."

She laughs a beautiful and hearty laugh, full of life. After a few seconds I'm laughing along with her.

"What if I don't want to take a break?"

She gives me a smile to convey that she anticipated that question. "If I sent you back home only to return in two weeks, you'd sit with the same painful memories, which in turn would undo all of our progress, and end up with us back at square one."

This is a valid observation. While I'm feeling good now, there's four seasons of Breaking Bad sitting on the coffee table at home, itching to pull me back into the abyss. "So where do you want me to go?"

"You talked about the regret you have about not being a better spouse and father. It makes me wonder what other regrets you have?"

I lean back and ponder the question. Do I have any regrets? Sure, there were girls I had never slept with and job opportunities I had talked myself out of, but for the most part, nothing life changing enough to spend my "second chance" trying to rectify. The only thought that comes to mind is my stepsister Lily. After she came out of the closet and was disowned by our family, we lost touch. Last I heard, she was at grad school in New York.

"I have a sister ... Lily."

Her eyes lit up like a Christmas tree, happy that I'd picked up what she'd hinted at in her notes. "Go on," she tells me.

"When she told our family she was gay, they flipped out on her and our relationship got lost in the shuffle."

"It's not a deck of cards Miles, this is one person who clearly means something to you. I think you owe it to each other to reconcile that relationship."

"I thought this hundred bucks covered my emotions, I wasn't aware you offered pricing in bulk."

She can sense the apprehension and goes in for the kill. "What's stopping you?" she asks. "You've got the resources, and more importantly, the time to make things right."

Now she's a motivational speaker. A slightly insensitive one, but nonetheless effective. She gets up from the table and pulls a laptop from a messenger bag in the corner. After sitting in a house observing technology that was manufactured when Cher had her last hit, it was refreshing to see something made in the post industrial era.

Sandra is clicking furiously on different links before turning the laptop to me. An American Airlines stewardess smiles at me, the page set to a red eye flight to New York City.

"You gotta be shitting me."

"This is your point of launch, Miles. Not sitting at home feeling sorry for yourself, or coming in here every week, dredging up the past and putting off the inevitable." She leans forward and the table creaks, a warning that it wasn't as spry as it used to be. "The truth is, you don't need me anymore, you just have to trust in your grief and let it guide you to be the man you want to become."

"Anything else?"

"Yes. Don't pack anything, just head to the airport," she says, getting up from the table. "Let the spontaneity consume you."

I feel a rush of excitement in my chest—that, or an oncoming panic attack. Before I can think of a rebuttal, my wallet is out and the flight is booked. As Sandra puts the laptop away, I lean back and rub my temples, coming to terms with the ending of our working relationship. We banter on for awhile, like friends do when they're trying to prolong the goodbye. Each of us coming up with new subjects to talk about to buy time, knowing when I leave, it will never be the same. I lose track of time and realize I have to get on the road if I'm going to make the flight. We share a long embrace, and I feel the lump growing in my throat, my tear ducts warming up for another water show. But I hold firm, because if she saw me cry, I'd have to stay and talk, and I've done enough of that already.

It was time for action.

"You alright?" she asks.

"Yeah, I just ... thank you ... for everything."

She released me and holds the door open, "You're welcome."

As I step out, I turn to look into her eyes again, remembering the first time she answered the door. But I see that her smile isn't the same, and I know that she's cared about me beyond the parameters of her job. It was then I made myself a promise, that even if it took the next ten years, I would figure out my life as my way of saying thank you for everything she'd done for me.

I chuckle, "Everything I love, I lose."

"You're not losing me, Miles. You're just going to find yourself," she replies, profound to the very end.

She watches me back out of the driveway, never moving, one hand shielding herself from the sun so she could watch me drive away. I honk twice and pulled off, watching her grow smaller in the rearview before she's gone, fading out of my life as peacefully as she entered it.

NINETEEN

UNSCHEDULED OPENINGS

"I DON'T KNOW why I'm doing this, because I know you'll try to talk me out of it," I say into the phone. "I don't need a therapist right now, but I could really use a friend."

There's silence on the other end of the phone as Dr. Felt mulls my offer while surely trying to find a loophole that'll allow her to slip back into the therapist role. The intercom in my terminal announces that my flight will begin boarding shortly. Unfortunately, because I bought my ticket at the last minute, I'm at the end of the final boarding group.

After an eternity, she agrees to be a friend, though we both know that it won't last long. "Talk to me, Miles. What's going on?"

"What—" I struggle to convey the words, "what do you do when you've fucked everything up?"

She lets out a long whistle, like the one a mother makes when you wreck the car but haven't told dad yet. The voice over the intercom announces that my flight is now boarding, so I take the long walk to the back of the line.

"Where are you?" Dr. Felt asks. She knows where I am, like she knows why I'm calling. But having me speak my line of thinking out loud is part of what makes her so great at her job.

"I'm at the airport." I say. "Look, I don't have long, my flight is boarding as we speak."

"Alright, but at least let me talk to you before you get on the plane, can you agree to that?" she asks, sounding more like Dr. Felt and less like Susan.

"Deal."

"Ok, let's start with the obvious. How did you fuck everything up?"

"The pain is still too fresh, and I don't wanna relive it. I just want you to know I did what I set out to do, but I'm coming back home."

"Your goal was to reconnect with your sister," she presses further. "If you did that, why are you calling me after midnight from an airport terminal?"

"Because it got complicated."

"I'm flying blind here, no pun intended. Tell me what's going on."

"I see her face everywhere, Dr. Felt, literally every time I close my eyes, all I see is her crying on the floor." The people in my part of the line are staring, and on instinct, I look down to make sure I don't have an erection. "She was willing to take me as I am, with all I've been through, and I walked away from her."

"From Lily?"

"Melody."

"Melody," she says, trying to recall where the name fits in my journey. "The girl from the coffee shop?"

"Yes."

"Oh...Wow. Man I wasn't expecting that." She hums for a few seconds. "Ok, you gotta start from the beginning."

I break everything down, starting with going to Lily's

school and the bribed security guard. Not the most pertinent detail, but it's a kick ass starting point. Lily's apartment comes next, the falling debris and potential accessory to property destruction charge getting their moment to shine. Next, I talk about my mothers appearance, and the WWE style entrance to boot. Finally, I tell her about Melody. I start with the number on the cup, and then the dates, leaving out the erection in the ice cream shop, but explaining how my feelings changed over time. I explain the night in her apartment, and the remark about not replacing Sara, which naturally leads to the fight with my mother and Lily. Lily's last words sting even worse hearing them come out of my mouth.

There is a long silence as the line I'm standing in moves at a snails pace. The first group has just finished boarding, with three more coming before they get to my group.

"You've been busy," she finally says. "I know we don't have much time, but I wanna work through this with you. If you didn't call me, what was your plan, and why?"

This is one of the reasons I love having her as my therapist. She never gets too high, approaching issues with a calmness that brings you back down to earth. It's from that level place that she helps you find a solution. At her price she's an absolute steal.

"Honestly? I saw there's seven seasons of a show called Shameless on Netflix."

"That's a great show," she says.

"Yeah, and I found the premise to be right in the wheelhouse of my current situation. So I figured, maybe get through a couple seasons of that—"

"And end up in the same environment that put you in my office in the first place. Not a good plan."

I laugh loudly, not because its funny, but because Dr.

Felt has done this shit enough that I should've seen it coming. The airline has made it through the next boarding group, and now it's moving at a brisker pace with all the strollers and families out of the way.

"I don't wanna feel anymore, Dr. Felt. This whole trip was a failure, even though I'm feeling different than when I got here."

"That's an interesting choice of words."

"What?"

"You said you felt differently than you did when you got there. Not that you felt worse, that you felt different."

"I didn't say I felt better—"

"But you also don't feel worse," she interjects. "That alone is confirmation that your trip wasn't a failure. I'd argue that it was a success, even if you refuse to give yourself credit. You're doing well Miles."

"Doing? You mean done. I'm through with this, the only reason I called is out of respect for the journey we've been on together."

"I think we both know that's a lie," she says, swatting my bullshit down in a hurry. "You called because you're scared, and I'm not talking about your mother and sister."

Beep.

Beep.

Beep.

They've finally reached my boarding line, the beeping of the boarding pass scanner growing closer by the second as the airline employee finally starts to hit her stride.

"I'm not scared," I say. Sounding weak and scared.

Twelve people stand between me and the bridge to the plane, with the scanner so loud that even Dr. Felt can hear it.

"I'm not gonna tell you what to do, you know I don't

work that way." Her tone is soft but focused now that she knows I'm almost to the front of the line. "And I will support whatever decision you make."

"Thank you, I appreciate that," I say.

Beep.

Beep.

Beep.

"But..."

Shit, here it comes.

"I'll leave you with this: I know getting on that plane feels like the right thing to do—and in some ways that might be true—but it's also the easy thing to do."

"I thought you said you weren't gonna tell me what to do, because right now, it sounds like you're telling me what to do."

Beep.

Beep.

Beep.

"I'm not telling you to stay ... and I'm not telling you to go," she says. "But the biggest regret in your life was watching Sara walk out the door. If you come back home, you're walking away from everything you've done to live the life she would've wanted you to. And I promise you, one regret won't replace the other."

Beep.

Beep.

"I'll see you soon Doc," I finally say, reaching the counter.

"Will I?" she shoots back. One last dig, for old times sake.

"I gotta go." I end the call with her in mid-sentence. I stare at the phone, my boarding delayed by the person in front of me complaining about his seating arrangement. I realize I never took my ticket out, and I empty my pockets trying to find it. It's finally my turn at the counter and I hand her my boarding pass.

"Thank you, Mr. Alexander" the stewardess says. "Enjoy your flight."

"Actually, something's come up. I won't be making the flight."

"Oh my God," she says, her face morphing into concern. "Is there anything I can do for you?"

"No, nothing is wrong," I assure her. "I'm just an idiot."

She smiles and I turn to leave. "Actually" I turn back, "can you toss this out for me?"

I take off the hospital band, freezing for a second as I consider if I really wanna throw it away. During my recovery, I could always look down at that wrist band to remind myself how far I'd come. But too much of a good thing eventually turns bad, and it's become a crutch. The stewardess takes it apprehensively, sensing there's more to the story with the wristband.

As I'm walking through the terminal, I shoot a quick text to Dr. Felt.

Looks like you win again.

TWENTY

TAILS NEVER FAILS

FOR BEING one of the busiest airports in the country, I'm impressed with the efficiency of the taxi stand. By this point I shouldn't be surprised with how quickly things move in this city, but it's worth noting.

That's also bullshit because I'm stalling with the decision at hand.

In the span of six hours, I'd managed to napalm the only relationships that still mattered in my life, laying waste to each in such brutal fashion that I'm questioning if it's even worth trying to figure it out. But something—for my sake I'm going with growth— wouldn't let me get on that plane. I feel like a gambler that's down to his last few dollars, who decides to go all-in on an eight team parlay that stands no chance of hitting, but also carries a reward large enough to cover all losses.

I just need to find a starting point.

My heart wants to go after Melody first, partly because it seems to be the path of least resistance. There wasn't a blowup, no words spoken that would take time to mend. In fact, had I not freaked out, I would've realized what she actually said relieved one of the mental hurdles I had about dating in the first place. My only hope is that when I find her, she'll remember how great it felt when we were together, and give me a chance to explain everything. We're just two people with an incredible amount of baggage trying to fit it all in the same overhead compartment.

Lily, on the other hand, is a different kind of beast. The venom of our words will have residual effects for years to come. But then again, nothing about our relationship follows the pattern of your average siblings. Some would even call it unhealthy, but it's ours and we've learned to operate within the prism. When our fight is viewed through the lens of our past, I know she didn't actually want me to kill myself, just as she knew I wasn't in opposition to her lifestyle. We only know how to communicate through raw emotion, with a filter being optional and, in most cases, absent. That's why Dr. Felt said to start with Melody. She knew Lily and I can pick up right where we left, just like we did upon my arrival.

I'll let fate decide who I should start with, removing any bias by flipping a coin. If it lands on heads, Lily, and if it's tails, Melody. The coin flip is harder than I meant for it to be, and the quarter hangs in the air like there's no urgency to the situation. No biggie, just a potential romantic relationship and family reunion at stake. It lands in my hand, where I quickly flip it onto my other hand and cover it like it some big secret. A quick glance at the folks in the terminal reminds me that nobody gives a shit.

It's heads, and I'd be lying if I said my stomach didn't drop. Melody's been running a marathon through my mind from the first time I saw her, but she's gonna be running a little longer because the gods have spoken. I pull out my phone and dial Lily's number, but it goes straight to voicemail.

"Hey, it's Lily. Leave a message and if I like you then maybe, possibly, I'll give you a call back."

Beep

"Lily, it's me. Look, we both know what our relationship is, but that doesn't make any of the things I said to you ok. I'm not leaving the city until we talk, so if you want me out of your life, you're going to have to look me in the eye and tell me that. I love you. See you soon, I hope."

That might've been the weirdest voicemail ever recorded—and I've left voicemails for my deceased wife. In some ways it sounds like something Sting would have written for The Police, but it was honest, and I think it'll have the intended affect. I've never done cocaine, but the rush I have right now has gotta be in the same ballpark. I don't know where she's staying, so I wonder where she could be. Where would someone with a fucked up family history go after telling their brother to kill himself? A place with alcohol is a given, but that can only numb so much of the pain.

A grin comes across my face because it's almost too brilliant.

But...

What if that place had alcohol *and* beautiful women that will tell you exactly what you want to hear? I just so happen to know of such an establishment.

The cab driver greets me like an old friend when I get in the car. Now *this* is a true New York City taxi. The dashboard is decorated with 'I Love New York' stickers, the radio is is tuned into the local sports station, and hanging from the mirror is the Met's mascot, Mr. Met. I give him the address to Rouge and we head off into the city. Because I'm selfish, I decide to send Melody a text.

I understand if you never wanna talk to me again. But can I just have a chance to explain myself?

I stare at the words on the screen, angry that I can't find the words to convey how I really feel, but unsure that they'd work even if I could fine them. I hit send before I give myself the chance to overthink it.

"You flew all the way here with no luggage for a stripper?" my driver asks. He doesn't tell me how he knows it's a strip club.

"Not exactly."

"Man, you gotta be in my top five strangest pickups," he continues. "I get guys cheating on their wives, dope dealers, and prostitutes that charge anything from five to five thousand dollars. Where you fall in?'

"I think I'd fall somewhere between the prostitute and the philanderer."

"You a funny motherfucker man," he says between laughs. "The name's Trent."

His voice is one of a true New Yorker, a booming baritone of someone that had to learn how to be heard in a city with so much noise. He kinda sounds like Raekwon of the Wu-Tang Clan. Adverbs are an exception instead of the rule.

"I'm Miles." I notice he's wearing a Giants beanie, and decide to have conversation that takes my mind away from everything. "You think it's time to move on from Eli?"

He scoffs, "It's been time. Every cat from Long Island to Yonkers know it was that time three years ago, my guy. He brought us two chips, and I got love for my man, so I'm not gonna call him the B word."

"Bitch?"

"Bum. I can't do my man like that after all he did for us."

He shakes his head in despair, like he's watching a friend wither away. "Who's' your team?"

"I'm an Eagles fan."

He blows out his lips, spraying mist all over the steering wheel before laughing. "You gotta be kidding me son. The bum-ass Eagles?"

"You mean the eight and one Eagles," I correct him. For the first time since I was in high school the Eagles have legitimate Super Bowl aspirations, history be damned.

"You right. Y'all doing your thing right now. That Wentz kid is a stud, reminds me of a young Eli."

"That's not the compliment you think it is."

"True, True, but I'm rooting for you guys. Anybody but the Cowboys."

I'm liking this guy more and more. "Amen to that." We share a pound and the conversation switches gears. "So, is this your only job Trent?"

"I do this on the side for a little extra bread. Wife ain't working, and my son loves baseball, so I gotta do what needs to be done. I make as many games as I can, but it's hard sometimes. You got seeds?"

"Seeds?"

"Kids man, kids."

I knew the question was coming, it was only logical, but nevertheless, I wasn't prepared to answer. There should be a course that trains you on how to reenter society after the loss of a loved one. Specifically for situations like this. Maybe some role playing exercises and a nifty certificate when you pass the final exam. You could even play on the subject matter by calling the graduation a 'Pity Party'—a burgeoning marketing career awaits me.

We just met and the conversation was going better than any I'd had in months, I didn't wanna make it awkward. But,

I can't live in a shell forever so I might as well get used to this new normal.

"I did have kids..."I finally say. The words hang there as I listen to the taxi roll over small bumps in the pavement. "they passed away."

No tears.

No heavy breathing.

No panic attack.

No pain.

Just the simple acceptance of a reality I've been been running from; and an acknowledgment that I was finally comfortable enough to deal with it. I can't help but think of Dr. Felt in this moment and the dedication she showed, so that I could have little moments like this, even though she'd probably deflect all credit.

"That's heavy man, I'm sorry," Trent says.

His tone is softer, which I've found is common when I tell people about the accident. Their voices get lower and, depending on seating, eye contact ceases. At that point we both start looking for an out; me because it hurts too much to talk about, and them because they can't help but be curious.

But I understand it completely.

Everyday we're bombarded with indications of the future—from the next iPhone, to our favorite sports teams planning drafts and contracts years down the line, even political elections. We assume that we'll be around to see it, and we take things for granted in the process. But then you meet someone that's terminally ill, or someone with a story like mine, and it humbles you because it makes you stop and realize your mortality. My story is clearly weighing on Trent because we're riding in silence, which I find happens anytime I tell my story.

"Does your son follow the Mets like you do?" I ask, trying to signal that it's alright to keep talking.

He smiles at the question. "You wondering if he jumped on the Yankee bandwagon instead of pouring his life into this sorry ass team? He wanted to follow the team I follow. Shit, maybe he'll see a parade during his lifetime, but I'm not counting on it."

He won't.

Sports was one of the things I was most excited about as a father. My childhood friends had two parent families and Dads that would take them to games. Lily's Dad, Greg, used to do stuff like that with me. I always appreciated the time we spent together, even secretly kept in contact with him after the divorce. Even though the time was fleeting, I welcomed the escape.

I saw myself picking Harry up from school early on a random day and hitting a ballpark for a day game, and seeing the look in his eyes the first time he saw a baseball stadium.

"I always wanted to see the new stadium, you been over there yet?"

"I went the first year and it's nice, but it ain't Shea Stadium." He rubs his beard. "Don't get me wrong, the old stadium was a shit hole, but it was *our* shit hole. New stadium just don't got the same character, and the Wilpons priced out guys like us. Two tickets run higher than my gas bill in the winter, and it ain't like we putting out the best product. You believe that shit? Can't even take my boy to the fucking game."

"Are the views that bad up top?"

He takes a long sip of his coffee, savoring it like a pinot before swallowing it and smacking his lips. "They really aren't, and any other game I'm all about sitting up there, but I want his first game to be special. Know what I mean?"

"Yes, but since we're in bumper to bumper traffic, let me hear it?"

"Alright. Dom pitches and plays third base on his off days, so I wanted him to be close for that first one, see Syndergaard drop that heater up close, maybe get an autograph before the game. You know, see that there's more to life than this shit here." he gestures to the world around us. "I also wanna drive there and do the tailgate thing, throw on the Daryl Strawberry throwback joint and play catch while we grill."

He speaks with such passion and attention to detail, I can tell this was something he thinks about often, adding layers every time he replays it in his mind throughout the day. Every step of the day is planned out, down to which team store they'd hit inside the stadium to purchase Dom the jersey of his choice—starting pitcher Noah Syndergaard.

"He saves his allowance every week to get that jersey, got a flow chart in his room that tells him when he'll have enough. He don't know it, but I'm checking all the ticketing apps, and one day I'm gonna make that shit happen," he says, taking another sip. "On my mother, it's gonna happen Miles."

I believe him. "When I was Dad, I dreamed of doing stuff like—"

"—are a Dad."

"Huh?"

"Listen to me man," he shifts his weight and finishes his coffee "you're a Dad, whether they here or not. That shit don't ever leave you. Your time might have been short but, look at me," our eyes meet in the rearview, "you'll always be a father, so wear that badge proudly, and be thankful for the time you did have."

"You'll never know how much I needed to hear that, Trent. Thank you."

"No doubt."

"The Mets still not finishing better than my Phillies this year though."

We share a long laugh and spend the next few minutes trading insults, talking about sports, and swapping stories about fatherhood. The surroundings start to look familiar from the first time I came here, signaling that the ride will be coming to an end soon. He takes a call from his wife while I play around on my phone for the last stretch of the trip. A new security guy I don't recognize from my first visit is at the door, and I wonder if it's a wasted trip. But something tells me I need to be here.

"What's your cell number, Trent?"

"I'm probably gonna be in a different part of the city by the time you leave here."

"It's not for a ride, what's the number."

He gives it to me in exchange for my credit card, and I type away furiously as the printer slowly prints out my receipt. His phone dings just as he hands me the card and receipt to sign. It takes him a moment to realize what he's reading.

"Miles, you bugging son. Three rows behind home plate? I can't accept this man."

After signing the tip receipt I hand it to him. "Should be enough there to cover jerseys, popcorn ... the whole nine."

He gets out of the car quicker than me, pulling me into a bear hug before I can close the door.

"I know money is important, but try to make all the games you can," I tell him. "Take it from me, you don't wanna sit around wishing you could have it back."

"No doubt. I don't know what to say man, thank you."

I turn to leave and start for the door.

"Yo, Miles," Trent calls, he's hanging over the roof of the car. "I hope you find whatever it is you looking for my guy."

I thank him, tell him to let me know how the game goes, and with a tip of his Giants cap, he hops back in the car and takes off.

Now I'm back in the real world, and I can honestly say I'm not scared of whatever the consequences might be. Three overpriced and watered down airport drinks are known to have that effect. Neither of them has answered to my messages, so I feel like I'm back at square one.

But I'm back.

And that's a win in and of itself.

* * *

Rogue is more lively this time around, with roughly double the amount of dancers and a large customer base diverse enough to make a music festival look like a Klan rally. According to a leaflet handed to me by a hostess, it's 'Pies and Thighs' night, a clever play on words that carries good value. If I order at least ten wings, it come with a free slice of pie, which is a pretty sweet deal. The amount of traffic in here is problematic because my plan—which is looking shittier by the second— revolved around finding three dancers in particular. Harmony, Nikki, and the third dancer Lily had sex with. As I watch the swarm of people move around the floor, I realize my plan has major flaws.

They're all wearing masks, which is cute and erotic when it's your first time, but doesn't help when trying to find someone. After a while, they all start to look the same, the only difference being the lingo used to lure you in. Another complication, and one that I didn't consider, is that Lily might not even be here. It just seemed like the perfect place for her to be after our argument. We both posses self destructive qualities, matching the bad moments in our lives with even worse situations, each running parallel with the other until they somehow collide dramatic fashion.

I find a table above the main floor and spend the next twenty minutes scanning for anybody that looks familiar.

"Well, if it isn't Mr.Dickpill," a familiar voice says from behind me. "You clean up well."

I turn to find one of Lily's trysts from the other night— Nikki, if I remember correctly. The purple tips of her spiked hair glows in the neon lights, just like it did the morning she found me on the bathroom floor. She's twirling an empty drink tray, stopping to use a familiar face as a brief refrain from the madness in the rest of the club.

"Hey, Nikki," I reply. "You're not dancing tonight?"

"No, the menstrual gods decided I deserved the night off," she says, frustrated to be missing out on easy money. "Where's Lily?"

"I was hoping you could help me out with that."

"Sorry, man, I haven't seen her since I left your hotel."

"Damnit. Is the other girl from that night here?"

"Summer has the night off." She scans the main floor for someone. "Harmony is around here somewhere, maybe she can help you. Just look for the girl with the heels that light up when she walks. It'll be awhile before you get a server, you want something to eat?"

I order ten lemon pepper wings, two beers, and a slice of apple pie. Nikki wishes me well and scampers away to enter my order. I check my phone and find no missed calls or text messages, feeling more like a failure by the second. I'm drawing a blank on my next move, a consequence of putting all my eggs in one basket. The Dj announces a buy one get one on lap dances, causing a mini stampede of drunk and horny men to engage their most primal desires in a frantic race to find their favorite dancer. I notice Amy about five feet from my table, apprehensive about what's going on, and I can't say I blame her.

"Hey, Amy," I call out. She turns and looks at me, and I swear for a second she's gonna run away. "I'll take the two for one if you just sit and keep me company, no dancing. It'll be the easiest twenty bucks you'll make tonight."

She ponders my offer for a second before agreeing with me and taking a seat.

"You lost the hospital band," she says, motioning to my wrist.

"Yeah. As it turns out, it's a conversation starter for all the wrong reasons." Amy laughs at this, the weirdness of the other night melting away faster than the ice in the drinks from the bar. "You still trying to find your footing here?"

"I actually put my two weeks in last night. This just isn't my thing ... being used as an object in someone else's fantasy and then giving half my money away. At least as a waitress, I have managers that get rid of the creeps."

"I could see that."

"But you still come here?"

"Point taken, but it's not what you think. First time I met you, it was my sister that dragged me here. She was the one determined to hook up with your cohorts. Tonight, I'm trying to find her, but she's not here. I'm just waiting on my food and then I'll head out. Strip clubs aren't my thing."

"You seem different than the rest of guys that come in here."

"Was that a compliment? Can I record it as a voice memo in my phone? You can't be the same girl from the other night."

"It's easier to be yourself when there's a light at the end of the tunnel."

This resonates with me, but telling her that would lead to more questions I'm not in the mood to answer.

Nikki comes back with my order and chastises Amy for wasting her time while there was easy money to be made. I slide a bill across the table in a dramatic fashion, and Nikki takes the hint and disappears. The Dj introduces Harmony and the place erupts. T-Pain has been replaced with Kanye West, and she struts out to the keys of 'Blood on the Leaves.' Like the other night, I've heard the song before, but seeing her routine in sync with it feels like I'm hearing it for the first time again.

But, something is amiss. She seems disinterested, like she's going through the motions. Not that the guys lining the stage could tell, as they take turns throwing cash in the air.

"Seems like a different girl tonight," I say aloud.

"She's dealing with stuff in her personal life, poor girl," Amy explains. "Some guy she was crushing on left her hanging. To be honest, I'm surprised she's even here tonight."

I take a drink and ponder this. Harmony didn't seem like the type to bring her personal life to work. From what Lily told me, and my own experience with her, she seemed completely detached from her line of work.

"You think I'm not cut out for this? She *really* doesn't belong in this line of work, but she's mastered the art of balancing who she really is and who she has to be here."

Something about that makes me stop eating, the hunger for an explanation superseding the one for food.

"She didn't talk much during our conversation. I figured it was part of her persona."

"You're not wrong, but getting to know her like I have, the person behind the mask is the real gem."

We watch her routine in silence for a little bit. Like the other night, she times her descent down the pole with the bass drop, and dollar bills fly through the air like they came out of a machine. One guy in particular is trying his damnedest to stand out, throwing wads of cash so aggressively it comes off as demeaning. Harmony crawls over and once she's close enough, he throws a stack of bills right in her face, slapping hands with his boys in celebration as she picks it up and saunters off stage. Seeing that takes my appetite, and I push my food away,

"Since we're talking, I can tell you that she convinced me you weren't a creeper."

"Really?"

"I guess she caught you after the liquor set in and you'd mellowed out a bit. Told me you were going through some things, but that you were one of the good ones."

"Is there such thing as a good one in a place like this?"

"You'd be surprised how many of them are decent guys just looking for an escape from everyday life. Some are emasculated in their personal lives and are just looking for a place to be appreciated. This business is an exercise in contradictions."

Amy tells me she's due on stage soon, wishes me luck and disappears into the crowd, leaving me alone in my thoughts. I sit for a long time, drinking my frustrations away while men live out their most erotic desires around me, and all I can think about is Melody.

My whole life I'd played it safe, chasing security and convincing myself that I was living. But it was all a facade, an illusion created to mask my fear of rejection, giving just enough of myself to bring the people I loved into my orbit but still keeping them at arms length. I've window shopped my emotions, glancing at the ones I want but never committing to them. Melody pushed me to embrace emotions I've wanted my whole life, and I did. But they hit with such force, rattling my core and fostering the same fear that had wrecked my marriage and any other relationship I'd cared about. I've never been content with just running away, that was too easy. I had to burn it down on the way out, a defense mechanism developed to protect myself from the temptation to make things right. I could've just told her I wasn't ready, leaving the door open to reconciliation. But I chose the word *distraction*, knowing it would extinguish our flame that was burning out of control.

It had come so easy to me because it always worked. But, this week I found that it wasn't as effective as I thought. Lily and my mother are examples of that. Two relationships left for dead, yet resurrected over the span of two days. Not because of luck, but because it's what we wanted all along. Our feelings for people we truly care about don't have an expiration date.

I can only hope that what Melody felt was real enough for her to let me explain. My phone buzzes in my pocket. Excitement rushes through me as I fumble around in my pocket trying to find it.

It's Lily, and though she won the coin toss, my heart drops because it's not Melody.

"Lily, Lily can you hear me?" I yell into the phone.

"Miles, where the fuck are you?"

"I'm at Rouge, looking for you. Hold on." I race from my seat, dodging dancers and customers on my way to the restroom. "Hold on, Lily," I say again, before I come face to face with Harmony. I move left and she follows, blocking my path. I go the other way and she follows, never breaking eye contact.

"Can you, like, move out of the way?" I ask. She doesn't

budge, instead just stands there, eyes glued to me. "I don't want a dance from you right now."

She still doesn't say anything, instead coming close enough that I can make out the specks of glitter on her mask. "Let me guess, you want another forty dollars?" I ask. She takes my hand and places it on her neck, her pulse so furious it feels like something is gonna jump out of her neck. She places her other hand on my chest, her eyes never leaving mine.

I finally decide I've had enough of the games. "I don't have time for this right now." I brush past her and tell her to find another easy mark for good measure, feeling bad right after I said it. I really don't understand how people can be sociopaths.

The bathroom is empty and I take the handicap stall at the end. Bass from the main floor rattles the bathroom, but it's quiet enough to talk.

"Sorry about that, Lily," I say. "This place is way more crowded than the last time we were here."

"It's a Saturday night in Manhattan, were you expecting a fucking library?" she replies. "That was uncalled for, I'm sorry."

"You don't have to apologize, it was actually perfect timing. Did you get my message?"

"I did, and for once, I'm the one that needs to apologize."

This wasn't how I pictured the start of our conversation, but I'm gonna roll with it, excited to watch somebody else work the shit shovel for once.

"Even if I was angry, I didn't mean any of the horrible things I said to you," she says. "There was a time when we would've taken a bullet for one another, and I've spent years chasing that connection, jumping in and out of relationships trying to find a bond that felt like that."

"You could've just picked up the phone, Lily. I would've answered."

"From afar, I watched you run away and build the life you always talked about, and I couldn't have been prouder. Even if I wasn't part of your life, it felt like I'd won too. Not to mention, I had to hear it filtered through Mom, and the quality of her information depends on how long she's been on a bender."

"You don't have to—"

"Can you *please* shut the fuck up and let me finish?"

"You're right," I say. "Continue."

"My point is, there's been a piece of me missing since I walked out on you."

It's a good thing we're on the phone, because if I were in front of her, she'd see my jaw drop. I'm not sure I heard that right—actually, I am, I just can't believe it. But three things have been guaranteed in my life; death, taxes, and all fault for the estrangement from my sister. I'd just come to accept it as fact, and when I was angry, a badge of honor. It was too complicated to view it any other way, and though she's being nice, we both made mistakes. But she also told me not to interrupt her anymore, and who am I to be disobedient?

"And then you lost everything. I wanted to call, but I figured you had enough shit going on that I didn't wanna add to it. But I was gonna reach out, Miles. I need you to know that." Her voice is starting to crack. It's getting harder to hold my tongue. "When Mom told me about your suicide attempt ..."

"Lily, please don't—"

"It sent me into a spiral, knowing you felt so alone in this world that killing yourself was your only option. I should've been there from the moment they died, I should've been there Miles. I missed the most meaningful time of your life, and when you lived, I decided I was gonna be a part of your redemption. And when you found Melody—who is perfect for you, by the way— I was jealous. I finally had you back in my life, and I felt like I was losing you again. But, I understand that I have to let you live your own life, I just wanna be part of it this time."

Someone enters the bathroom in a hurry, a female by the sound of her heels. I dawns on me that I've walked into the Women's restroom. Even when I try to do right, I still can't do right. The tapping is getting closer, and I can see that it's Harmony, her glowing heels shining off the tiles. She wants my stall, but sees my feet and takes one two stalls over. I can hear her sobbing, and now I feel even worse about how I treated her.

"I know you blame yourself," I say into the phone. "But the truth is, if the tables were turned, I'd feel the same way."

"So, we're good?" She asks, and I let it hang their while I silently count five Mississippis—not for the drama, but because I'm an asshole.

"We always have been," I finally tell her.

"Whew, that's a fucking relief," she says, morphing back into the Lily I'm more familiar with. I actually like this version of her better than the emotional one, she keeps me grounded. "Also, I lied to you. I didn't tell Melody about your family."

"It's ok if you did, we're good either way."

"But I didn't," she says. "You were ripping me apart, I had to say something to turn the tables. Mom didn't do it either, we've been trying to figure it out ourselves. Nothing makes sense. I'm staying with Mom, but do you want me to meet you at Rogue?"

The offer is enticing, because it feels like we're finally on stable ground, but there's more pressing business to attend to. As relieved as I am to have resolved differences with Lily, every part of me has been aching to find Melody. She's been the pursuer since I met her, and I'm excited to play the role this time around.

"I'd love to do that, Lily," I say, "But ,I gotta find Melody. You told me to kill myself, and that still is the second most disastrous conversation I had that night."

"That's a hell of an accomplishment. What did you say to her.?"

"You get the assist on this one, I used your word for her."

She finds this hilarious. "What a fucking idiot," she says, ignoring her role as creator completely. I swear my mother's influence on our social skills will live on forever.

"But here's the kicker, she makes me *feel*." The sobs from the next stall are starting to get distracting, but I've said enough hurtful shit to Harmony already. "Everything I thought I lost with Sara has come back. But Melody's so different that I don't feel like I'm replacing Sara, if that makes any sense. Melody just ... *gets* me."

"Then tell her that."

"I texted her, but she didn't reply. I'm just gonna head over to her apartment and—"

"Yeah, don't do that. It doesn't sound as romantic as you think."

"Ok, Cupid. What do you suggest I do?"

"Oh, I don't know. Maybe pick up the fucking phone and call her like a human being. Yeah, I think that sounds logical. Wouldn't you agree, little brother?"

"And what if she tells me to go to Hell?"

She sucks her teeth, my pessimism starting to wear thin on her. "Then I meet you at Rogue and we drown your sorrows in alcohol and chicken wings." I'm not against this, because the wings were better than they had any right to be.

"Wow. You have got to be the worst motivational speaker that I've ever come across. I'm just gonna go to her place, some things need to be done in person."

She laughs, "Either way, you won't have to deal with it alone. I promise. I love you."

We've never said I love you to each other. Ever. We have a love that's just understood, mostly through sarcasm and shoulder bumps. Any other time I would've laughed her off the phone, but tonight it just feels right. "I love you too."

After I hang up I sit on the toilet, staring at the ceiling, paralyzed by fear of calling Melody. It's the same fear I had in the airport bar a week ago. Even when you know the step needs to be taken, it doesn't make it any less scary. I view our week together as a success, even if she rejects me. Learning to feel again, after shutting all of your emotions down, is a bittersweet exercise. It hurts at the beginning, having to constantly remind yourself that human connection is a two-way street, requiring both effort and commitment. Like the first day at the gym, there's pain and the disappointment of not seeing immediate results. But once the initial tears are healed, and the pain reveals itself to be a necessary part of the process, it almost becomes an addiction. I'm tired of channeling my grief into self-destruction, it's more fun turning it to growth.

"I'm sorry for the things I said to you, Harmony," I say through the wall of the stall. We're the only ones in the bathroom, giving me the courage to speak freely. "I dehumanized you, and there's no excuse for that. You have value as a person, and Amy spoke highly of you." She doesn't respond, and I can't blame her.

The fear comes rushing back as my finger hovers above Melody's contact. I walk to the sink and rinse my face, but alas, the water doesn't rinse away the fear. My Uber's esti-

mated arrival time is six minutes, so I fix myself in the mirror
—trying to at least create the illusion that I have my shit
together—before heading for the door.

"Miles, wait," a voice calls out from the stall.

The door to the stall unlocks, and Harmony steps out of
the stall, still in her stage gear but carrying a small handbag
like my mother's. I really need to stop subconsciously
comparing dancers to the dominant females in my life. She's
at the far end of the restroom, but close enough that I could
tell she's breathing heavily. I dial Melody's number and wait
for the dial tone. I step toward Harmony as 'Pictures of You'
by The Cure starts blaring from her purse. Either somebody
else in the world has impeccable timing, or I'm finally realizing something that's been standing right in front of me the
whole time. I reach her just as the phone stops ringing, and I
can hear her breaths, slow and fast, partially muffled by the
mask.

I reach behind her and untie the mask, and my heart
jumps like it did the first time I saw her. Melody looks
apprehensive, unsure of my thoughts, and maybe a little
scared that I'm gonna walk away.

But I try not to make the same mistakes twice, and I pull
her into a long embrace.

There's a lot to work through, and stories to swap as we
put together the pieces of the puzzle; each of us missing
pieces that are held by the other. But, I just wanna live in
this moment. She whispers over and over how sorry she is,
and each time, I tell her she has nothing to be sorry about.
It's not the most ideal place to reconcile, but nothing about
us is ideal, and that's what makes it work. My phone buzzes,
a message that my Uber driver is waiting for me. We both
look at the notification, and I can tell she's scared that I'm
gonna leave.

"You think you—"

"Meet me out back in two minutes," she says, before grabbing her mask and leaving the bathroom.

I leave right behind her and find the Toyota Highlander waiting for me by the valet. He agrees to switch the destination to my hotel and pulls around the back. Melody bursts out the backdoor, her stage attire replaced with a black tracksuit, and if I didn't tell the driver the plan, he would've assumed we robbed the place. Melody jumps in and we head off into uncertainty, but together nonetheless. None of that matters right now, because for once, I actually made a decision to do something because I *wanted* to, and it didn't bite me in the ass.

I guess this is it feels like to be on cloud nine.

TWENTY-ONE

ALL THE PIECES MATTER

BEING on cloud nine is a lot like drinking coffee.

The rush is initially satisfying, numbing you from the world and the responsibilities that come with it. But, if you ever watch a coffee commercial, upon closer review you realize it all takes place no later than noon. It's hard to convince people to buy your product when they know a crash is inevitably coming. Riding a wave of emotion is no different.

I don't know what the plan was when Melody came running out of the backdoor of Rogue. It didn't matter, because in that moment, in spite of everything, we'd found our way back to each other. But, as we sat in the back of the car in Manhattan traffic, the adrenaline levels out and reality buckles up in the front seat. We're holding hands and looking out of our respective windows, occasionally glancing at each other, unsure of where to start. But, since Lady Luck seems to be in my corner tonight, I start out with the only question I had.

"How did you know?" I ask. Her eyes meet mine, both of us understanding the question, and I feel her grip soften on my hand. "Not that it'll change my opinion of you," I reassure her. "But I feel like it's a good place to start."

She smiles, relishing the opportunity to spill the beans. "About a year ago, Lily started coming in to the club," she begins. *I knew it.* "She became a regular, and slept with about half of my coworkers. But, she could never convince me to come home with her."

"Because you don't like women?"

"I've played around before," she says with a smirk, which makes my mind race with possibilities. "But she wasn't my type, and I vowed to be done with toxic relationships. Once she knew it wasn't happening, we developed a mutual respect for one another. She stopped being pushy, unlike most of my customers, and I think she started to view me in a different light from the other dancers. Anyway, she'd come in and vent, telling me about her life, and that's when I learned about you."

Mentally I'm putting the pieces together, feeling even worst about the accusations I lobbed at Lily knowing that she played it straight. "This was before they died?"

Melody nods. "Yeah. She'd get really drunk and talk about how much she missed you, and the bond you two had. Then a day later she'd be complaining about you. I got the vibe that your relationship was complicated, but eventually she would've made the call. But, whatever happened between you guys didn't stop her from keeping up with your life. I mean, she showed me your whole Facebook profile."

"I can't believe she opened up to you like that."

"You'd be surprised how comfortable people are talking to someone wearing a mask."

She's not lying. It was different than any strip club I'd ever been to, but it was perfect for New York City. Adding masks to the mixture of dancers and alcohol created something like an exotic confessional, a place anybody with a few dollars to spill their darkest secrets, and create new ones as well.

"Six months ago," she continued, "she came in on a slow night, and she was a different person. Usually people come to the club to have a good time, see a little skin. You know, live the fantasy."

The timeline she's laying out lines up with their deaths, and hearing Melody describe it feels like I'm reliving it all over again, but through the eyes of someone else—like one of those Guy Ritchie movies where it shows different points of view of the same event.

"But sometimes, there are customers that give off a certain ..." she struggles to find the word. "... vibe. Like, you can tell they wanna go to a dark place, and take dancers along for the ride. I try to avoid those types, but most of the girls have a price tag."

I think back to earlier, about the customer throwing money at her face, getting rid of his own demons by projecting them onto somebody else, not realizing that putting it on someone else doesn't numb them.

"That must've been the night she found out what happened," I say.

"It was. She took it bad, coming in high, which wasn't like her. Lily always talked about reconciling with you, but she thought your life was going so well, she didn't wanna complicate things by pulling you back into your past. She thought the world of your kids though, and always admired that you managed to get away from your mother and create the life you wanted. Lily was rooting for you, Miles, and so was I."

Our eyes meet, and she squeezes my hand. "But you didn't even know me."

"I'd never met you, but I felt a strange connection to you. You had every excuse to become a terrible human being, think about it. But you turned your childhood into something beautiful. It's inspiring."

Hearing her describe my life as 'something beautiful' is an example of the dangers of social media. My Facebook profile was a digital snapshot of my life, cropped and shaped to my liking, masking my insecurities as I soaked in compliments from friends on how great of a family man I was.

"You're such a great Dad," one person would write, usually under a picture of me at an event with the kids.

"Sara is lucky to have a man like you," one of her friends wrote on an anniversary post.

Each comment was a rung on a ladder of bullshit, one that I gladly climbed with each post, before tipping over with their deaths. And since I was at the top of the ladder, the pain of the fall was harder. Anybody that knew us—and not many people did— would have seen my life for what it was; a group project I contributed the least amount of work to, but still came out with the same grade as everyone else. It's one thing for acquaintances to leave random comments under your photos, it's another to know that your previously estranged sister and future budding love interest thought you had your shit together.

"Melody," I say. "I know what it looked like, but I wasn't that great of a father, and even worse as a spouse."

"Maybe so, but you recognize that you should've been better, and that counts for something."

I'm starting to wonder what I'd have to say for Melody to walk away. Not that I want her to, it's more wanting to know where the line is, so I could go nowhere near it. I've called her a distraction, and outed myself as an average parent and spouse. But she keeps building me up, seeing the best in me when I don't see it in myself. This is so foreign to me that if the car suddenly pulled over, and the driver revealed it all to be an elaborate prank, I'd thank them for casting me and exit stage left.

"So, you knew about the suicide attempt before we talked about it?" I ask.

"Yeah, I pretty much heard about it in real time. I'd been prodding her to visit you anyway, but when she found out about that, everything went off the rails. I didn't see her again until the night she showed up with you, I figured she jumped on a plane and you guys figured it out."

Hearing Melody tell me how my suicide attempt had an effect on Lily is oddly comforting. Yes, a big reason for trying to kill myself was living without my family, but with therapy I can admit that it wasn't the catalyst.

I was afraid of being alone.

My whole life I've convinced myself that I didn't need anybody, and that train of thought served me well for many years. But as people, we can only function on self-love and stubbornness for so long, life and its obstacles make the road too treacherous. The human spirit is meant to be part of a village, sharing in the joys and sorrows, never letting the next person be overwhelmed. But relationships take effort, and I treated them like fire extinguishers, leaving them unattended until I needed them. When that emergency finally came, I was unprepared, frustrated because I had nobody to turn to. My entire life revolved around my family—at least when I wasn't being an idiot—and when they were gone, friends revealed themselves as acquaintances, and I learned what it felt like to truly be alone.

"I'd think about you a lot," she says. "Whenever I was having a bad day, I'd think of you out there, alone, trying to figure it out and it made me stop feeling sorry for myself.

Then I'd realize how stupid it was, dreaming of someone I'd never met. I repeated that cycle for months, and it drove me crazy."

"That would explain your face the first time I saw you," I say, remembering the shocked look she had that day in the coffee shop.

"I tried to forget you," she admits. "And then one day, I look up while working the morning rush and you were there, and I swear my heart almost jumped out of my chest." I laughed and mutter *universe* and she cut me off. "Exactly," she agrees. There was no reason we ever should've ever crossed paths, so I took it as a sign and stepped into the universe. I'm sorry I never told you I was a dancer, I thought you'd run ... like they all do."

"You don't have to be sorry," I say. "You're the first thing that's gone right for me in a long time. I should've trusted you and told you about my family, even though you already knew. Wait...you said they all run?"

"Its a running joke at the job between the dancers," she says. "Everyone wants to lay with you, but nobody wants to stay with you. It's almost impossible to have a healthy relationship when you're a stripper. Men are possessive by nature, so the idea that someone else getting to touch what a guy feels is rightfully his is a non starter for most."

I'm not sure how to respond to this, so I stay silent, hoping the silence will allow the thought to pass.

"I don't enjoy being a stripper, and I don't turn tricks like some of the other girls. You just get so tired of being hurt, you do anything to make sure you don't have to ask anyone for anything."

I'd never heard anything that resonated with me more in my life.

"After I left your place, I had a huge fight with Lily and

my Mother. I thought I lost you ... and I needed somebody else to feel that pain." The night replays in my mind, seeing my mother walk out without even putting up a fight plays over and over. "I told my mom it made me sick to know I needed her. Then Lily told me I should finish the job next time."

She laid her head on my shoulder, her way of letting me know she was there, but wouldn't pry if it was to uncomfortable.

"I packed my clothes and left for the airport, didn't even check out of my room. It's so easy to run away and start over when you spend most of your life being alone."

"You don't have to explain yourself to me, I get it," she assures me. "Why'd you come back?"

I place her hand on my wrist, now bare without the constant reminder of how far I'd fallen after Sara died. "I called my therapist in the boarding line," I say, laughing because Dr. Felt had won again. "I called her because I knew she'd talk me into staying, which I wanted to do anyway, and she made me realize leaving would only make the pain worse."

"Sounds like a great therapist."

"She is, she really is."

The Freedom Tower looms over us, which means the hotel is getting closer. The driver lets us out at the front and I make it a point to tip extra in appreciation for him not chiming in during our conversation. Things starts getting heavy about halfway up the elevator ride to my room as I took in every scent of her, neither of us burdened by the skeletons of our respective pasts. As I unlock the door she stops me, a look of fear paralyzed her while scaring me.

Does my breath stink?

Am I moving too fast?

Should we have gotten dinner first?

"It's alright if you can't stay because you have work in the morning."

"It's not that, I'm actually working the open mic tomorrow, it's just..." She's nervous, like whatever she's gonna say could ruin the night. "...just for tonight, can you forget that I'm Harmony?" she asks. "Please?"

The door beeps and a clicking sound echoes through the deserted hallway. My foot holds the door open as I look her in the eyes, and I can see the fear. Fear that I would be like the rest, that she'd be discarded in the morning to rebuild the wall she'd taken down for me.

"Melody..." I say her name, "I have no fucking idea what you're talking about."

She smiles and jumps into my arms, picking up where we left off in the elevator. I flicked the lights on as I carried her through the doorway. The auto close mechanism of the door does its job.

I'll remember to leave a five star Yelp review because of it.

TWENTY-TWO

LUCID DREAMS

"IS HE AWAKE?" *a voice whispers gently.*

"Touch his nose," another voice says, from a further distance than the first.

A warm hand clamps my nose shut, and when I open my eyes, my daughter Grace squeaks and jumps back. I realize I'm not in New York, but in my bedroom back in Colorado.

"Daddy, Daddy, Daddy!" Harry, exclaims as he bursts through the door, revealing himself as the second voice. "Daddy, you're awake, you're awake."

He always sends his sister to wake me, figuring I wouldn't be as angry with her.

Some things never change.

Harry spins in circles yelling my name, his body trying to keep pace with his mind. He tires himself out before joining his sister in my lap, jockeying for position with Grace before I convince them there's enough room for both of them. I embrace them both tightly, unsure of how I got here, but determined to hold onto them as long as I can.

"Daddy, why are you crying?" Harry asks, running his

fingers through the streak of tears I didn't realize we're falling.

"I'm just so happy to see you guys," I say, running my fingers through his curls, still in disbelief that I'm holding them again in our home. They're both in the footsie pajamas, prepared for both a playdate at home and a Walmart run.

"Daddy," Grace says. "We...um... made breakfast for you, and want to eat as a family. Please Daddy, please."

"Of course princess."

It always made me chuckle when she talked like that. Her little mouth so excited to say what was in her heart that it would come out in spurts, and in my head, I'd insert commas and periods. But she wasn't lying about breakfast, the scent of maple sausage , a staple in our family, wafts into the room. There will be a side of cinnamon raisin toast and cheese eggs to go along with it. To pass the time, they take turns being flipped on the bed, each giving demand on how they want to be flipped.

"Put me on your shoulders, put me on your shoulders," Grace screams and I oblige, her little hands gripping my ears for stability.

"I'll save you Wonder Woman," Harry says, using a running start to hit a drop kick to my stomach. He helps her off my shoulders and I slump onto the bed, letting them pile on, burying me under anything they can find.

I lay still under the mess of pillows as they celebrate slaying the monster, taking turns peeking under to make sure I'm not moving.

My heart is full right now. In this moment I'm being the father I should have been all along, instead of the one they saw in spurts. It's too late to make it right, but I can make this moment last, and for that I'm thankful.

I burst out from under their pile, roaring like a lion and

sending them running for cover. Grace hides on the side of the bed, waiting for her brother to emerge from his usual spot in the closet. Their unity during these battles was always a fascinating look into their relationship. They'd be thick as thieves one moment, then at each others throats the next.

"Morning there sunshine," a voice says from the doorway.

I turn and find Sara there, as beautiful as she was on our wedding day, a cup of coffee in hand, smiling like she always did in these moments.—when she finally saw the father she knew I could be all along. If I had to guess, she'd been standing there awhile. Whenever I'd have playtime with the kids, she gave us space, allowing me to stay in the moment, and not get distracted talking about things married couples talk about. I joked that whenever her love for me would run empty, she'd use these moments to recharge herself.

"Breakfast will be ready soon kids," she says to them. "Paw Patrol is on in the living room, gives us a few ok?"

They put everything back in its place and head out, racing to see who could get to the couch first.

"Bye babies," I say, feeling like the breakfast they spoke of isn't gonna happen. "I love you."

Sara jumps in the bed, placing her leg over my torso, our hands finding each other like they always did. She breathes deep into my neck, the Tahitian vanilla from her shampoo teasing my senses. There's much to be said between us, but I don't know how much time I have, so I take her in one last time.

"I've missed you," she says, before kissing me, starting from my neck and working her way up.

"I'm sorry," I tell her, "I'm sorry I didn't figure it out until it was too late."

She kisses me softly, and I notice she has tears streaming down her face, mixing with mine to flow down my neck. My *foot finds the waistband of the fleece pajama pants I got her our last Christmas together, the ones she swore she'd never get back into after she had our third child. I slide them down, the warmth of her skin reminding me of the first time we made love.*

I was so nervous back then, just the awkward guy from her chemistry class with a weird sense of humor. It was my first time, but she guided me through it, like she would do once we were married.

Sara guides my hand on her body, shivering as I run my fingertips up her spine. She holds my hand to her face, pecking softly, her shallows breaths warming my palm. The breeze of the ceiling fan meets the tears, creating a cold that makes me shiver. Sara smiles, rubbing my head and kissing my hand, never breaking eye contact.

"Miles," a voice calls.

Sara looks up in a panic, trying to figure out where the voice came from. It wasn't the kids, and the look on her face tells me we're the only ones in the house.

"Miles," the voice calls again, this time louder.

Sara is staring up, still in a panic, before a smile eventually forms on her lips. It's a sad smile, one I would normally see after she'd realize she couldn't talk me out of something. A smile of acceptance, of understanding that fate was at hand. She grips my hand tighter, tears fully streaming as it dawns on me what's happening.

"Miles, come on. Please, Miles," the voice pleads even louder.

"It's ok, Miles," Sara says. "We're ok, I promise."

The room suddenly turns bright, and I can barely make out her silhouette, the touch of her skin slowly fading away.

"Don't go," I cry out. "Please don't leave me again, I'm sorry."

"It's alright Miles," she says, fading away.

"I can be better, just don't leave yet," I beg, struggling to convey every regretful thought I've had since they walked out the door. "I'm sorry Sara. Can you hear me? I'm sorry, please come back."

"We're alright." It's almost in a whisper.

"Come back."

The room becomes too bright to make anything out as Sara keeps repeating assurances, softer and softer until she fades away.

"Miles, please wake up," the voice says.

A room is coming back into focus, but it's not my bedroom. The shape of a woman is coming into view. My hotel room begins to take shape, the sharpness of the lighting gleaning off the chandelier, illuminating the woman. She's holding my wrists, trying frantically to get my attention. I'm pulled into an embrace as she rocks me back and forth, whispering words I can't understand into my ear. It's a touch I have never known before, both comforting and reassuring. The woman isn't Sara, and she isn't Melody.

The woman is my mother.

TWENTY-THREE

THE TRAILS WE TAKE

I JUMP BACK without a thought to my position and crash into the night stand. As nice as this room is, I'm beginning to think it's bad luck.

The two times I woke up expecting Melody to be there I was greeted by a stripper and now my mother.

My heart pounds rapidly as Sara's last words replay I my head. She wanted me to know they were alright.

"Christ, Miles, are you alright?" my mother asks, rushing to help me up off the floor. "What the hell are you jumping for?"

"I saw them. I was back in Colorado, and I saw them." I get up from the floor, covering myself with a blanket before moving through the hotel suite, looking for Melody. "It was like they never left."

"Saw who?" she asks.

"Your grandchildren, Mom," I shoot back, annoyed that she isn't keeping up. But the dream is second to me finding Melody. Two rooms down in my search and not a sign of her.

"Miles, what are you doing?" She asks, staying right on

my heels.

As my brain reboots I remember that technically I'm still angry with her. "How about we start with ... oh, I don't know ... maybe, how the hell did you get in here is a good starting point," I continue to wander from room to room, hoping Melody just stepped away to make a phone call, or is enjoy the view. Panic takes hold with every room I find empty.

"She's gone Miles," my mother says, her tone carrying an authority that ends my search. "She let me in, interesting girl that Melody."

"You talked to her?"

She nods, "We chatted for a bit, she was in tears when I got here, so I gave her an ear."

The one person I have sex with woke up and had a conversation with *my mother* before disappearing. The best writers in Hollywood couldn't make this shit up. I run my fingers through my hair, dropping the blanket in the process.

"I forgot you were uncircumcised," she says conversationally, looking at my genitals. "Sorry about that."

"Mom, can I get a second?" I ask. "Just add it to the list of everything else you did wrong when I was growing up."

She gives me some time to get dressed, and I can hear her from the bedroom defending her skills as a mother. I'm sitting on the floor trying to collect my thoughts. Last night somehow surpassed my expectations, and not in the way one would think. It felt like a first date, with both of us free from the burdens we carried. I told her everything, filling in the blanks while being genuinely surprised at how much Lily knew about my situation. We talked about her night job, and all the weird things the customers would say to her.

"Does the stripper thing bother you? You can be honest," she asked.

"No, I mean, I'm the guy carrying a tragic past. At the very least, we're even."

"But does it change the way you see me?"

"It doesn't, but this is all new to me," I told her. "The feelings I have for you, my own insecurities, it's a lot to process. But there's something here Melody, and whatever it is, I wanna stick around for it."

After making love we laid out in the main room overlooking Central Park, the darkness of the park pockmarked by flickers of lights throughout. It was the first time since they died that I didn't feel alone in the world, and it was a feeling I thought was lost forever when Sara died. We opened another bottle and made love again, but it was different. Free from any secrets, we explored every part of each other, never breaking eye contact. If I never woke up, I would've died a happy man.

My mother joins me after awhile and takes a seat next to me on the floor. Despite all that we've been through, I'm happy she's here. Even if she's not the ideal person, it's nice having someone to process this with.

"What did Melody say, Mom?"

"She talked about the time you guys spent together, and how you made her feel. That reminds me," she says, pulling a piece of paper out of her handbag. "She had to run, but she said to give you this."

It was a letter, written on the hotel stationary from the nightstand. The handwriting is scribbled but legible, written in haste before I could wake up. I open it without a thought, desperate for information:

Dear Miles,
I'll start with an apology. Please don't take me
leaving as a sign of me not caring about you. In fact, I

actually care about you too much, and it's why I'm doing this. I was starting to wonder if my idea of following the Universe's signs was a cop out for not wanting to be vulnerable. But, then you showed up and helped me understand that I was just waiting for the right person. I'm used to men only wanting sex before using my job as an excuse to rid themselves of me. But you showed me that I have worth beyond the stage, and for that, I could never repay you. Spending time with you this week has made me feel emotions I've never felt before. To be seen as a human being, with feelings that matter, allows me to believe in people again. To believe in love again. You did that Miles. No matter how many regrets you have in your past, know that you're a good person (and a great lover too :-)). But, in my excitement to validate my view of the world and experience intimacy, I ignored your recovery in the process. I cast you unknowingly into a role you aren't ready for, and I'm sorry for that. If we never see each other again, I'll always look back on our time together as the moment my life started to make sense. This isn't goodbye. At least I hope it's not. This is me trusting that when the time is right, the universe will lead us back to each other.

Love, Melody

I fold the letter up and fall into my mother's lap. She takes the letter and reads it, smiling for whatever reason and chuckling after handing it back to me. I join in the laughter, because life has reached the point where that's all I can do.

"What made you come back?" I ask, trying to avoid talking about Melody.

"Because I felt you needed someone in your corner."

"Great timing," I reply, immediately wishing I could take it back.

She moves my head and goes to the window, staring out in silence. "Why do you hate me so much?" she finally asks.

I was expecting a snarky remark like usual, but the question and the weariness of her tone catches me off guard. It hurts to know she feels this way, because I've never hated her. But, all the jabs I've thrown at her over the years clearly had an effect.

"I don't hate you, mom..." I trail off, unsure if the time is right for this conversation—or if I'm in the emotional space to have it. But, the alternatives are talking about last night with Melody and my dream, so it wins by default.

"Then what is it?"

"I just—I just don't know how to love you."

She shakes her head. "Wow, you know the absolute worst things to say to a person."

"Well, I learned at the foot of the master."

She opens her mouth for a rebuttal, but her heart gets the better of her mind. "That's fair."

In our minds, we build these moments with relatives into epic confrontations. I always imagined confronting my mother over the phone, drunk of course, because that's the only way to get through a conversation like that. But, over the last couple of days I've come to see her in a different light, and I'm still not sure if I'm buying it. That's unfair to her because she's really making an effort, even if her delivery isn't perfect.

"Now, isn't the time for this conversation," I tell her.

"Actually it is," she replies with a tone of authority reserved for parents. "I think we both know we should've talked a long time ago, and if we don't have it now, we never will. So, I'm gonna give you the chance to say anything you've ever felt, and while I hope it's not disrespectful, I understand it's been building inside of you for years, and I'm prepared for it."

Did she really just give me a license to curse her out? If Sara and the kids were still alive, I might've taken her up on it. But I can feel her sincerity, and the opportunity to build the relationship we should've had all along—the one I swore I never wanted but knew I did, the one that she apparently wanted as well. I wish Dr. Felt was here right now, because I don't even know where to begin. It's like walking into a messy bedroom, and there's so much junk you don't know where the cleanup should start. But you have to start somewhere, so you grab the first piece of trash and go from there.

"Alright, but where is this coming from?"

"You tell me, from what Lily and Melody told me, you've been pouring your emotions out all over the city this week. And you know, I'm always up for trying a new drink, especially when it's the talk of the town," she says. "Stop trying to change the subject, we're having this conversation."

"Fine," I say. I've thought about this conversation for the last fifteen years, even had a game plan going in, but my mind goes blank. This is going to be a difficult conversation either way, so I start with the biggest gripe I have. "I never felt like you really loved me."

Not the best start, I know, but I can tell by the look on her face this wasn't unexpected. She nods at this, and joins me on the floor.

"Do you remember what life was like before Greg?" she asks. "How I worked all the time, and the nights we had to eat at the shelter?"

We never talked about those times, they were something like our own little Great Depression. Mom worked two jobs during that time, doing everything she could, but always coming up just short. Our grocery money was dependent on tips from her waitressing gig, and when they didn't come in, we made the ten block trek to the shelter—where in exchange for listening to a sermon and helping with the cleanup, we got to eat.

"I buried those."

"I don't blame you, but dig them back up, because it's important. What was the best day to visit the shelter? I know you remember that."

"Monday," I said. "The broth was always better on Monday."

Mom smiles at this. "It really was."

Monday was delivery day, so everything was fresh. Even Lori, the chef, had a pep in her step on Monday. You could taste her passion for culinary on Mondays. Her food was always great, but on Monday, she cooked like she was competing for a Michelin Star. Lori was my first real friend, even though it was just her taking pity on my situation. She made me feel like I mattered, giving me important jobs and constantly building my confidence through positive affirmation, telling me I would rise above everything so many times I actually believed her. Lori knew the sermons held no value for me, so she'd sneak me out the back to make store runs with her to pick up little odds and ends for the kitchen. My shoes had holes in them, a hazard for working in the kitchen. So she bought me a new pair to keep in her locker, and after every store run, she'd give me five dollars with the promise of more if I could save it until the next time I saw her. That was how I learned the value of a dollar.

"I remember you running around that kitchen," Mom says. "You wore that little chef hat, as cute as you could be. But I was thankful for those moments, because you were able to get away from our situation and just be a kid." She rubs my head, and I don't pull away, both of us navigating new waters cautiously, but finding a new normal in the process.

"You know, I don't remember thinking about it like that."

"Why would you? You were a child. I can tell you this now, but I envied your relationship with Lori."

"Really?" I'm intrigued by this. I wanna chime in, but I'm mesmerized by the woman in front of me, processing emotions without sarcasm. The years before she married Greg were bleak, but they were also when we were closest, because all we had was one another.

"Yeah. When you were at home with me, all we talked about was survival. What bills were past due, if we were gonna be evicted..."

She averts eye contact, staring into the distance as she talks, and I'm trying not to move, using one of Dr. Felt's tricks. In the moments when I was reaching a breaking point, Dr. Felt was deliberate in her movements, knowing that if I broke concentration, I'd default to going into survival mode to finish out the session, making her job twice as hard next time.

"I put a lot of stuff on you that I shouldn't have. My drinking didn't help either. But when you got around Lori, you became a different kid, and I was thankful that she helped you forget why we were there to begin with. Sometimes I felt like you wanted her to be your mom, like you gave up on me."

"I didn't mean to make you feel that way."

"I know you didn't, Miles." She moves closer to me. "But all I'd known was broken relationships, and though I wasn't the best Mother, I knew I couldn't tell you that. You were just a kid. When Greg came along with Lily, I tried to build the relationship with her that I wanted with you, because I thought that ship had sailed for us already."

You can love someone your whole life, and realize you never really knew them at all. She's been Helen, a woman I loved, but didn't like. I'm realizing we'd spent all this time revealing our true selves to everyone but each other. But I don't feel any pain, because for once, I'm figuring something out before it's too late. The regret fades away a little easier.

"Well, you were right and wrong," I say. Mom looks puzzled by this. "I did give up on you, but it was later than you expected. Much later."

"How much later?"

I couldn't help laughing, sitting here like two detectives piecing together together the timeline of a crime. "Sophomore year."

"You're kidding right? High School?"

"Yeah. At some point, I stopped trying. Seeing how close you were with Lily made me start counting the days until I could head off for college."

"Some of that was done to spite you, but I wanted you to see I could be a mother."

"But I'd already seen it, mom. You kept us afloat when we had nothing. I might have been young, but I could understand you were doing what you could." The awkwardness is gone, replaced by a curiosity as I try to process everything. "Since we're being charitable with our memories, I'll tell you something I've never told anybody else."

"I like where this is going. What?"

"Sometimes, I'd wish we were poor again. Crazy as it sounds, I missed the time when it was us against the world."

This revelation affects her. She just nods her head awhile, staring out into nowhere, trying to process everything. "I pushed you away," she says, shifting the tone of the conversation. "I tried to change, Miles, but I got scared and pushed you away. Even convinced myself I was teaching you how to deal with life. Every time I got it in my head to have this conversation with you, I'd panic."

"You still could've tried."

"And what would you have said?" she asks. I don't have a response because she's right. I would've blown her off, or made up an excuse to get off the phone. She was my antagonist, even more than my deadbeat father. I could force her to watch my growth in real time, using her grandkids to keep her hostage in the audience. I spent so much time trying to flaunt this persona to her, that I neglected them because I needed her to believe I was something I wasn't. Cutting her off was too easy. But keeping her on the fringes of my life— close enough to peek, but far enough to feel excluded— gave me an intimate look at the effects, like she did to me in high school. But that's the tricky part of harboring resentment, it damages everyone but its intended target.

"I'm sorry too, Mom," I say. "I've said some hurtful things to you over the years—"

"Water under the bridge," she interjects. "Life's too fragile to chase things we can't change. Let's just move forward."

"Done."

She caresses my face, and I give her the moment. "Can I ask you something?"

"You can ask me anything."

"How was last n—"

"You can ask me *almost* anything," I say fore she can finish. Mom raises her hands to signal she's leaving it alone. *Oh, what the hell.* "It was awesome."

"Ok, so what's next?"

Fuck. I couldn't let good enough be, I had nineteen on the blackjack table and got greedy. I fall into her lap, wishing I could've woken up and caught Melody. She slipped out of my life just as gracefully as she entered it, leaving feelings behind that I'll never forget. I spent the week chasing Melody around the city, and it's easy to think it was all for nothing. But in the process—from the bar to the record shop, and up until the moment I slid the mask off her face—I found something I didn't know I was looking for.

I found myself.

But in the process of finding myself, I lost her. The guy that walked in that coffee shop, with the heavy heart and shoe full of dog shit was gone ... or should I say fixed? Either way, he's better because of her, but she'll never see the fruits of her labor because he figured it out too late. A cruel twist of irony that I'll never get over.

"It's over, Mom," I say. She glares at me like I'm an idiot before grabbing Melody's letter and clearing her throat. She begins to read it out loud line by line, pausing at passages she thinks are relevant, punctuating them with a quick glance that drives home her insistence that I'm an idiot. During certain sections, she smiles, and I imagine Dr. Felt would smile while reading it as well. I'll imagine her face with every milestone I reach for the rest of my life.

"*'This isn't goodbye. At least I hope it's not. This is me trusting that when the time is right, the universe will lead us back to each other. Love, Melody.'*" Mom folds the letter and puts it back in the envelope. "Now—" she places the letter firmly on my chest. "—exactly what part of that letter says that it's over? Because I can't find it."

"You wanna be my mother, or you wanna be my therapist?" I ask.

"I wanna be whatever you need me to be, Miles."

The sincerity in her voice makes me regret the years I spent believing she was the bane of my existence. But, I think she's a little too optimistic about this situation.

"It's not as simple as it sounds," I say. "She's telling me to work myself out, and *maybe* it'll work out."

"What's there to work out?" She gives the rundown on my life. "Lily's been taken care of, I was never part of the equation to begin with, but we worked that out. If you left the city right now, the only thing you'd regret is Melody."

"You're not getting it," I say, frustrated. "She doesn't see the world like everyone else. I appreciate what you're trying to do, but she said the universe would lead us back to each other. That doesn't happen overnight."

She distorts her face in disgust. "The universe could drop that fucking chandelier on top of us too." She moves from under me, stand over me and puts her foot on my chest. "Listen, I talked to that girl for an hour, and she cares about you in a way that most people spend their lives searching for."

"But she—"

She balls her fist up to silence me. "This is the part where you shut the fuck up, and let me be a mother." She seems determined to make up for lost time, even though we agreed to move forward. "Listen, the universe did bring you together, and I'm thankful for it because she's perfect for you."

I don't know what they talked about, but it clearly had an effect on my mother. In my lifetime I've brought home six girls to meet her, and until now, only Sara has gotten the stamp of approval.

"But bringing you together isn't enough to sustain it. You watched me struggle for years trying to find what you're walking away from." She bends and takes my head in her hands. "Love is too precious to be left to chance. Do you understand me?" she pleads, shaking my head.

She continues before I can agree.

"You can't trust that it's just gonna work out. Relationships are too complex. And yes, luck got you to the door, but it can't make you step inside." She recites the last line of Melody's letter one more time. "That isn't telling you to wait, Miles. She's telling you to trust your feelings. If you don't go find her, what do you expect her to do? What does that tell her?"

"That she doesn't matter," I say. Mom nods, and moves her foot so I can get up. There's a knock on the door from room service, and Mom leaves to deal with it.

I find my clothes and jump in the shower, using every minute of this solitary time to summon the courage to go talk to Melody. The hot water gets the blood pumping to my brain and panic starts to set in.

What if I'm wrong?

It's easy for my mom and everyone else to tell me how stupid I'm being. They weren't on our dates. They never looked into her eyes as she told the story of her upbringing, the events that led her to believe what she does. If she turns me away, it's me—not them—that's going to have to deal with the heartbreak. Sure, they'll be there to support me and say the right things, like my other friends after the car accident, but they won't have to deal with the fallout. The late nights when you do a mental play-by-play of every moment spent together, wondering what you missed that made it all go wrong. They don't have to avoid certain places because the memories are too painful, or skip songs on a playlist because it opens the wound again.

But at the same time, I know I have to see her again. I could ignore it, convince myself that it wouldn't have worked out any way, but I know myself. Loose ends are fertile ground for self destructive behavior, and knowing I walked away without even trying will haunt me, casting a shadow over any relationship in the future. If I don't have the heart to go after her, then I wasn't worthy of having her to begin with. The fear of rejection is strong, but with a solid playlist and a night out, I'd eventually get over it. But I've lived with regret—it's practically been my roommate for the past six months—and the feeling of knowing you didn't do everything you could is one that I don't wish upon anybody.

The water is getting cooler, a reminder that I've taken long enough, and I get dressed quickly. Mom asks me if I want a shot for my nerves and I consider it, but politely decline, wanting my mind as clear as possible.

Mom gives me a once over, licking her fingers and pinning down wayward eyebrow hairs.

"Alright," she says once she's satisfied, "let's go find your girl."

TWENTY-FOUR

COFFEE AND CONDOLENCES

"You're officially on the list, Little Brother," Lily says triumphantly, returning to the table from the bathroom. "You're in the show."

"Just like that?" I ask, impressed. "How'd you manage that?"

"Even got you the prime time spot at the end of the night. So, don't ever say I didn't do anything nice for you."

"That's not what I asked, Lily."

She realizes I'm serious and comes clean, "Alright, I know the guy that runs it. His name is Mark, and he kinda has a thing for me."

"And?"

"And ... I might've told him I'd suck his dick if he put you on the performance list tonight. So, no pressure."

"No pressure? You don't even like men," I remind her.

"Yeah, I could see how that might be a problem. Unfortunately, telling him that didn't seem conducive to what we're trying to accomplish." She grabs my cheeks. "So, maybe you should stop worrying about what I'm doing with my mouth, and focus a little bit more on what you're about to be doing with yours. Ok, Shakespeare?"

Before I can respond, our mother returns from the hostess stand. I think she's annoyed, judging by her pursed lips. "Can you believe they charged us gratuity ... on three people?"

"Really?" Lily replies. "That's what's pissing you off? Not the twenty-one dollar Bud Light?"

Mom shoots her a look of disgust."I can handle New York City prices, but it's understood that gratuity is only on parties of eight or more," she complains.

"I guess you're right," Lily concedes. "Who are we if we don't stand by our morals?"

"You just conned someone out of an open mic slot by pretending that you'd give him a blow job," I remind her.

"I believe I did that to help my little brother find his muse," Lily says. "But, as always, you're more concerned with the methods instead of the results."

"Will you two give it a rest?" Mom practically begs. "We haven't been back together a whole day and you guys are already at each other's throats."

We leave the restaurant and walk through Central Park, passing the spot where Melody and I had our first date. It feels like a million years ago when I think of how our relationship has grown since then. I laugh looking at the bench I hid behind, unsure if I could go through with the date. Or the bike stand, where I thought she was nuts for asking me to ride through the city.

"You guys go on ahead," I say. "I'm gonna hang out here for awhile, get ready for tonight."

They exchange glances of uneasiness, probably thinking I'm gonna use it as an opportunity to skip out on the open mic, but I assure them I just need some time to prepare for tonight. We agree to meet at Romancing the Bean and they head off, leaving me on a bench in the company of the squirrels.

I spend some time jotting down notes of things to say tonight. I haven't written a poem since high school. I lack the coordination to make a beat poem, so I settle on something like a letter. The words come flowing out of me. Narrating the last few months of my life as a spectator helps me appreciate the journey. Panic creeps in and out, fear of humiliating myself, or Melody telling me that the timing isn't right.

I find solace in the fact that if it goes wrong, I can shave my head and move to Thailand, where the exchange rate will allow me to live comfortably for the rest of my life as a bartender named Paco.

* * *

Under normal circumstances, I would enjoy the open mic night at Romancing the Bean. The clientele is more diverse than the morning regulars, with the hurried young professionals being replaced by middle age dreamers looking for fun night out without the stress of going to a bar. Lily is outside smoking when I arrive, and I can tell she's already had a couple drinks.

"I bet Mom you wouldn't show up," she says. "It wouldn't be the first time I lost out on something I was sure about. How you feeling?"

"Not as nervous as I thought I would be," I tell her. "Where's Mom?"

"She had to use the restroom. Don't worry, I'm making sure to run interference if she goes near your girl. She looks sad by the way, your girl."

I'm not sure if this bodes well for my chances or not, but

I'm happy to know the four bowel movements I had due to butterflies weren't for nothing. "We should go inside," I say. My spot was in the next fifteen minutes, assuming it's running on time.

"Hey," she says, "before we go in, and I mean this in all sincerity, I'm proud of you. If she turns you down, know that you won't have to deal with it alone." I pull my phone out and hold it up. "What are you doing?"

"Say what you just said one more time, but do it real slow," I tell her. She frowns and gives me the bird. "What? If I told mom you said something that beautiful, she'd never believe me."

We go inside and find our mother with a table close to the door. I see Melody, but I'm at an angle where she can't see me. I could tell something was off, but she was still efficient in her work. Somehow, she's even more beautiful tonight than the morning I met her. Maybe it's because I know her story, the scars that made her who she is, or the tender moments when she lets her guard down—like the moment right before I carried her into my room. People are much more beautiful when they're flawed, I think.

The act on stage finishes to polite applause and is relieved by the MC, Mark. He tells some lame jokes and has an arrogant persona. I make a mental note to have Lily record the moment she tells him she's not holding up her end of the bargain. He introduces the next act, a middle aged guy, Jerry, who comes to the stage with his acoustic guitar. He kinda looks like an out of shape Tom Hanks, but he has surprising range in his voice. He play three Beatles songs, closing with 'Hey Jude,' extending his time by singing the chorus multiple times. Mark appears on stage again and takes the mic.

"Give it up one more time for Jerry." The crowd gives

him a respectable ovation and Mark moves on. "Alright, we're down to our last performer of the evening, and for the first time in awhile, we've got prose poetry." The crowd starts snapping their fingers in unison. "Give a nice welcome to Mr. Miles Alexander."

I made sure to keep my eyes on Melody during my introduction to gauge her reaction. Hearing my name, she immediately looks up, and we lock eyes as I walk toward the stage. She's shocked. But, I still can't tell if it's the good kind. The applause from the crowd brings back the butterflies, and internally I start to panic as I fiddle with the mic stand. I'm breathing heavily, with a heart rate that's doubled in the past forty-five seconds. I sound like a pervert as my breathing blares over the PA system. My eyes find Melody's again and I remember that moment by the water, the first time I realized I was falling for her. I take my phone from my pocket, close my eyes, take a deep breath, and exhale slowly. I get a few laughs but when I open my eyes, I can see Melody has moved closer to the stage.

"Sorry, I'm a little nervous about this, so bear with me."

"You got this," someone calls from the audience.

"This piece is called Coffee and Condolences." I tell them, taking a deep breath and diving in.

"I've loved Coffee for most of my life. The smell of of a fresh pot, the jolt it provides to otherwise average mornings. I felt all of that before I ever had my first cup, and when I did, I was hooked. You see, I've always been a runner—jumping from one thing to the next, never satisfied, never appreciating what was in front of me. And Coffee fueled those runs, keeping me alert, eyes forever trained on what's next. It was an

*unhealthy relationship where I was giving more than
I was receiving."*

I sneak quick glances at Lily, Mom, and Melody, each of
them glued to me. I continue:

*"It wasn't until the crash—when I was forced to slow
down—that I understood how toxic the relationship
had become. All the events I missed, people I had
taken for granted, because I didn't wanna slow down.
Ashamed and heartbroken, I went looking for something to replace it, and that's when I met Condolences. It was a whirlwind romance; the Condolences
came so swift, flattering me and giving me a place of
comfort to feel sorry for myself, until she revealed
how fickle she could be, almost killing me. So here I
am, a life spent running, now on the brink of death
because the one I replaced was worse than the other."*

I can see Lily and Mom crying, but I don't look at
Melody. I can't look at her, so once again, I continue:

*So I have two vices, each pulling at my soul from
opposite directions, each offering its own tragic
ending. I needed help, but all those years running left
me with nobody. So, I had to settle for something I
never saw coming. I had to settle for a distraction.
She was everything I ever needed, even though
Condolences had told me I'd never be happy. When
Coffee told me I was ready to run again, she laced up
her shoes too. I guess what I'm trying to say is, I'm
thankful for the Coffee and Condolences, because*

without them, I'd be too blind to see what's right in front of me."

The applause is surprising, but appreciated. My breathing returns to normal as I lock eyes with Melody.

We gaze at each other for seconds, but it feels like forever.

Finally, through my tears I can see it, the faintest hint of a smile.

So I take my cue, say a silent prayer for luck, and step into the Universe.

ACKNOWLEDGMENTS

Truth be told, my list of acknowledgments for this book could run as long as the book itself. First off I wanna thank my wife Paula. At times she's had to keep our three children occupied so I could chase this dream of being a writer. To Xander, Naomi, and Chase, everything I do is so that your smiles can shine brighter everyday.

For Ms. Andie Hartz, in 7th grade you fostered my love for reading and writing as my English teacher and all these years later I hope this book makes you proud.

To Dr. Iver Arnegard and Juan Morales, you guys were the best writing professors a guy could ask for. Thank you for teaching me how to channel the pains and emotions of life and turn it into something creative.

Matthew Hanover, I don't think there's enough words to express my gratitude to you. I was inspired by your work and you've taken the time to help me through the entire process, treating this project as if it were your own. Our conversations and debates about everything under the sun have been one of the highlights of this process. Ian Shane and Matthew Norman are two other authors that took the time to offer advice and encouragement. I promise to always pay it forward if another author comes along looking for an ear.

To my editor Sarah Jane Villanueva, I expected an editor and found a lifelong friend. Thank you for taking on the duel role of editor and therapist.

Jennifer Fleming, you were the first person to believe in this project, thank you for always encouraging me to keep writing.

Thank you to my team of authors and beta readers. Angelique Bosman, Sarah Neofield, Amy Noelle Smith, Maryann Tippett, Ava January, Kristen Granata, Nikki Lamers, Anngie Perez, Melizza Khan, Ric Lucero, Hannah Pearson, Segan Falconer, Jeremy Reed, Leighann Hart, Lauren Mae, Natalie Wright, Nikki Carter, Ethan Rodriguez, and Noelle Davenport.

And finally, if you bought this book and made it this far I have to thank you, my readers. I hope you enjoyed my book and will leave a review. Knowing you took the time to purchase during a pandemic no less) and read my work means the world to me. If you enjoy it, feel free to drop me a line on Instagram.

ABOUT THE AUTHOR

Wesley Parker has enjoyed reading his entire life. When not writing he can either be found making a mixtape, engaging his fandom of Philadelphia sports, or hanging with his wife and three children.

He can be reached on Instagram @weswritesforfun and on Twitter @arigold710.